Hans of Iceland
Vol. 1

by

Victor Hugo

Hans of Iceland
Vol. 1
by Victor Hugo

ISBN: 978-93-62204-70-7

Published by

DOUBLE 9 BOOKS
2/13-B, Ansari Road
Daryaganj, New Delhi – 110002
info@double9books.com
www.double9books.com
Tel. 011-40042856

ABOUT THE AUTHOR

A politician and writer of the French Romantic movement, Victor-Marie Hugo. He is acknowledged as one of France's greatest writers of all time. The Hunchback of Notre-Dame (1831) and Les Misérables are two of his most well-known compositions (1862). In his lifetime, he created more than 4,000 drawings and advocated for social concerns including the repeal of the death penalty. On February 26, 1802, Victor-Marie Hugo was born in Besançon. He was the youngest child of Sophie Trébuchet and Joseph Léopold Sigisbert Hugo. Against the desires of his mother, he fell in love with Adèle Foucher, and in 1816 they secretly were married. François-René de Chateaubriand had a significant impact on him. At the age of 20, Hugo's first book of poetry, Odes et poésies diverses, was released. With the dramas Cromwell (1827) and Hernani (1830), Hugo rose to prominence as the representative of the Romantic literary movement (1830). After being published in 1831, his book Notre-Dame de Paris (The Hunchback of Notre Dame) was swiftly translated into various languages throughout Europe. Hugo's best-known work, Les Misérables, was released in 1862. Hugo's pneumonia-related death on May 22, 1885, at the age of 83, sparked protracted national sorrow. In addition to being admired as a literary giant, he was a statesman who helped establish the Third Republic and democracy in France.

CONTENTS

INTRODUCTION

"HANS of Iceland" is the work of a young man,—a very young man.

As we read it, we see clearly that the eighteen-year old boy who wrote "Hans of Iceland" during a fever fit in 1821 had no experience of men or things, no experience of ideas, and that he was striving to divine all this.

Every intellectual effort, be it drama, poem, or romance, must contain three ingredients,—what the author has felt, what he has observed, and what he has divined.

In a romance particularly, if it is to be a good one, there must be plenty of feeling and plenty of observation; and those things which are divined must be derived logically, simply, and with no solution of continuity, from those things which are observed and felt.

If we apply this law to "Hans of Iceland," we shall readily grasp the chief defect of the book.

There is but one thing felt in "Hans of Iceland," the young man's love; but one thing observed, the young girl's love. All the rest is a matter of divination,—that is, of invention; for youth, having neither facts nor experience nor models behind it, can only divine by means of its imagination. "Hans of Iceland," therefore, admitting that it deserves classification, is hardly more than a fanciful romance.

When a man's prime is past, when his head is bowed, when he feels compelled to write something more than strange stories to frighten old women and children, when all the rough edges of youth are worn away by the friction of life, he realizes that every invention, every creation, every artistic divination, must be based upon study, observation, meditation, science, measure, comparison, serious reflection, attentive and constant imitation of Nature, conscientious self-criticism; and the inspiration evolved from these new conditions, far from losing anything, gains broader influence and greater strength. The poet then realizes his true aim. All the vague revery of his earlier years is crystallized, as it were, and converted into thought. This second period of life is usually that of an artist's greatest works. Still young, and yet mature,—this is the precious phase, the intermediate and culminating point, the warm and radiant hour of noon, the moment when there is the least possible shade, and the most light. There are supreme artists who maintain this height all their lives, despite declining years. These are the sovereign geniuses. Shakespeare and Michael Angelo left the impress of youth upon some of their works, the traces of age on none.

To return to the story of which a new edition is now to be published: Such as it is, with its abrupt and breathless action, its characters all of a piece, its barbarous and bungling mannerism, its supercilious and awkward form, its undisguised moods of revery, its varied hues thrown together haphazard with no thought of pleasing the eye, its crude, harsh, and shocking style, utterly destitute of skill or shading, with the countless excesses of every kind committed almost unwittingly throughout, this book represents with tolerable accuracy the period of life at which it was written, and the particular condition of the soul, the imagination, and the heart of a youth in love for the first time, when the commonplace and ordinary obstacles of life are converted into imposing and poetic impediments, when his head is full of heroic fancies which glorify him in his own estimation, when he is already a man in two or three directions, and still a child in a score of others, when he has read Ducray-Duminil at eleven years of age, Auguste la Fontaine at thirteen, Shakespeare at sixteen,—a strange and rapid scale, which leads abruptly, in the matter of literary taste, from the silly to the sentimental, from the sentimental to the sublime.

We give this book back to the world in 1833 as it was written in 1821, because we feel that the work, ingenuous, if nothing else, gives a tolerably faithful picture of the age that produced it.

Moreover, the author, small as may be his place in literature, having undergone the common fate of every writer, great or small, and seen his first works exalted at the expense of the latest, and having heard it declared that he was far from having fulfilled the promise of his youth, deems it his duty, not to oppose to a criticism, perhaps wise and just, objections which might seem suspicious from his lips, but to reprint his first works simply and literally as he wrote them, that his readers may decide, so far as he is concerned, whether it be a step forward or backward that divides "Hans of Iceland" from "Nôtre-Dame de Paris."

Paris, May, 1833.

PREFACE TO THE FIRST EDITION

THE author of this work, from the day he wrote its first page to the day when he placed the happy word "End" at the bottom of the last page, was a prey to the most absurd illusion. Fancying that a composition in four parts deserved some consideration, he wasted his time in seeking a fundamental idea, in working it out, well or ill, according to a plan good or bad, as the case may be, in arranging scenes, combining effects, studying manners and customs as best he might, — in a word, he took his work seriously.

It is only now, when, as it is the wont of authors to end where the reader begins, he was about to elaborate a long preface, which should be the shield of his work, and contain, together with a statement of the moral and literary principles upon which his conception rests, a more or less hasty sketch of the various historical events which it embraces, and a more or less clear picture of the country in which the scene is laid, — it is only now, I say, that he perceives his error; that he recognizes all the insignificance and all the frivolity of the species of work in behalf of which he has so solemnly spoiled so much paper, and that he feels how strangely he was misled when he persuaded himself that this romance was indeed, up to a certain point, a literary production, and that these four fragments formed a book.

He therefore sagely resolved, after making a proper apology, to say nothing at all in this so-called preface, which the publisher will consequently be careful to print in large letters. He will not tell the reader his name or surname, whether he be old or young, married or a bachelor; whether he has written elegies or fables, odes or satires; whether he means to write tragedies, dramas, or comedies; whether he be the patrician member of some great literary association, or whether he holds a position upon some newspaper, — all things, however, which it would be very interesting to know. He confines himself to stating that the picturesque part of his story has been the object of his especial care; that K's, Y's, H's, and W's abound in it, although he uses these romantic letters with extreme temperance, witness the historic name of Guldenlew, which some chroniclers write Guldenloewe, — a liberty which he has not ventured to allow himself; that there will also be found numerous diphthongs varied with much taste and elegance; and finally, that each chapter is preceded by a strange and mysterious motto, which adds singularly to the interest and gives more expressiveness to each part of the composition.

January, 1823.

PREFACE TO THE SECOND EDITION

THE author has been informed that a brief preface or introduction to this second edition of his book is absolutely essential. In vain he declared that the four or five paragraphs which escorted the first edition, and with which the publisher persisted in disfiguring it, had already drawn down upon his head the anathemas of one of the most distinguished and honorable of French writers,[1] who accused him of assuming the sour tones of the illustrious Jedediah Cleishbotham, schoolmaster and sexton of the parish of Gandercleugh; in vain he alleged that this brilliant and sensible critic, from dealing severely with an error, would doubtless become merciless, upon a repetition of the same mistake,—in a word, he presented countless equally good reasons for declining to fall into the trap; but better ones must have been brought to bear against them, since he is now writing a second preface, after so bitterly repenting that he wrote the first. While executing this bold resolve, his first thought was to open the second edition with those general and particular views on the subject of romance-writing with which he dared not burden the first. Lost in meditations on this literary and didactic treatise, he was still a prey to that strange intoxication of composition, that brief instant when the author, feeling that he is about to grasp an ideal perfection which, alas, he can never reach, is thrilled with delight at his task; he was, we say, enjoying that period of mental ecstasy when labor is a delight, when the secret possession of the muse seems sweeter than the dazzling pursuit of fame, when one of his wisest friends waked him suddenly from his dream, his ecstasy, his intoxication, by assuring him that several very great, popular, and influential men of letters considered the dissertation which he was preparing utterly flat, insipid, and unnecessary; that the painful apostleship of criticism with which they were charged in various public pages, imposing upon them the mournful duty of pitilessly hunting down the monster of "romanticism" and bad taste, they were even then busily preparing for certain enlightened and impartial journals a conscientious, analytical, and spicy criticism of the aforesaid forthcoming dissertation. Upon hearing this terrible news, the poor author *obstupuit; steteruntque comæ, et vox faucibus hæsit,*—that is to say, nothing remained but to leave in the limbo whence he was about to rescue it the essay, "virgin and yet unborn," as Jean Jacques Rousseau has it, of which such just and such severe critics had fallen foul. His friend advised him to replace it by a few simple preliminary remarks from the publishers, as he could very properly put into those gentlemen's mouths all the sweet nothings which so delicately tickle an author's ear; nay, he even offered him certain models, taken from highly successful works, some beginning with the words, "The immense popular success of this book," etc.; others thus, "The European fame which this work has won," etc.; or, "It is now superfluous to praise this book, since popular opinion declares that no praise can equal its merit," etc. Although these various formulæ, according to the discreet adviser, were not without their attested virtues, the author did not feel sufficient humility and paternal indifference to expose his work to the disappointment or the demands of the reader who should peruse these magnificent apologies, nor sufficient effrontery to imitate those rustic mountebanks who attract the curious public by displaying a painted crocodile upon a curtain, behind which, on paying their fee, they find nothing but a lizard. He therefore rejected the idea of sounding his own praises through the obliging lips of his publishers. His friend then suggested that he should put into the mouth of his villanous Icelandic outlaw, by way of a passport, phrases suited to popularize him and render him congenial with the age,—such as delicate jests directed against the nobility, bitter sarcasms upon the clergy, ingenious invectives against nuns, monks, and other monsters of the social order. The author asked nothing better; but it scarcely seemed to him that nobles and monks had any very direct connection with the work in hand. He might, it is true, have borrowed other colors from the same palette, and thrown together a few highly philanthropic pages, in which—always keeping at a prudent distance from the dangerous shoals hidden under the waters of philosophy, and known as the shoals of the Court of Misdemeanors—he might have advanced certain of those truths discovered by the wise for the glory of mankind and the consolation of the dying; namely, that man is but a brute, that the soul is a gas of greater or less density, and that God is nothing; but he thought these incontestable truths very trivial and very hackneyed, and he could scarcely add a drop to the deluge of reasonable morality, atheistic religion, maxims, doctrines, and principles with which we have been flooded for our good for thirty years, in so monstrous a fashion that we might, if it be not irreverent, apply Regnier's verses on a shower,—

"From out the clouds the rains in such vast torrents pour,
That thirsty dogs can drink and not their foreheads lower."

Moreover, these lofty themes had no very visible connection with the subject of his story, and he might have been puzzled to find any bond of union leading up to it, although the art of transitions has been singularly simplified, since so many great men have discovered the secret of passing from a stable to a palace direct, and of exchanging without incongruity the policeman's cap for the civic crown.

Recognizing, therefore, that neither his talent nor his learning, "neither his wings nor his beak," as the ingenious Arab poet has it, could furnish him with a preface which would interest his readers, the author resolved merely to offer them a serious and frank account of the improvements introduced in this second edition.

He must first inform them that the words "second edition" are incorrect, and that the term "first edition" should really be applied to this reprint, inasmuch as the four variously sized bundles of grayish paper blotted with black and white, which the indulgent public has hitherto kindly consented to consider as the four volumes of "Hans of Iceland," were so disfigured with typographic errors by a barbarous printer that the wretched author, on looking over his own production, altered as it was beyond all recognition, was perpetually subjected to the torments of a father whose child returns to him mutilated and tattooed by the hand of an Iroquois from Lake Ontario.

For instance, the type turned a "lion's" voice into a "line," robbed the Dovrefield Mountains of their "peaks" and bestowed upon them "feet," and when the Norse fishers hoped to moor their boat in various "creeks," the printer drove them upon "bricks." Not to weary the reader, the author will pass by in silence all the outrages of this kind which his wounded memory recalls,—

"Manet alto in pectore vulnus."

Suffice it to say that there is no grotesque image, no strange meaning, no absurd idea, no confused figure, no burlesque hieroglyph, which the sedulously stupid ignorance of this enigmatical proof-reader did not make him utter. Alas! every one who ever printed a dozen lines, were it only an invitation to a wedding or a funeral, will feel the deep bitterness of such a sorrow!

The proofs of this reprint have accordingly been read with sedulous care; and the author now ventures to hope, in which he is sustained by one or two close friends, that this romance *redivivus* is worthy to figure among those splendid writings before which "the eleven stars bow low,' as before the sun and moon."[2]

Should journalists accuse him of making no corrections, he will take the liberty of sending them the proof-sheets of this regenerate work, blackened by minute scrutiny; for it is averred that there is more than one doubting Thomas among them.

The kindly reader will also observe that several dates have been corrected, historical notes added, one or two chapters enriched with new mottoes,—in a word, he will find on every page changes whose extreme importance is to be measured only by that of the entire book.

An impertinent adviser desired a translation in foot-notes of all the Latin phrases with which the learned Spiagudry sprinkles the book, "for the comprehension," adds this personage, "of those masons, tinkers, or hairdressers who edit certain journals wherein 'Hans of Iceland' may chance to be reviewed." The author's anger at such insidious counsel may be imagined. He instantly begged to inform the would-be joker that all journalists, without distinction, are mirrors of courtesy, wisdom, and good faith, and requested him not to insult him by believing him to be one of those ungrateful citizens who are ever ready to address those dictators of taste and genius in this poor verse of an old poet,—

"Keep your own skins, my friends, nor other folk condemn,"

for he is far from thinking that the lion's skin is not the true skin of those popular gentlemen.

Still another friend implored him—for he must conceal nothing from his readers—to put his name on the titlepage of this story, hitherto the neglected child of an unknown father. It must be owned that beyond the pleasure of seeing the half-dozen capital letters which spell out one's name printed in fine black characters upon smooth white paper, there is also a certain charm in displaying it in solitary grandeur upon the back of the cover, as if the work which it adorns, far from being the only monument of the author's genius, were but one of the columns in the imposing temple wherein his genius is some day to spread its wings, but a slight specimen of his hidden talent and his unpublished glory. It proves that at least he hopes to be a noted and admired writer some day. To triumph over this fresh temptation, the author was forced to muster all his fears lest he should never break through the crowd of scribblers who, even though they waive their anonymity, must ever remain unknown.

As for the hint thrown out by certain amateurs with very delicate ears regarding the uncouth harshness of his Norwegian names, he considers it well founded. He therefore proposes, so soon as he shall be made a member of the Royal Society at Stockholm or the Bergen Academy, to invite the Norwegians to change their language, inasmuch as the hideous jargon which they are whimsical enough to employ wounds the ears of Parisian ladies, and their outlandish names, as rugged as their rocks, produce the same effect upon the sensitive tongue that utters them, as their bear's grease and bark bread would probably have upon the delicate nervous filaments of our palate.

It only remains for him to thank the few persons who have been good enough to read his book through, as is proved by the really tremendous success which it has won; he also expresses his gratitude to those of his fair readers who, he is assured, have formed a certain ideal of the author of "Hans of Iceland" from his book; he is vastly flattered that they should attribute to him red hair, a shaggy beard, and fierce eyes; he is overcome with confusion that they should condescend to do him the honor to suppose that he never cuts his nails; but he entreats them on his knees to rest assured that he never carries his ferocity so far as to devour little children alive; moreover, all these facts will become fixed when his renown has reached the level of that of the authors of "Lolotte and Fanfan" or of "Monsieur Botte," —men of transcendent genius, twins alike in talent and in taste, *arcades ambo*; and when his portrait, *terribiles visu formæ*, and his biography, *domestica facta*, are prefixed to his works.

He was about to close this long epistle, when his publisher, on the point of sending the book to the reviews, requested that he would add a few complimentary notices of his own work, adding, to remove all the author's scruples, that "his writing should not be the means of compromising him, as he would copy these articles himself." This last remark struck the author as extremely touching. Since it seems that in this most luminous age every man considers it his duty to enlighten his neighbor as to his own qualities and personal perfections, concerning which none can be so well informed as their possessor, as, moreover, this last temptation is a strong one, the author thinks it his duty, in case he should yield to it, to warn the public not to believe more than half of what the press may say of his work.

April, 1828.

HANS OF ICELAND

I

Did you see it? did you see it? did you see it? Oh! did you
see it?—Who saw it? Who did see it? For mercy's sake, who
saw it?

Sterne: *Tristram Shandy.*

"THAT'S what comes of falling in love, Neighbor Niels. Poor Guth
Stersen would not be stretched out yonder on that great black slab, like
a starfish forgotten by the tide, if she had kept her mind on mending her
father's boat and patching his nets. Saint Usuph, the fisher, console our old
friend in his affliction!"

"And her lover," added a shrill, tremulous voice, "Gill Stadt, that fine
young man beside her, would not be there now, if instead of making love to
Guth and seeking his luck in those accursed Roeraas mines, he had stayed
at home and rocked his little brother's cradle, under the smoky cross-beams
of his mother's hut."

Neighbor Niels, whom the first speaker addressed, interrupted: "Your
memory is growing old along with yourself, Mother Olly. Gill never had
a brother, and that makes poor Widow Stadt's grief all the harder to bear,
for her home is now left utterly desolate; if she looks up to heaven for
consolation, she sees nought but her old roof, where still hangs the cradle of
her son, grown to be a tall young man, and dead."

"Poor mother!" replied old Olly, "it was the young man's own fault.
Why should he go to Roeraas to be a miner?"

"I do believe," said Niels, "that those infernal mines rob us of a man for
every escalin's[3] worth of copper which we get out of them. What do you
think, Father Braal?"

"Miners are fools," replied the fisherman. "If he would live, the fish
should not leave the water. Man should not enter the bowels of the earth."

"But," asked a young man in the crowd, "how if Gill Stadt had to work
in the mines to win his sweetheart?"

"A man should never risk his life," interrupted Olly, "for affections which are far from being worth a life, or filling it. A pretty wedding-bed Gill earned for his Guth!"

"So then that young woman," inquired a curious bystander, "drowned herself in despair at the death of this young man?"

"Who says so?" loudly exclaimed a soldier, pushing his way through the crowd. "That young girl, whom I knew well, was indeed engaged to marry a young miner who was lately crushed by falling rocks in the underground tunnels of Storwaadsgrube, near Roeraas; but she was also the sweetheart of one of my mates, and as she was going to Munkholm secretly, day before yesterday, to celebrate with her lover the death of her betrothed, her boat capsized on a reef, and she was drowned."

A confused sound of voices arose: "Impossible, master soldier," cried the old women. The young ones were silent; and Neighbor Niels maliciously reminded fisher Braal of his serious statement: "That's what comes of falling in love!"

The soldier was about to lose his temper with his opponents; he had already called them "old witches from the cave of Quiragoth," and they were not disposed to bear so grave an insult patiently, when a sharp and imperious voice, crying "Silence, silence, you old fools!" put an end to the dispute. All was still, as when the sudden crow of a cock is heard amid the cackling of the hens.

Before relating the rest of the scene, it may be well to describe the spot where it occurred. It was—as the reader has doubtless guessed—one of those gloomy structures which public pity and social forethought devote to unknown corpses, the last asylum of the dead, whose lives were usually sad ones; where the careless spectator, the surly or kindly observer gather, and friends often meet tearful relatives, whom long and unendurable anxiety has robbed of all but one sad hope. At the period now remote, and in the uncivilized region to which I have carried my reader, there had as yet been no attempt, as in our cities of gold and mud, to make these resting-places into ingeniously forbidding or elegantly funereal edifices. Daylight did not fall through tomb-shaped openings, into artistically sculptured vaults, upon beds which seem as if the guardian of the place were anxious to leave the dead some of the conveniences of life, and the pillow seems arranged for sleep. If the keeper's door were left ajar, the eye, wearied with gazing upon hideous, naked corpses, had not as now the pleasure of resting upon elegant furniture and happy children. Death was there in all its deformity, in all its horror; and there was no attempt to deck its fleshless skeleton with ribbons and gewgaws.

The room in which our actors stood was spacious and dark, which made it seem still larger; it was lighted only by a broad, low door opening upon the port of Throndhjem, and a rough hole in the ceiling, through which a dull, white light fell, mingled with rain, hail, or snow, according to the weather, upon the corpses lying directly under it. The room was divided by an iron railing, breast-high, running across it from side to side. The public entered the outer portion through the low door; in the inner part were six long black granite slabs, arranged abreast and parallel to each other. A small side door served to admit the keeper and his assistant to either section, their rooms occupying the rear of the building, close to the water. The miner and his betrothed occupied two granite beds; decomposition had already begun its work upon the young woman's body, showing itself in large blue and purple spots running along her limbs on the line of the blood-vessels. Gill's features were stern and set; but his body was so horribly mutilated that it was impossible to judge whether his beauty were really so great as old Olly declared.

It was before these disfigured remains, in the midst of the mute crowd, that the conversation which we have faithfully interpreted, began.

A tall, withered old man, sitting with folded arms and bent head upon a broken stool in the darkest corner of the room, had apparently paid no heed until the moment when he rose suddenly, exclaiming, "Silence, silence, you old fools!" and seized the soldier by the arm.

All were hushed; the soldier turned and broke into a burst of laughter at the sight of his strange interrupter, whose pale face, thin greasy locks, long fingers, and complete costume of reindeer leather amply justified this mirthful reception. But a clamor arose from the crowd of women, for a moment confounded: "It is the keeper of the Spladgest![4]—That infernal doorkeeper to the dead!—That diabolical Spiagudry!—That accursed sorcerer!"

"Silence, you old fools, silence! If this be the witches' Sabbath, hasten away and find your broomsticks; if you don't, they'll fly off without you. Let this worthy descendant of the god Thor alone."

Then Spiagudry, striving to assume a gracious expression, addressed the soldier: "You say, my good fellow, that this wretched woman—"

"Old rascal!" muttered Olly; "yes, we are all 'wretched women,' to him, because our bodies, if they fall into his claws, only bring him thirty escalins' reward, while he gets forty for the paltry carcass of a man."

"Silence, old women!" repeated Spiagudry. "In truth, these daughters of the Devil are like their kettles; when they wax warm, they must needs sing. Tell me, my valiant king of the sword, your comrade, this Guth's lover, will doubtless kill himself in despair at her loss, won't he?"

Here burst forth the long-repressed storm. "Do you hear the miscreant,— the old Pagan!" cried twenty shrill, discordant voices. "He would fain see one less man living, for the sake of the forty escalins that a dead body brings him."

"And what if I would?" replied the keeper of the Spladgest. "Doesn't our gracious king and master, Christian V.,—may Saint Hospitius bless him!—declare himself the natural guardian of all miners, so that when they die he may enrich his royal treasury with their paltry leavings?"

"You honor the king," answered fisher Braal, "by comparing the royal treasury to the strong-box of your charnel-house, and him to yourself, Neighbor Spiagudry."

"Neighbor, indeed!" said the keeper, shocked by such familiarity. "Your neighbor! say rather your host! since it may easily chance some day, my dear boat-dweller, that I shall have to lend you one of my six stone beds for a week. Besides," he added, with a laugh, "if I spoke of that soldier's death, it was merely from a desire to see the perpetuation of the custom of suicide for the sake of those great and tragic passions which ladies are wont to inspire."

"Well, you tall corpse and keeper of corpses," said the soldier, "what are you after, with your amiable grimace, which looks so much like the last smile of a man who has been hanged?"

"Capital, my valiant fellow!" replied Spiagudry. "I always felt that there was more wit beneath the helmet of Constable Thurn, who conquered the Devil with his sword and his tongue, than under the mitre of Bishop Isleif, who wrote the history of Iceland, or the square cap of Professor Shoenning, who described our cathedral."

"In that case, if you will take my advice, my old bag of leather, you will give up the revenues of the charnel-house, and go and sell yourself to the viceroy's museum of curiosities at Bergen. I swear to you, by Belphegor, that they pay their weight in gold there for rare beasts; but say, what do you want with me?"

"When the bodies brought here are found in the water, we have to give half the reward to the fisherman. I was going to ask you, therefore, illustrious heir to Constable Thurn, if you would persuade your unfortunate comrade not to drown himself, but to choose some other mode of death; it can't matter much to him, and he would not wish to wrong the unhappy

Christian who must entertain his corpse, if the loss of Guth should really drive him to that act of despair."

"You are quite mistaken, my charitable and hospitable friend. My comrade will not have the pleasure of occupying an apartment in your tempting tavern with its six beds. Don't you suppose he has already consoled himself with another Valkyria for the death of that girl? He had long been tired of your Guth, by my beard!"

At these words, the storm, which Spiagudry had for a moment drawn upon his own head, again burst more furiously than ever upon the luckless soldier.

"What, miserable scamp!" shrieked the old women; "is that the way you forget us? And yet we love such good-for-nothings!"

The young girls still kept silence. Some of them even thought—greatly against their will, of course—that this graceless fellow was very good-looking.

"Oh, ho!" said the soldier; "has the witches' Sabbath come round again? Beelzebub's punishment is frightful indeed if he be condemned to hear such choruses once a week!"

No one can say how this fresh squall would have ended, if general attention had not at this moment been utterly absorbed by a noise from without. The uproar increased steadily, and presently a swarm of little ragged boys entered the Spladgest, tumultuously shouting and crowding about a covered bier carried by two men.

"Where does that come from?" the keeper asked the bearers.

"From Urchtal Sands."

"Oglypiglap!" shouted Spiagudry.

One of the side doors opened, a little man of Lappish race, dressed in leather, entered, and signed to the bearers to follow him. Spiagudry accompanied them, and the door closed before the curious crowd had time to guess, by the length of the body on the bier, whether it were a man or a woman.

This subject still occupied all their thoughts, when Spiagudry and his assistant reappeared in the second compartment, carrying the corpse of a man, which they placed upon one of the granite couches.

"It's a long time since I've handled such handsome clothes," said Oglypiglap; then, shaking his head and standing on tiptoe, he hung above the dead man the elegant uniform of a captain in the army. The corpse's head was disfigured, and his limbs were covered with blood; the keeper sprinkled the body several times from an old broken pail.

"By Saint Beelzebub!" cried the soldier, "it is an officer of my regiment. Let me see; can it be Captain Bollar, —from grief at his uncle's death? Bah! he is the heir. Baron Randmer? He lost his estate at cards yesterday, but he will win it back to-morrow, with his adversary's castle. Can it be Captain Lory, whose dog was drowned, or Paymaster Stunck, whose wife was unfaithful to him? But, really, I don't see why he should blow out his brains for that!"

The crowd steadily increased. Just at this instant, a young man who was crossing the wharf, seeing the mob of people, dismounted from his horse, handed the bridle to the servant behind him, and entered the Spladgest. He wore a simple travelling dress, was armed with a sword, and wrapped in a large green cloak; a black plume, fastened to his hat by a diamond buckle, fell over his noble face and waved to and fro upon his lofty brow, shaded by chestnut hair; his boots and spurs, soiled with mud, showed that he had come a long distance.

As he entered, a short, thick-set man, also wrapped in a cloak and hiding his hands in huge gloves, replied to the soldier.

"And who told you that he killed himself? That man no more committed suicide, I'll be bound, than the roof of your cathedral set itself on fire."

As the double-edged sword makes two wounds, this phrase gave birth to two answers.

"Our cathedral!" said Niels; "it is covered with copper now. It was that miserable Hans who set it on fire to make work for the miners, one of whom was his favorite Gill Stadt, whom you see lying yonder."

"What the devil!" cried the soldier, in his turn; "do you dare tell me, the second musketeer in the Munkholm garrison, that that man did not blow out his brains!"

"He was murdered," coldly replied the little fellow.

"Just listen to the oracle! Go along with you. Your little gray eyes can see no better than your hands do under the big gloves with which you cover them in the middle of the summer."

The little man's eyes flashed.

"Soldier, pray to your patron saint that these hands may never leave their mark upon your face!"

"Oh!—enough of this!" cried the soldier, in a rage. Then, pausing suddenly, he said: "No, there must be no word of a duel before dead men."

The little man growled a few words in a foreign tongue, and vanished.

A voice cried out: "He was found on Urchtal Sands."

"On Urchtal Sands?" said the soldier; "Captain Dispolsen was to land there this morning, from Copenhagen."

"Captain Dispolsen has not yet reached Munkholm," said another voice.

"They say that Hans of Iceland haunts those sands just now," added a fourth.

"Then it is possible that this may be the captain," said the soldier, "if Hans was the murderer; for we all know that the Icelander murders in so devilish a fashion that his victims often seem to be suicides."

"What sort of man is this Hans?" asked some one.

"He is a giant," said one.

"He is a dwarf," said another.

"Has nobody seen him, then?" put in a voice.

"Those who see him for the first time, see him for the last time also."

"Hush!" said old Olly; "they say there are but three persons who ever exchanged human speech with him,—that reprobate of a Spiagudry, Widow Stadt, and—but he had a sad life and a sad death—that poor Gill, who lies yonder. Hush!"

"Hush!" was repeated on all sides.

"Now," suddenly exclaimed the soldier, "I am sure that this is indeed Captain Dispolsen. I recognize the steel chain which our prisoner, old Schumacker, gave him when he went away."

The young man with the black plume broke the silence abruptly: "Are you sure it is Captain Dispolsen?"

"Sure, by the merits of Saint Beelzebub!" said the soldier.

The young man left the room hurriedly.

"Get me a boat for Munkholm," he said to his servant.

"But, the general, sir?"

"Take the horses to him. I will follow to-morrow. Am I my own master, or not? Come, night is falling, and I am in haste. A boat!"

The servant obeyed, and for some time stood watching his young master as he moved away from the shore.

II

I will sit by you while you tell me some pleasant tale to pass away the time.—Maturin: *Bertram.*

THE reader is already aware that we are at Throndhjem, one of the four chief cities in Norway, although not the residence of the viceroy. At the date of this story (1699) the kingdom of Norway was still united to Denmark, and governed by a viceroy whose seat was in Bergen, a larger, handsomer, and more southerly town than Throndhjem, in spite of the disagreeable nickname attached to it by the famous Admiral Tromp.

Throndhjem offers a pleasant prospect as you approach it by the fjord to which the city gives its name. The harbor is quite large, although it cannot be entered easily in all weathers. At this time it resembled nothing so much as a long canal, lined on the right by Danish and Norwegian ships, and on the left by foreign vessels, as prescribed by law. In the background lay the town, situated on a well-cultivated plain, and crowned by the lofty spires of the cathedral. This church—one of the finest pieces of Gothic architecture, as we may judge from Professor Shoenning's book, so learnedly quoted by Spiagudry, which describes it as it was before repeated fires had laid it waste—bore upon its highest pinnacle the episcopal cross, the distinctive sign that it was the cathedral of the Lutheran bishop of Throndhjem. Beyond the town, in the blue distance, were the slender white peaks of the Kiölen Mountains, like the sharp-pointed ornaments on an antique crown.

In the middle of the harbor, within cannon-shot of the shore, upon a mass of rocks lashed by the waves, rose the lonely fortress of Munkholm, a gloomy prison which then held a prisoner celebrated for the splendor of his long prosperity and for his sudden disgrace.

Schumacker, born in an obscure station, was loaded with favors by his master, then hurled from the chair of the Lord High Chancellor of Denmark and Norway to the traitor's bench, dragged to the scaffold, and thence by royal clemency cast into a lonely dungeon at the extreme end of the two kingdoms. His creatures had overthrown him, but gave him no right to inveigh against their ingratitude. How could he complain if the steps gave way beneath him, which he had built so high for his own aggrandizement only?

The founder of the Danish nobility, from the depth of his exile, saw the grandees whom he had created share his own dignities between them. Count d'Ahlefeld, his mortal enemy, succeeded him as chancellor; General Arensdorf, as earl-marshal, distributed military titles, and Bishop Spollyson took the position of inspector of universities. The only one of his foes who did not owe his rise to him was Count Ulric Frederic Guldenlew, natural son of King Frederic III, and now viceroy of Norway. He was the most generous of all.

Toward the sombre rock of Munkholm the boat of the youth with the black plume now slowly moved. The sun sank rapidly behind the lonely fortress, whose walls cut off its last beams, already so horizontal that the peasant on the distant eastern hills of Larsynn might see beside him on the heather the faint shadow of the sentinel keeping his watch on Munkholm's highest tower.

III

Ah! my heart could receive no more painful wound!... A young man destitute of morals.... He dared gaze at her! His glance soiled her purity. Claudia! The mere thought drives me mad.—Lessing.

"ANDREW, go and order them to ring the curfew bell in half an hour. Let Sorsyll relieve Duckness at the portcullis, and Malvidius keep watch on the platform of the great tower. Let a careful lookout be kept in the direction of the Lion of Schleswig donjon. Do not forget to fire the cannon at seven o'clock, as a signal to lift the harbor chain. But no, we must wait a little for Captain Dispolsen; better light the signals instead, and see if the Walderhog beacon is lighted, as I ordered to-day. Be sure to keep refreshments ready for the captain. And, I forgot,—give Toric-Belfast, the second musketeer of the regiment, two days' arrest; he has been absent all day."

So said the sergeant-at-arms beneath the black and smoky roof of the Munkholm guard-house, in the low tower over the outer castle gate.

The soldiers addressed left their cards or bed to carry out his orders; then silence was restored. At this moment the measured beat of oars was heard outside.

"That must be Captain Dispolsen at last!" said the sergeant, opening the tiny grated window which looked out upon the gulf.

A boat was just landing at the foot of the iron gate.

"Who goes there?" cried the sergeant in hoarse tones.

"Open!" was the answer; "peace and safety."

"There is no admittance here. Have you a passport?"

"Yes."

"I must make sure of that. If you lie, by the merits of my patron saint, you shall taste the waters of the gulf!" Then, closing the lattice and turning away, he added: "It is not the captain yet."

A light shone behind the iron gate. The rusty bolts creaked, the grating rose, the gate opened, and the sergeant examined a parchment handed him by the new-comer.

"Pass in," said he. "But stay," he added hastily, "leave your hat-buckle outside. No one is allowed to enter the prisons of the State wearing jewels. The order declares that 'the king and the members of the royal family, the viceroy and members of the vice-regal family, the bishop, and the officers of the garrison, are alone excepted.' You come under none of these heads, do you?"

The young man, without reply, removed the forbidden ornament, and flung it to the fisherman who brought him thither, in payment of his services; the latter, fearing lest he might repent his generosity, made haste to put a broad expanse of sea between the benefactor and his benefit.

While the sergeant, grumbling at the chancellor's imprudence in being so prodigal with his passes, replaced the clumsy bars, and while the lingering sound of his heavy boots still echoed on the stairs leading to the guard-house, the young man, throwing his mantle over his shoulder, hurriedly crossed the dark vault of the low tower, the long parade-ground, and the ordnance-room, where lay a few old dismantled culverins, still to be seen in the Copenhagen museum, all nearer approach to which was forbidden by the warning cry of a sentinel. He reached the great portcullis, which was raised on sight of his parchment. Thence, followed by a soldier, he crossed diagonally, without hesitation, and like one familiar with the place, one of the four square courts which skirt the great circular yard, in whose midst rose the huge round rock upon which stood the donjon, called the castle of the Lion of Schleswig, from the forced sojourn there of Jotham the Lion, Duke of Schleswig, held captive by his brother, Rolf the Dwarf.

It is not our purpose to give a description of Munkholm keep, the more so that the reader, confined in a State prison, might fear that he could not escape through the garden. He would be mistaken; for the castle of the Lion of Schleswig, meant for prisoners of distinction only, among other conveniences affords them the pleasure of a walk in a sort of wild garden of considerable extent, where clumps of holly, a few ancient yews, and some dark pines grow among the rocks around the lofty prison, inside an enclosure of thick walls and huge towers.

Reaching the foot of the round rock, the young man climbed the rude winding steps which lead to the foot of one of the towers of the enclosure, having a postern below, which served as the entrance to the keep. Here he blew a loud blast on a copper horn handed to him by the warder of the great portcullis. "Come in, come in!" eagerly

"He blew a loud blast on a horn."

Photo-Etching.—From drawing by Démarest.

exclaimed a voice from within; "it must be that confounded captain!"

As the postern swung open, the new-comer saw, in a dimly lighted Gothic apartment, a young officer stretched carelessly upon a pile of cloaks and reindeer-skins, beside one of the three-beaked lamps which our ancestors used to hang from the rose-work of their ceilings, and which at this moment stood upon the ground. The elegance and indeed excessive luxury of his dress was in strong contrast with the bare walls and rude furniture; he held a book, and turned slightly toward the new-comer.

"Is it you, Captain? How are you, Captain? You little suspected that you were keeping a man waiting who has not the pleasure of your acquaintance; but our acquaintance will soon be made, will it not? Begin by receiving my commiseration upon your return to this venerable castle. Short as my stay here may be, I shall soon be about as gay as the owl nailed at donjon doors to serve as scarecrow, and when I return to Copenhagen, to my sister's wedding feast, the deuce take me if four women out of a hundred will know me! Tell me, are the knots of pink ribbon at the hem of my doublet still in fashion? Has any one translated a new novel by that Frenchwoman, Mademoiselle Scudéry? I have 'Clelia;' I suppose people are still reading it in Copenhagen. It is my code of gallantry, now that I am forced to sigh remote from so many bright eyes; for, bright as they are, the eyes of our young prisoner—you know who I mean—have never a message for me. Ah! were it not for my father's orders!... I must tell you in confidence, Captain, that my father,—but don't mention it,—charged me to—you understand me—Schumacker's daughter. But I have my labor for my pains; that pretty statue is not a woman; she weeps all day long and never looks at me."

The young man, unable thus far to interrupt the officer's extreme volubility, uttered an exclamation of surprise:—

"What! What did you say? Charged you to seduce the daughter of that unfortunate Schumacker!"

"Seduce? Well, so be it, if that is the name you give it now in Copenhagen; but I defy the Devil himself to succeed. Day before yesterday, being on duty, I put on for her express benefit a superb French ruff sent direct from Paris. Would you believe that she never even raised her eyes to look at me, although I passed through her room three or four times clinking my new spurs, whose rowels are no bigger than a Lombardy ducat? That's the newest fashion, is n't it?"

"Heavens! Heavens!" said the young man, striking his forehead; "but this confounds me!"

"I thought it would!" rejoined the officer, mistaking the meaning of the remark. "Not to take the least notice of me! It is incredible, and yet it is true."

The young man strode up and down the room in violent excitement.

"Won't you take some refreshment, Captain Dispolsen?" cried the officer.

The young man started.

"I am not Captain Dispolsen."

"What!" said the officer angrily, sitting up as he spoke; "and pray who are you, then, that venture to introduce yourself here at this hour?"

The young man displayed his papers.

"I wish to see Count Griffenfeld,—I would say, your prisoner."

"The Count! the Count!" muttered the officer in some displeasure. "But, to be sure, this paper is in order; here is the signature of Vice-Chancellor Grummond de Knud. 'Admit the bearer to visit all the royal prisons at any hour and at any time.' Grummond de Knud is brother to old General Levin de Knud, who is in command at Throndhjem, and you must know that this old general had the bringing up of my future brother-in-law."

"Thanks for these family details, Lieutenant. Don't you think you have told me enough of them?"

"The impertinent fellow is right," said the lieutenant, biting his lips. "Hullo, there, officer, officer of the tower! Escort this stranger to Schumacker, and do not scold if I have taken down your lamp with three beaks and but one wick. I was curious to examine an article which is doubtless the work of Sciold the Pagan or Havar the giant-killer; and besides it is no longer the fashion to hang anything but crystal chandeliers from the ceiling."

With these words, as the young man and his escort crossed the deserted donjon garden, the martyr to fashion resumed the thread of the love adventures of the Amazonian Clelia and Horatius the One-eyed.

IV

Benvolio. Where the devil should this Romeo be? Came he
not home to-night?
Mercutio. Not to his father's; I spoke with his man.
Shakespeare: *Romeo and Juliet.*

A MAN and two horses entered the courtyard of the palace of the
governor of Throndhjem. The horseman dismounted, shaking his head with
a discontented air. He was about to lead the two animals to the stable, when
his arm was seized, and a voice cried: "How! You here alone, Poël! And
your master,—where is your master?"

It was old General Levin de Knud, who, seeing from his window
the young man's servant and the empty saddle, descended quickly, and
fastened upon the groom a gaze which betrayed even more alarm than his
question.

"Your Excellency," said Poël, with a low bow, "my master has left
Throndhjem."

"What! has he been here, and gone again without seeing his general,
without greeting his old friend! And how long since?"

"He arrived this evening and left this evening."

"This evening,—this very evening! But where did he stay? Where has
he gone?"

"He stopped at the Spladgest, and has embarked for Munkholm."

"Ah! I supposed he was at the antipodes. But what is his business at that
castle? What took him to the Spladgest? Just like my knight-errant. After all,
I am rather to blame, for why did I give him such a bringing up? I wanted
him to be free in spite of his rank."

"Therefore he is no slave to etiquette," said Poël.

"No; but he is to his own caprice. Well, he will doubtless return. Rest
and refresh yourself, Poël. Tell me," and the general's face took on an
expression of solicitude, "tell me, Poël, have you been doing much running
up and down?"

"General, we came here direct from Bergen. My master was melancholy."

"Melancholy! Why, what can have occurred between him and his father? Is he averse to this marriage?"

"I do not know. But they say that his Serene Highness insists upon it."

"Insists! You say, Poël, that the viceroy insists upon this match! But why should he insist unless Ordener refused?"

"I don't know, your Excellency. He seems sad."

"Sad! Do you know how his father received him?"

"The first time, it was at the camp, near Bergen. His Serene Highness said, 'I seldom see you, my son.' 'So much the better for me, my lord and father,' replied my master, 'if you take note of it.' Then he gave his Grace certain details about his travels in the North, and his Grace said: 'It is well.' Next day my master came back from the palace and said: 'They want me to marry; but I must consult my second father, General Levin.' I saddled the horses, and here we are."

"Really, my good Poël," said the general, in trembling tones, "did he really call me his second father?"

"Yes, your Excellency."

"Woe to me if this marriage distresses him, for I will sooner incur the king's displeasure than lend myself to it. And yet, the daughter of the Lord High Chancellor of both kingdoms—By the way, Poël, does Ordener know that his future mother-in-law, Countess d'Ahlefeld, has been here incognito since yesterday, and that the count is expected?"

"I don't know, General."

"Oh, yes," thought the old governor, "he knows it; for why else should he beat a retreat the instant that he arrived?"

Upon this, the general, with a friendly wave of the hand to Poël, and a salute to the sentinel who presented arms to him, returned in anxious mood to the quarters which he had left in anxious mood.

V

It seemed as if every emotion had stirred his heart, and
had also deserted it; nothing remained but the mournful,
piercing gaze of a man thoroughly familiar with men, who
saw, at a glance, the aim and object of all things.—Schiller:
The Visions.

WHEN, after leading the stranger along the winding stairs and lofty
halls of the donjon of the Lion of Schleswig, the officer finally threw open
the door of the room occupied by the man he sought, the first words that fell
upon his ear were once more these: "Has Captain Dispolsen come at last?"

The speaker was an old man, seated with his back to the door, his elbows
on a writing-table, his head buried in his hands. He wore a black woollen
gown, and above a bed at one end of the room hung a broken escutcheon,
around which were grouped the broken collars of the orders of the Elephant
and the Dannebrog; a count's coronet, reversed, was fastened under the
shield, and two fragments of a hand of Justice, tied crosswise, completed
the strange ornamentation. The old man was Schumacker.

"No, my Lord," replied the officer; then he said to the stranger, "This
is the prisoner;" and leaving them together, he closed the door, without
heeding the shrill voice of the old man, who exclaimed: "If it is not the
captain, I will see no one."

At these words the stranger remained by the door; and the prisoner,
thinking himself alone,—for he had turned away,—fell back into his silent
revery. Suddenly he exclaimed: "The captain has assuredly forsaken
and betrayed me! Men,—men are like the icicle which an Arab took for a
diamond; he hid it carefully in his wallet, and when he looked for it again
he found not even a drop of water."

"I am no such man," said the stranger.

Schumacker rose quickly. "Who is here? Who overhears me? Is it some
miserable tool of that Guldenlew?"

"Speak no evil of the viceroy, my lord Count."

"Lord Count! Do you address me thus to flatter me? You have your
labor for your pains; I am powerful no longer."

"He who speaks to you never knew you in your day of power, and is none the less your friend."

"Because he still hopes to gain something from me; those memories of the unhappy which linger in the minds of men are to be measured by the hopes of future gain."

"I am the one who should complain, noble Count; for I remember you, and you have forgotten me. I am Ordener."

A flash of joy lit up the old man's sad eyes, and a smile which he could not repress parted his white beard, as when a sunbeam breaks through a cloud.

"Ordener! Welcome, traveller Ordener! A thousand prayers for the happiness of the traveller who remembers the prisoner!"

"But," inquired Ordener, "had you really forgotten me?"

"I had forgotten you," said Schumacker, resuming his sombre mood, "as we forget the breeze which refreshes us and passes by; we are fortunate if it does not become a whirlwind to destroy us."

"Count Griffenfeld," rejoined the young man, "did you not count upon my return?"

"Old Schumacker did not count upon it; but there is a maiden here, who reminded me this very day that it was a year on the 8th of last May, since you went away."

Ordener started.

"Heavens! Can it be your Ethel, noble Count?"

"Who else?"

"Your daughter, my Lord, has deigned to count the months of my absence! Oh, how many dreary days I have passed! I have traversed Norway from Christiania to Wardhus; but my journeyings always tended back toward Throndhjem."

"Use your freedom, young man, while you may. But tell me who you are. I would like, Ordener, to know you by some other name. The son of one of my mortal foes is called Ordener."

"Perhaps, my lord Count, this mortal foe feels greater kindness for you than you for him."

"You evade my question; but keep your secret. I might learn that the fruit which quenches my thirst is a poison which will destroy me."

"Count!" cried Ordener, angrily; "Count!" he repeated, in tones of pity and reproach.

"Why should I trust you," replied Schumacker, — "you who to my very face defend the merciless Guldenlew?"

"The viceroy," gravely interrupted the young man, "has just ordered that for the future you shall be free and unguarded within the entire precinct of the Lion of Schleswig keep. This news I learned at Bergen, and you will doubtless soon hear it from headquarters."

"This is a favor for which I dared not hope, and I thought you were the only person to whom I had mentioned my wish. So they lessen the weight of my chains as that of my years increases; and when old age renders me helpless, they will probably tell me, 'You are free.'"

So saying, the old man smiled bitterly, and added: "And you, young man, do you still cling to your foolish ideas of independence?"

"If I had not those same foolish ideas, I should not be here."

"How did you come to Throndhjem?"

"Why, on horseback."

"How did you reach Munkholm?"

"By boat."

"Poor fool! You think yourself free, and yet you only leave a horse for a boat. It is not your own limbs that carry out your wishes; it is a brute beast, it is material matter; and you call that free will!"

"I force animate beings to obey me."

"To assume a right to the obedience of certain beings is to give others a right to command you. Independence exists only in isolation."

"You do not love mankind, noble Count?"

The old man laughed sadly. "I weep that I am a man, and I laugh at him who would console me. You will yet learn, if you do not already know, that misfortune creates suspicion as prosperity does ingratitude. Tell me, since you come from Bergen, what favoring winds blow upon Captain Dispolsen. Some good fortune must have befallen him, that he forgets me."

Ordener looked grave and embarrassed.

"Dispolsen, my lord Count? I come here to-day to talk to you of him. I know that he possessed your entire confidence."

"You know?" broke in the prisoner, uneasily. "You are mistaken. No one on earth has my confidence. Dispolsen has, it is true, my papers, and very important papers too. He went to Copenhagen, to the king, for me. I may even confess that I reckoned more surely upon him than upon any one else, for in the days of my prosperity I never did him a service."

"Well, noble Count, I saw him to-day—"

"Your distress tells me the rest; he is a traitor."

"He is dead."

"Dead!"

The prisoner folded his arms and bent his head, then looking up at the young man, said: "I told you some good fortune must have befallen him!"

His eye turned to the wall, where the signs of his former grandeur hung, and he waved his hand, as if to dismiss the witness of a grief which he strove to conquer.

"I do not pity him; 'tis but one man the less. Nor do I pity myself; what have I to lose? But my daughter,—my unfortunate daughter! I shall be the victim of this infernal plot; and what is to become of her, if her father is taken from her?"

He turned quickly to Ordener. "How did he die? Where did you see him?"

"I saw him at the Spladgest. No one knows whether he died by suicide or by the hand of an assassin."

"That is now all-important. If he was murdered, I know who dealt the blow. Then all is lost. He bore proofs of the conspiracy against me. Those proofs might have saved me and ruined them! Unhappy Ethel!"

"My lord Count," said Ordener, bowing, "to-morrow I will tell you whether he was murdered."

Schumacker, without answering, cast on Ordener, as he left the room, a look of quiet despair more terrible than the calm of death.

Ordener found himself in the prisoner's empty antechamber, not knowing which way to turn. Night was far advanced and the room was dark. He opened a door at haphazard and entered a vast corridor lighted only by the moon, which moved rapidly through pale clouds. Its misty beams fell now and again upon the long, narrow glass windows, and painted on the opposite wall what seemed a procession of ghosts, appearing and disappearing simultaneously in the depths of the passage. The young man slowly crossed himself, and walked toward a light which shone faintly at the end of the corridor.

A door stood ajar; a young girl knelt in a Gothic oratory, at the foot of a bare altar, reciting in low tones litanies to the Virgin, — simple and sublime aspirations, in which the soul that rises toward the Mother of Seven Sorrows asks nothing but her prayers.

The young girl was dressed in black crape and white gauze, as if to show at a glance that her days had hitherto been passed in grief and innocence. Even in this modest attitude she bore the impress of a strange nature. Her eyes and her long hair were black (a very rare beauty in the North); her eyes, raised to heaven, seemed kindled with rapture rather than dimmed by meditation. She seemed a virgin from the shores of Cyprus or the banks of the Tiber, clad in the fanciful disguise of one of Ossian's characters and prostrate before the wooden cross and stone altar of Christ Jesus.

Ordener started and almost fell, for he recognized the devotee.

She was praying for her father, for the mighty who had fallen, for the old and desolate prisoner; and she recited aloud the psalm of the deliverance out of Egypt. She prayed for another as well, but Ordener did not hear his name. He did not hear it, for she did not utter it; she merely recited the canticle of the Sulamite, the bride who awaits her bridegroom and the return of her beloved.

Ordener stepped back into the gallery; he respected the maiden holding converse with the sky. Prayer is a great mystery, and his heart was involuntarily filled with unknown but profane ecstasy.

The door of the oratory was gently closed. Soon a light borne by a white figure moved toward him through the darkness. He stood still, for he felt one of the strongest emotions of his life; he leaned against the gloomy wall; his body was weak, and his limbs trembled beneath him. In the silence of his entire being the beating of his heart was plainly audible to his own ear.

As the young girl passed, she heard the rustle of a garment, and a quick, sudden gasp, and cried out in terror.

Ordener rushed forward. With one arm he supported her, with the other he vainly tried to grasp the lamp which she had dropped, and which went out.

"It is I," he said softly.

"It is Ordener!" said the girl; for the last echo of that voice, which she had not heard for a year, still rang in her ear.

And the moon, passing by, revealed the joy of her fair face. Then she repeated, in timid confusion, freeing herself from the young man's arms, "It is my lord Ordener."

"Himself, Countess Ethel."

"Why do you call me countess?"

"Why do you call me my lord?"

The young girl smiled, and was silent. The young man was silent, and sighed. She was first to break the silence.

"How came you here?"

"Pardon me, if my presence disturbs you. I came to see the count, your father."

"Then," said Ethel, in a changed tone, "you only came for my father's sake."

The young man bent his head, for these words seemed to him unjust.

"I suppose you have been in Throndhjem a long time," she continued reproachfully, "I suppose you have been here a long time already? Your absence from this castle cannot have seemed long to you."

Ordener, deeply wounded, made no reply.

"You are right," said the prisoner, in a voice which trembled with anger and distress; "but," she added, in a haughty tone, "I hope, my lord Ordener, that you did not overhear my prayers?"

"Countess," reluctantly replied the young man, "I did hear you."

"Ah! my lord Ordener, it was far from courteous to listen."

"I did not listen, noble Countess," said Ordener in a low voice; "I overheard you accidentally."

"I prayed for my father," rejoined the girl, looking steadily at him, as if expecting an answer to this very simple statement.

Ordener was silent.

"I also prayed," she continued uneasily, and apparently anxious as to the effect which her words might produce upon him, "I also prayed for some one who bears your name, for the son of the viceroy, Count Guldenlew. For we should pray for every one, even our persecutors."

And she blushed, for she thought she was lying; but she was offended with the young man, and she fancied that she had mentioned him in her prayer; she had only named him in her heart.

"Ordener Guldenlew is very unfortunate, noble lady, if you reckon him among the number of your persecutors; and yet he is very fortunate to possess a place in your prayers."

"Oh, no," said Ethel, troubled and alarmed by his cold manner, "no, I did not pray for him. I do not know what I did, nor what I do. As for the viceroy's son, I detest him; I do not know him. Do not look at me so sternly; have I offended you? Can you not forgive a poor prisoner,—you who spend your days in the society of some fair and noble lady, free and happy like yourself?"

"I, Countess!" exclaimed Ordener.

Ethel burst into tears; the young man flung himself at her feet.

"Did you not tell me," she continued, smiling through her tears, "that your absence seemed to you short?"

"Who, I, Countess?"

"Do not call me countess," said she, gently; "I am no longer a countess to any one, and far less to you."

The young man sprang up, and could not help clasping her to his heart in convulsive delight.

"Oh, my adored Ethel, call me your own Ordener! Tell me,"—and his ardent glances rested on her eyes wet with tears,—"tell me, do you love me still?"

The young girl's answer went unheard, for Ordener, carried away by his emotions, snatched from her lips with her reply that first favor, that sacred kiss, which in the sight of God suffices to make two lovers man and wife.

Both were speechless, because the moment was one of those solemn ones, so rare and so brief in this world, when the soul seems to feel something of celestial bliss. These instants when two souls thus converse in a language understood by no other are not to be described; then all that is human is hushed, and the two immaterial beings become mysteriously united for life in this world and eternity in the next.

Ethel slowly withdrew from Ordener's arms, and by the light of the moon each gazed into the other's face with ecstasy; only, the young man's eye of fire flashed with masculine pride and leonine courage, while the maiden's downcast face was marked by that modesty and angelic shame which in a virgin beauty are always blended with all the joys of love.

"Were you trying to avoid me just now," she said at last, "here in this corridor, my Ordener?"

"Not to avoid you. I was like the unfortunate blind man who is restored to sight after the lapse of long years, and who turns away from the light's first radiance."

"Your comparison is more applicable to me, for during your absence my only pleasure has been the presence of a wretched man, my father. I spent my weary days in trying to comfort him, and," she added, looking down, "in hoping for your coming. I read the fables of the Edda to my father, and when he doubted all men, I read him the Gospel, that at least he might not doubt Heaven; then I talked to him of you, and he was silent, which shows that he loves you. But when I had spent my evenings in vainly watching the arrival of travellers by various roads, and the ships which anchored in the harbor, he shook his head with a bitter smile, and I wept. This prison, where my whole past life has been spent, grew hateful to me; and yet my father, who until you came was all-sufficient for my wants, was still here; but you were not here, and I longed for that liberty which I had never known."

There was a charm which no tongue can express, in the maiden's eyes, in the simplicity of her love, and the sweet hesitation of her confession. Ordener listened with the dreamy delight of a being who has been removed from the world of reality to enjoy an ideal world.

"And I," said he, "no longer desire that liberty which you do not share!"

"What, Ordener!" quickly exclaimed Ethel, "will you leave us no more?"

These words recalled the young man to all that he had forgotten.

"My Ethel, I must leave you this very night. I will see you again to-morrow, and to-morrow I must leave you again, to remain until I may return never more to leave you."

"Alas!" mournfully broke in the girl, "must you leave me again?"

"I repeat, my beloved Ethel, that I will come back soon to wrest you from this prison or bury myself in it with you."

"A prisoner with him!" she said softly. "Ah! do not deceive me. Must I only hope for such happiness?"

"What oath do you require? What would you have me do?" cried Ordener; "tell me, Ethel, are you not my wife?" And in a transport of affection he pressed her to his heart.

"I am yours," she whispered.

The two pure and noble hearts throbbed rapturously together, and were but purer and nobler for the embrace.

At this moment a violent burst of laughter was heard close by. A man wrapped in a cloak opened a dark lantern which he had concealed, and the light suddenly revealed Ethel's alarmed, confused face and Ordener's proud but astonished features.

"Courage, my pretty pair! Courage! It strikes me that after so short a walk in the regions of Romance you can scarcely have followed all the windings of the stream of Sentiment, but that you must have taken a short-cut to reach the village of Kisses so quickly."

Our readers have doubtless recognized the lieutenant, who so cordially admired Mademoiselle de Scudéry. Roused from his reading of "Clelia" by the midnight bell, which the two lovers had failed to hear, he started on his nightly rounds. As he passed the end of the eastern corridor, he caught a few words, and saw what seemed two ghosts moving in the gallery by the light of the moon. Being naturally bold and curious, he hid his lantern under his cloak, and advanced on tiptoe to the two phantoms, so disagreeably awakened from their ecstasy by his sudden burst of laughter.

Ethel made a movement to escape from Ordener; then, returning to his side as if instinctively, and to ask his protection, she hid her burning blushes on her lover's breast.

He raised his head with all the dignity of a king.

"Woe," said he, "woe to him who has frightened and distressed you, Ethel!"

"Yes, indeed," said the lieutenant; "woe befall me if I am so unfortunate as to alarm so sensitive a lady!"

"Sir Lieutenant," haughtily exclaimed Ordener, "I command you to be silent!"

"Sir Insolent," replied the officer, "I command you to be silent!"

"Do you hear me?" returned Ordener in tones of thunder. "Buy pardon by your silence."

"*Tibi tua,*" responded the lieutenant; "take your own advice,—buy pardon by your silence!"

"Silence!" cried Ordener in a voice which made the windows shake; and seating the trembling girl in one of the old arm-chairs in the corridor, he grasped the officer rudely by the arm.

"Oh, clown!" said the lieutenant, half laughing, half angry; "don't you see that the doublet which you are so mercilessly crushing is made of the finest Abingdon velvet?"

Ordener looked him full in the face.

"Lieutenant, my patience is not so long as my sword."

"I understand you, my fine fellow," said the lieutenant with a sardonic smile. "You want me to do you the honor to fight with you. But do you know who I am? No, no, if you please! 'Prince with prince; clown with clown,' as the fair Leander has it."

"If he had added, 'Coward with coward,'" Ordener replied, "I should assuredly never have the distinguished honor of measuring weapons with you."

"I would not hesitate, most worthy shepherd, if you did but wear a uniform."

"I have neither lace nor fringes, Lieutenant; but I wear a sword."

The proud youth, flinging back his cloak, set his cap firmly on his head and grasped his sword-hilt, when Ethel, roused by such imminent danger, seized his arm and clasped his neck, with an exclamation of terror and entreaty.

"You are wise, my pretty mistress, if you do not want your young coxcomb punished for his temerity," said the lieutenant, who at Ordener's threats had put himself upon his guard without any show of emotion; "for Cyrus was about to quarrel with Cambyses,—if it be not too great an honor to compare this rustic to Cambyses."

"For Heaven's sake, Lord Ordener," said Ethel, "do not make me the cause and witness of such a misfortune!" Then lifting her lovely eyes to his, she added, "Ordener, I implore you!"

Ordener slowly replaced his half-drawn blade in its scabbard, and the lieutenant exclaimed,—

"By my faith, Sir Knight,—I do not know whether you be a knight, but I give you the title because you seem to deserve it,—let us act according to the laws of valor, if not of gallantry. The lady is right. Engagements like that which I believe you worthy to enter upon with me should not be witnessed by ladies, although—begging this charming damsel's pardon—they may be caused by them. We can therefore only properly discuss the *duellum remotum* here and now, and as the offended party if you will fix the time, place, and weapons, my fine Toledo blade on my Merida dagger shall be at the service of your chopping-knife from the Ashkreuth forges or your hunting-knife tempered in Lake Sparbo."

The "duel adjourned," which the officer suggested was usual in the North, where scholars aver that the custom of duelling originated.

The most valiant gentlemen offered and accepted a *duellum remotum.* It was sometimes deferred for several months, or even years, and during that space of time the foes must not allude by word or deed to the matter which caused the challenge. Thus in love both rivals forbore to see their sweetheart, so that things might remain unchanged. All confidence was put in the loyalty of a knight upon such a point; as in the ancient tournament, if the judges, deeming the laws of courtesy violated, cast their truncheon into the arena, instantly every combatant stayed his hand; but until the doubt was cleared up, the throat of the conquered man must remain at the selfsame distance from his victor's sword.

"Very well, Chevalier," replied Ordener, after a brief reflection; "a messenger shall inform you of the place."

"Good!" answered the lieutenant; "so much the better. That will give me time to go to my sister's wedding; for you must know that you are to have the honor of fighting with the future brother-in-law of a great lord, the son of the viceroy of Norway, Baron Ordener Guldenlew, who upon the occasion of this 'auspicious union,' as Artamenes has it, will be made Count Daneskiold, a colonel, and a knight of the Order of the Elephant; and I myself, who am a son of the lord high chancellor of both kingdoms, shall undoubtedly be made a captain."

"Very good, very good, Lieutenant d'Ahlefeld," impatiently exclaimed Ordener, "you are not a captain yet, nor is the son of the viceroy a colonel; and swords are always swords."

"And clowns always clowns, in spite of every effort to lift them to our own level," muttered the soldier.

"Chevalier," added Ordener, "you know the laws of duelling. You are not to enter this donjon again, and you are not to speak of this affair."

"Trust me to be silent; I shall be as dumb as Mutius Scævola when he held his hand on the burning coals. I will not enter the donjon again, nor permit any Argus of the garrison to do so; for I have just received orders to allow Schumacker to go unguarded in future, which order I was directed to convey to him to-night,—as I should have done had I not spent most of the evening in trying on some new boots from Cracow. The order, between you and me, is a very rash one. Would you like to have me show you my boots?"

During this conversation Ethel, seeing that their anger was appeased, and not knowing the meaning of a *duellum remotum,* had disappeared, first softly whispering in Ordener's ear, "To-morrow."

"I wish, Lieutenant d'Ahlefeld, that you would help me out of the fortress."

"Gladly," said the officer, "although it is somewhat late, or rather very early. But how will you find a boat?"

"That is my affair," said Ordener.

Then, chatting pleasantly, they crossed the garden, the circular courtyard, and the square court, Ordener escorted by the officer of the guard, meeting with no obstacle; they passed through the great gate, the ordnance-room, the parade-ground, and reached the low tower, whose iron doors opened at the lieutenant's order.

"Good-by, Lieutenant d'Ahlefeld," said Ordener.

"Good-by," replied the officer. "I declare that you are a brave champion, although I do not know who you are or whether those of your peers whom you may bring to our meeting will be entitled to assume the position of seconds, and ought not rather confine themselves to the modest part of witnesses."

They shook hands, the iron grating was closed, and the lieutenant went back, humming an air by Lully, to enjoy his Polish boots and French novel.

Ordener, left alone upon the threshold, took off his clothes, which he wrapped in his cloak and fastened upon his head with his sword-belt; then, putting into practice Schumacker's principles of independence, he sprang into the still, cold waters of the fjord, and swam through the darkness towards the shore, in the direction of the Spladgest, — a point which he was almost sure to reach, dead or alive.

The fatigues of the day had exhausted him, so that it was only with great difficulty that he landed. He dressed himself hastily, and walked towards the Spladgest, which reared its black bulk before him, the moon having been for some time completely veiled.

As he approached the building he heard the sound of voices; a faint light shone from the opening in the roof. Amazed, he knocked loudly at the square door. The noise ceased; the light disappeared. He knocked again. The light reappeared, and he saw a black figure climb out of the hole in the roof and vanish. Ordener knocked for the third time with the hilt of his sword, and shouted: "Open, in the name of his Majesty the King! Open, in the name of his Serene Highness the Viceroy!"

The door opened slowly, and Ordener found himself face to face with the pale features and tall, thin figure of Spiagudry, who, his clothes in disorder, his eyes fixed, his hair standing erect, his hands covered with blood, held a lamp, whose flame trembled less visibly than his long and lanky figure.

VI

Pirro. Never!

Angelo. What! I believe you would try to play the virtuous man. Wretch! If you utter a single word —

Pirro. But, Angelo, I beseech you, for the love of God —

Angelo. Do not meddle with what you cannot prevent.

Pirro. Ah! When the Devil holds one by a single hair, as well yield him the entire head. Unhappy that I am!

Emilia Galotti.

AN hour after the young traveller with the black plume left the Spladgest, night fell, and the crowd dispersed. Oglypiglap closed the outer door of the funereal structure, while his master, Spiagudry, gave the bodies deposited within a final sprinkling. Then both withdrew to their scantily furnished abode, and while Oglypiglap slept upon his wretched pallet, like one of the corpses intrusted to his care, the venerable Spiagudry, seated at

a stone table covered with old books, dried plants, and fleshless bones, was buried in grave studies which, although really very harmless, had done no little to give him a reputation among the people, for sorcery and witchcraft, — the disagreeable consequence of science at this period.

He had been absorbed in his meditations for some hours, and, ready at last to exchange his books for his bed, he paused at this mournful passage from Thormodr Torfesen: "When a man lights his lamp, death is beside him ere it be extinguished."

"With the learned doctor's leave," he muttered, "he shall not be beside me to-night."

And he took up his lamp to blow it out.

"Spiagudry!" cried a voice from the room where the corpses lay.

The old man shook from head to foot. Not that he believed, as another might have done in his place, that the gloomy guests of the Spladgest had risen in revolt against their master. He was enough of a scholar to be proof against such imaginary terrors; and his alarm was genuine, because he knew the voice which called him only too well.

"Spiagudry!" angrily repeated the voice, "must I come and pull off your ears before I can make you hear me?"

"Saint Hospitius have mercy, not on my soul, but on my body!" said the terrified old man; and with a step both hastened and delayed by fear, he moved towards the second side door, which he opened. Our readers have not forgotten that this door led into the mortuary.

His lamp lit up a strange and hideous scene, — on the one hand, the thin, tall, stooping figure of Spiagudry; on the other, a short, stout man, dressed from head to foot in the skins of wild beasts, still stained with dried blood, standing at the feet of Gill Stadt's corpse, which, with the dead bodies of the young girl and the captain, occupied the background. These three mute witnesses, buried in shadow, were the only ones who could behold, without flying in horror, the two living beings who now entered into conversation.

The features of the little man, thrown into vivid relief by the light, were singularly wild and fierce. His beard was red and bushy, and his forehead, hidden under an elkskin cap, seemed bristling with hair of the same color; his mouth was large, his lips thick, his teeth white, sharp, and far apart, his nose hooked like an eagle's beak; and his grayish-blue eyes, which were extremely quick, flashed a side glance at Spiagudry, in which the ferocity of a tiger was only tempered by the malice of a monkey. This singular character was armed with a broadsword, an unsheathed dagger, and a stone axe, upon whose long handle he leaned; his hands were covered with thick gloves made of a blue fox-skin.

"That old ghost keeps me waiting a long time," said he, as if talking to himself; and he uttered a sound like the roar of a wild beast.

Spiagudry would certainly have turned pale with fright, had he been capable of turning paler than he was.

"Do you know," continued the little man, addressing him directly, "that I come from Urchtal Sands? Do you want to change your straw bed for one of these beds of stone, that you keep me waiting thus?"

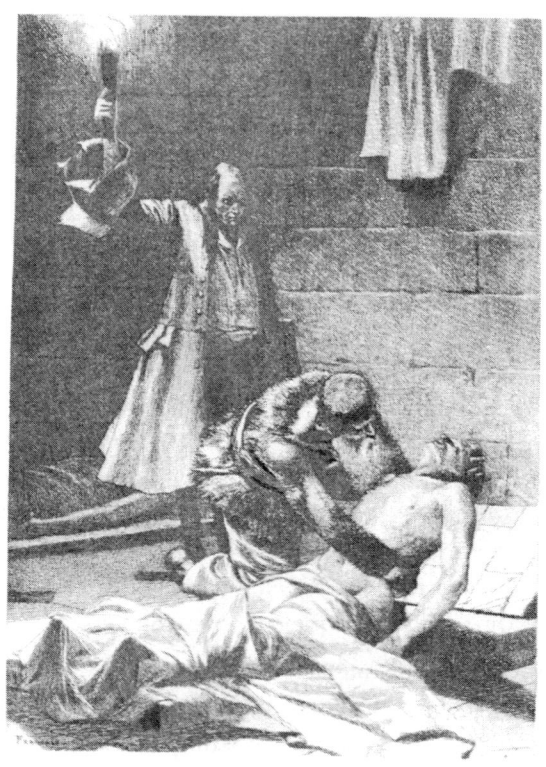

Hans of Iceland finding the Body of his Son, Gill Stadt.
Photo-Etching. — From drawing by François Flameng.

Spiagudry trembled more than ever; the two solitary teeth left to him chattered in his head.

"Excuse me, master," said he, bending his long back to a level with the little man; "I was asleep."

"Do you want me to make you acquainted with a far sounder sleep than that?"

Spiagudry's face assumed an expression of terror, the only thing which could be more comic than his expression of mirth.

"Well! what is it?" continued the little man. "What ails you? Is my presence disagreeable to you?"

"Oh, my lord and master!" replied the old keeper, "there can surely be no greater happiness for me than to see your Excellence."

And the effort which he made to twist his frightened face into a smile would have unbent the brow of any but the dead.

"Tailless old fox, my Excellence commands you to hand over the clothes of Gill Stadt."

As he uttered this name, the little man's fierce, mocking features grew dark and sad.

"Oh, master, pardon me, but I no longer have them!" said Spiagudry. "Your Grace knows that we are obliged to turn over the property of all workers in the mine to the Crown, the king inheriting by right of their being his wards."

The little man turned to the corpse, folded his arms, and said in a hollow voice: "He is right. These miserable miners are like the eider duck;[5] their nests are made for them, but their down is plucked from them."

Then raising the corpse in his arms and hugging it to his heart, he began to utter wild yells of love and grief, like the howls of a bear caressing her young. With these inarticulate sounds were blended, at intervals, a few words in a strange lingo, which Spiagudry did not understand.

He let the corpse drop back upon the stone, and turned towards the guardian.

"Do you know, accursed sorcerer, the name of the ill-fated soldier who was so unlucky as to be preferred by that girl to Gill?"

And he kicked the cold remains of Guth Stersen.

Spiagudry shook his head.

"Well! by the axe of Ingulf, the first of my race, I will exterminate every wearer of that uniform!" and he pointed to the officer's dress. "He on whom I must be avenged will surely be of the number. I will burn down the entire forest to consume the poisonous shrub that it contains. I swore it on the day that Gill died, and I have already given him a companion that will delight his corpse. Oh, Gill! so there you lie, lifeless and powerless,—you who outswam the seal, outran the deer; you who outwrestled the bear in the mountains of Kiölen. There you lie motionless,—you who traversed the province of Throndhjem, from the Orkel to the Lake of Miösen, in a single day; you who climbed the peaks of the Dovrefjeld as the squirrel climbs the oak. There you lie mute and dumb, Gill,—you who on the stormy summits of Kongsberg sang louder than the thunder's roar. Oh, Gill! so it is in vain that for your sake I filled up the Färöe mines; in vain for your sake I burned the Throndhjem cathedral. All my labor is in vain, and I shall never see the race of the children of Iceland, the descendants of Ingulf the Destroyer, perpetuated in you; you will never inherit my stone axe; but you leave me the legacy of your skull, from which I may henceforth drink sea-water and the blood of men."

With these words he seized the corpse by the head, exclaiming: "Help me, Spiagudry!" And pulling off his gloves, he displayed his broad hands, armed with long, hard, crooked nails, like the claws of a wild beast.

Spiagudry, seeing him about to hew off the corpse's head with his sword, cried out with unconcealed horror, "Good heavens! master! A dead man!"

"Well," calmly responded the little man, "would you rather have me sharpen my blade upon a living one?"

"Oh, let me entreat your Grace—How can your Excellency commit such profanation? Your Worship—Sir, your Serenity would not—"

"Are you done? Do I require all these titles, living skeleton, to believe in your deep respect for my sabre?"

"By Saint Waldemar! By Saint Usuph! In the name of Saint Hospitius, spare the dead!"

"Help me, and do not talk of saints to the devil!"

"My lord," continued the suppliant Spiagudry, "by your illustrious ancestor, Saint Ingulf—"

"Ingulf the Destroyer was an outlaw like myself."

"In the name of Heaven," said the old man, falling on his knees, "whose anger I would spare you!"

Impatience overcame the little man. His dull gray eyes flashed like a couple of live coals.

"Help me!" he repeated, flourishing his sword.

These words were uttered in the voice which might beseem a lion, could he speak. The keeper, shuddering and half dead with fright, sat down upon the black stone slab, and held Gill's cold, damp head in his hands, while the little man, by means of sword and dagger, removed the crown with rare skill.

When his task was done, he gazed at the bloody skull for some time, muttering strange words; then he handed it over to Spiagudry, to be cleaned and prepared, saying with a sort of howl,—

"And I, when I die, shall not have the comfort of thinking that an heir to the soul of Ingulf will drink sea-water and the blood of men from out my skull."

After a mournful pause, he added,—

"The hurricane is followed by a hurricane, each avalanche brings down another avalanche, but I shall be the last of my race. Why did not Gill hate every human face even as I do? What demon foe to the demon of Ingulf urged him into those fatal mines in search of a handful of gold?"

Spiagudry, who now returned with Gill's skull, interrupted him: "Your Excellency is right; even gold, as Snorri Sturleson says, may often be bought at too high a price."

"You remind me," said the little man, "of a commission I have for you; here is an iron casket which I found upon yonder officer, all of whose property, as you see, did not fall into your possession; it is so firmly fastened, that it must contain gold,—the only thing precious in the eyes of men. You will give it to widow Stadt, in Thoctree village, to pay her for her son."

He drew a small iron box from his reindeer-skin knapsack. Spiagudry received it with a low bow.

"Obey my orders faithfully," said the little man, with a piercing glance; "remember that nothing can prevent two demons from meeting; I think you are even more of a coward than a miser, and you will answer to me for that box."

"Oh, master, with my soul!"

"Not at all. With your flesh and bones."

At this moment the outer door of the Spladgest echoed with a loud knock. The little man was amazed; Spiagudry tottered, and shaded his lamp with his hand.

"Who is there?" growled the little man. "And you, old villain, how you will shake when you hear the last trump sound, if you shiver so now!"

A second and louder knock was heard.

"It is some dead man in haste to enter," said the little man.

"No, master," muttered Spiagudry, "no corpses are brought here after midnight."

"Living or dead, he drives me hence. You, Spiagudry, be faithful and be dumb. I swear to you, by the spirit of Ingulf and the skull of Gill, that you shall see the dead bodies of the entire regiment of Munkholm pass through your hostelry in review."

And the little man, binding Gill's skull to his belt, and drawing on his gloves, hurried, with the nimbleness of a goat, and by the help of Spiagudry's shoulders, through the opening in the roof, where he vanished.

A third knock shook the whole Spladgest, and a voice outside commanded him to open in the name of the king and viceroy. Then the keeper, moved alike by two different terrors,—one of which might be called the terror of memory, and the other of hope,—hurried toward the low door and opened it.

VII

In the pursuit of such pleasure as may be found in temporal felicity, she wore herself out, on rough and painful paths, without ever attaining her object. — *Confessions of Saint Augustine.*

RETURNING to his closet after leaving Poël, the governor of Throndhjem ensconced himself in a big easy-chair, and to distract his thoughts directed one of his secretaries to read over the petitions presented to the government.

Bowing low, the secretary began: —

"1. The Rev. Dr. Anglyvius prays that a substitute may be provided for the Rev. Dr. Foxtipp, the head of the Episcopal library, on account of his incompetency. The petitioner does not know who should take the place of the said incompetent doctor; he would merely state that he, Dr. Anglyvius, has for a long time exercised the functions of librari—"

"Send the rascal to the bishop," interrupted the general.

"2. Athanasius Munder, priest and chaplain to the prisons, asks pardon for twelve penitent convicts on the occasion of the glorious marriage of his Grace, Ordener Guldenlew, Baron Thorwick, Knight of the Dannebrog, son of the viceroy, and the noble lady Ulrica d'Ahlefeld, daughter of his Grace the lord high chancellor of the two kingdoms."

"Lay it on the table," said the general. "I pity convicts."

"3. Faustus-Prudens Destrombidès, Norwegian subject and Latin poet, asks leave to write the epithalamium for the said noble pair."

"Ah, ha! The worthy man must be growing old, for he is the same man who wrote an epithalamium in 1674, for the marriage planned between Schumacker, then Count of Griffenfeld, and Princess Louisa Charlotte of Holstein-Augustenburg, — a marriage which never took place. I fear," muttered the governor, "that Faustus-Prudens is destined to be the poet of broken matches. Lay his petition on the table, and go on. Inquire, on behalf of the said poet, if there be not a vacant bed at the Throndhjem hospital."

"4. The miners of Guldbrandsdal, the Färöe Islands, Sund-Moer, Hubfallo, Roeraas, and Kongsberg, petition to be released from the costs of the royal protectorate."

"These miners are restless. I hear that they are even beginning to grumble at our long delay in answering their petition. Let it be laid aside for mature consideration."

"5. Braal, fisherman, declares, in virtue of the Odelsrecht,[6] that he persists in his intention of buying back his patrimony.

"6. The magistrates of Nœs, Loevig, Indal, Skongen, Stod, Sparbo, and other towns and villages of Northern Throndhjem, pray that a price may be set upon the head of the assassin, thief, and incendiary, Hans, said to be a native of Klipstadur, in Iceland. Nychol Orugix, executioner for the province of Throndhjem, who claims that Hans is his property, opposes the petition. Benignus Spiagudry, keeper of the Spladgest, to whom the corpse should belong, supports the petition."

"That robber is a very dangerous fellow," said the general, "particularly now that we are threatened with trouble among the miners. Issue a proclamation offering a thousand crowns reward for his head."

"7. Benignus Spiagudry, doctor, antiquary, sculptor, mineralogist, naturalist, botanist, lawyer, chemist, mechanic, physicist, astronomer, theologian, grammarian—"

"Why," broke in the general, "is not this the same Spiagudry who keeps the Spladgest?"

"Yes, to be sure, your Excellency," replied the secretary,—"keeper, for his Majesty, of the institution of the Spladgest, in the royal city of Throndhjem, sets forth that he, Benignus Spiagudry, discovered that the stars called fixed are not lighted by the star called the sun; *item*, that the real name of Odin is Frigg, son of Fridulf; *item*, that the marine lobworm feeds on sand; *item*, that the noise of the inhabitants drives the fish away from the coast of Norway, so that the means of subsistence are growing less in proportion to the increase of the population; *item*, that the fjord known as Otte-Sund was formerly known as Limfjord, and only took the name of Otte-Sund after Otho the Red cast his spear into it; *item*, he sets forth that it was by his advice and under his direction that an old statue of Freya was changed into the statue of Justice, which now adorns the market-place in Throndhjem, and that the lion found at the feet of the idol has been turned into a devil, symbolizing crime; *item*—"

"Oh, spare me the rest of his eminent services! Let me see,—what does he want?"

The secretary turned over several pages, and went on:

"Your most humble petitioner feels that he may justly petition your Excellency, in return for so many useful labors in the domain of science and literature, to increase the reward to ten escalins for every corpse, male or female, which cannot but be gratifying to the dead, as proving the value set upon their bodies."

Here the door opened, and the usher in a loud voice announced, "The noble lady, Countess d'Ahlefeld."

At the same time a tall woman, wearing the small coronet of a countess, richly dressed in scarlet satin trimmed with gold fringe and ermine, entered, and accepting the hand which the general offered her, seated herself beside him.

The countess was perhaps fifty years old. Age had added little to the furrows with which pride and ambition had long since marked her face. She looked at the old governor haughtily, and with an artificial smile.

"Well, General, your ward delays. He should have been here before sunset."

"He would have been here, my lady Countess, if he had not gone to Munkholm upon his arrival."

"To Munkholm! I hope it was not to see Schumacker?"

"That may be."

"Could Baron Thorwick's first visit be to Schumacker!"

"Why not, Countess? Schumacker is unfortunate and unhappy."

"What, General! Is the viceroy's son on familiar terms with a prisoner of state?"

"When Frederic Guldenlew confided his son to my care, he begged me, noble lady, to bring him up as if he were my own. I thought that an acquaintance with Schumacker might be useful to Ordener, who is destined some day to wield such power; consequently, with the viceroy's permission, I obtained from my brother, Grummond de Knud, a permit to enter all the prisons, which I gave to Ordener. He often uses it."

"And how long, noble General, has Baron Ordener had the pleasure of this useful acquaintance?"

"Rather more than a year, Countess. It seems that Schumacker's society pleased him, for it kept him at Throndhjem for a long time; and it was only reluctantly, and by my express request, that he left the city last year to visit Norway."

"And does Schumacker know that his comforter is the son of one of his greatest enemies?"

"He knows that he is a friend, and that is enough for him, as for us."

"But you, General," said the countess, with a searching look, "when you tolerated—nay, encouraged—this connection, did you know that Schumacker had a daughter?"

"I knew it, noble Countess."

"And this fact seemed to you of no importance to your pupil?"

"The pupil of Levin de Knud, the son of Frederic Guldenlew, is an honest man. Ordener knows the barrier which separates him from Schumacker's daughter; he is incapable of winning the affection, unless his purpose was upright, of any girl, above all the daughter of an unfortunate man."

The noble Countess d'Ahlefeld blushed and paled. She turned away her head to avoid the calm gaze of the old man, as if it were that of an accuser.

"But," she stammered, "this connection strikes me, General,—let me speak my mind,—as strange and imprudent. It is said that the miners and tribes of the North are threatening to revolt, and that the name of Schumacker is mixed up with the affair."

"Noble lady, you surprise me!" exclaimed the governor. "Schumacker has hitherto borne his misfortunes calmly. The report is doubtless ill-founded."

At this moment the door opened, and the usher announced that a messenger from his Grace the lord high chancellor wished to speak with the noble countess.

The lady rose hurriedly, took leave of the governor, and while he continued his inspection of the petitions she hastened to her apartments in a wing of the palace, directing that the messenger should follow her.

She had been seated on a rich sofa in the midst of her women for a few instants only, when the messenger entered. The countess on seeing him made a slight gesture of aversion, which she hid at once by a friendly smile.

And yet the messenger's appearance was not at all repulsive. He was a man of somewhat diminutive stature, whose plumpness suggested anything else rather than a messenger. Still, a close study of his face showed it to be frank to the point of impudence, and his look of good-humor had a spice of deviltry and malice. He bowed low to the countess, and offered her a package sealed with silk thread.

"Noble lady," said he, "deign to permit me to venture to lay at your feet a precious message from his Grace your illustrious husband, my revered master."

"Is he not coming himself? And why did he choose you as his messenger?" inquired the countess.

"Important business delays the coming of his Grace, as this letter will inform you, Madam. For myself, I am by the orders of my noble master to enjoy the distinguished honor of a private interview with you."

The countess turned pale, and exclaimed in a trembling voice, "With me,—me, Musdœmon?"

"If it distresses the noble lady in the slightest degree, her unworthy servant will be reduced to despair."

"Distress me! No, of course not," returned the countess, trying to smile. "But is this conversation so essential?"

The messenger bowed down to the ground.

"Absolutely essential. The letter which the illustrious countess has deigned to receive from my hands probably contains a formal order to that effect."

It was strange to see the proud Countess d'Ahlefeld tremble and turn pale before a servant who paid her such profound respect. She slowly opened the package and read its contents. After a second reading she turned to her women, and said in a faint voice: "Go; leave us alone."

"I hope the noble lady," said the messenger, bending his knee, "will deign to pardon the liberty which I venture to take and the trouble which I seem to cause her."

"On the contrary," replied the countess, with a forced smile, "I assure you that I am very happy to see you."

The women withdrew.

"Elphega, have you forgotten that there was a time when you were not averse to being alone with me?"

It was the messenger who addressed the noble countess, and the words were accompanied by a laugh like that uttered by the Devil, at the instant that his compact expires and he seizes the soul which sold itself to him.

The great lady bowed her humbled head.

"Would that I had indeed forgotten it!" she murmured.

"Poor fool! Why should you blush for things which no human eye ever saw?"

"God sees what men do not see."

"God, weak woman! You are not worthy to deceive your husband, for he is less credulous than you."

"Your insults to my remorse are scarcely generous, Musdœmon."

"Well, if you feel remorse, Elphega, why insult it yourself by daily committing fresh crimes?"

The Countess d'Ahlefeld hid her face in her hands; the messenger continued: "Elphega, you must choose: remorse and more crimes, or crime and no more remorse. Do as I do: choose the second course; it is better—at least it is more cheerful."

"Heaven grant," said the countess, in low tones, "that those words may not be counted against you in eternity."

"Come, my dear, a truce to jest."

Then Musdœmon, seating himself behind the countess, and putting his arm about her neck, added: "Elphega, try to be, at least in imagination, what you were twenty years ago."

The unfortunate countess, the slave of her accomplice, strove to respond to his loathsome caresses. There was something too revolting, even for these degraded souls, in this adulterous embrace of two beings who scorned and despised each other. The illegal caresses which had once delighted them, and which some horrible and unknown expediency compelled them still to lavish upon each other, now tortured them. Strange but just change of guilty affections! Their crime had become their punishment.

The countess, to cut short this guilty torment, at last asked her odious lover, tearing herself from his arms, with what verbal message her husband had charged him.

"D'Ahlefeld," said Musdœmon, "just as he was about to see his power confirmed by the marriage of Ordener Guldenlew to our daughter—"

"Our daughter!" exclaimed the haughty countess; and she fixed her eye on Musdœmon with a look of pride and contempt.

"Well," coldly continued the messenger, "I think that Ulrica is at least as much mine as his. I was saying that the match would not be wholly satisfactory to your husband unless Schumacker could at the same time be destroyed. In his remote prison the old favorite is yet almost as much to be dreaded as in his palace. He has obscure but powerful friends at court,—

powerful because they are obscure; and the king, learning a month since that the chancellor's negotiations with the Duke of Holstein-Ploen were at a standstill, cried out impatiently: 'Griffenfeld knew more than all of them put together.' A schemer named Dispolsen, come from Munkholm to Copenhagen, had several secret interviews with him, after which the king sent to the chancellor's office for Schumacker's patents of nobility and title-deeds. No one knows the object of Schumacker's ambition; but if he desire nothing but his liberty, for a prisoner of state that is the same as to desire power! He must therefore die, and must die by authority of justice; we are now striving to invent a crime for him. Your husband, Elphega, on the plea of inspecting the northern provinces incognito, will assure himself of the result of our underhand dealings among the miners, whom we hope to incite to rebel, in Schumacker's name, which revolt we can easily put down later. What troubles us is the loss of certain important papers relating to this plot, and which we have every reason to believe have fallen into the hands of Dispolsen. Knowing that he had set out to return to Munkholm, carrying to Schumacker his parchments, his diplomas, and possibly these documents which might ruin, or at least compromise us, we posted certain faithful men in the gorges of Kiölen, directing them to rid us of him, after robbing him of his papers. But if, as we are assured, Dispolsen left Bergen by water, our efforts in that quarter are in vain. However, as I came along I gathered vague reports of the murder of a captain by the name of Dispolsen. We shall see. Meantime we are searching for a famous bandit, Hans, called Hans of Iceland, whom we wish to put at the head of the revolt in the mines. And you, my dear,—what news have you for me here? Has the pretty bird at Munkholm been caught in her cage? Has the old minister's daughter finally fallen a prey to our *falco fulvus*, our son Frederic?"

The countess, recovering her pride, again exclaimed: "Our son!"

"I' faith, how old may he be? Twenty-four. We have known each other some twenty-six years, Elphega."

"God knows," cried the countess, "my Frederic is the chancellor's lawful heir."

"If God knows it," laughingly replied the messenger, "the Devil does not. Moreover, your Frederic is but a presumptuous youngster, quite unworthy of me, and it is not worth our while to quarrel for such a trifle. He is only fit to make love to a girl. Has he at least succeeded?"

"Not yet, so far as I know."

"Oh, Elphega, do try to play a less passive part in our affairs. The count and myself, as you see, are tolerably active. I return to your husband to-morrow. For mercy's sake, do not confine yourself to praying for our sins, like the Madonna whom the Italians invoke when about to commit a murder! D'Ahlefeld, too, must see to rewarding me a little more munificently than he has hitherto done. My fortune is closely connected with yours; but I am tired of being the husband's servant when I am the wife's lover, and of being only the tutor, the teacher, the pedagogue, when I am almost the father."

At this instant midnight struck, and one of the women entered, reminding the countess that by the palace regulations all lights must be put out at that hour.

The countess, glad to end a painful interview, recalled her attendants.

"Permit me, gracious Countess," said Musdœmon, as he withdrew, "to retain a hope of seeing you to-morrow, and to lay at your feet my homage and sincere respect."

VIII

It cannot be but thou hast murdered him;
So should a murderer look; so dead, so grim!
Shakespeare: *Midsummer Night's Dream*.

"UPON my honor, old man," said Ordener to Spiagudry, "I began to think that the corpses who lodge in this building would have to open the door."

"Excuse me, sir," replied the keeper, in whose ears the names of king and viceroy still rang, as he repeated his trite excuse, "I was—I was sound asleep."

"Then I suppose your dead men do not sleep, and it was probably they whom I heard talking just now."

Spiagudry was confused.

"You—stranger,—you—heard?"

"Oh, yes! but what does it matter? I did not come here to meddle with your affairs, but to interest you in mine. Let us go inside."

Spiagudry was by no means anxious to allow the new-comer to see Gill's body, but these last words comforted him considerably; and besides, how could he prevent his entrance?

He accordingly allowed the young man to pass, and closing the door, said: "Benignus Spiagudry is at your service in all that relates to human science; yet if, as your unseasonable visit seems to show, you suppose that you are dealing with a sorcerer, you are wrong; *ne famam credas*; I am only a learned man. Enter my laboratory, stranger."

"Not at all," said Ordener; "my errand is with these corpses."

"These corpses!" said Spiagudry, beginning to tremble again. "But, sir, you cannot see them."

"What! I cannot see bodies which are placed here for the sole purpose of being seen! I repeat, that I wish to question you concerning one of them; it is your duty to answer. Obey cheerfully, old man, or you will be forced to obey."

Spiagudry had a sincere respect for swords, and he saw the flash of steel at Ordener's side.

"*Nihil non arrogat armis*," he muttered; and fumbling with his bunch of keys, he opened the grating, and admitted the stranger into the second section of the hall.

"Show me the captain's clothes," said the latter.

At this instant a ray from the lamp fell upon Gill Stadt's bloody head.

"Good God!" exclaimed Ordener, "what abominable sacrilege!"

"Great Saint Hospitius, pity me!" sighed the poor keeper.

"Old man," continued Ordener, in threatening tones, "are you so remote from the tomb that you can safely violate the respect which is its due? And do you not fear, wretched fellow, that the living will teach you what you owe to the dead?"

"Oh," cried the poor keeper, "mercy! It was not I! If you only knew—" And he stopped; for he remembered the little man's words: "Be faithful, be dumb." "Did you see any one escape through that aperture?" he asked faintly.

"Yes; was it your accomplice?"

"No; it was the guilty man, the only guilty man! I swear it by all the torments of hell, by all the blessings of heaven, by this same body so infamously profaned!" and he fell upon the pavement before Ordener.

Hideous as Spiagudry was, there was yet an accent of truth in his despair and protestations, which convinced the young man.

"Old man," said he, "rise; and if you did not outrage death, do not degrade age."

The keeper rose. Ordener continued: "Who is the culprit?"

"Oh, silence, noble youth! You know not of whom you speak. Silence!"

And Spiagudry mentally repeated: "Be faithful, be dumb."

Ordener answered coldly: "Who is the culprit? I must know!"

"In Heaven's name, sir, do not say so! Be silent, for fear—"

"Fear will not silence me, but shall make you speak."

"Excuse me; forgive me, young master!" said the agonized Spiagudry. "I cannot."

"You can, for I insist. Tell me the profaner's name!"

Spiagudry still strove to evade.

"Well, noble master, the profaner of this corpse is the assassin of that officer."

"Then that officer was murdered?" asked Ordener, reminded, by this abrupt transition, of the object of his search.

"Yes, undoubtedly, sir."

"And by whom,—by whom?"

"In the name of the saint on whom your mother called when she gave you birth, do not seek to know his name, young master; do not force me to reveal it."

"If my desire to know it required any spur, you would add it, old man, in the shape of curiosity. I command you to name the murderer."

"Well, then," said Spiagudry, "see these deep wounds, made by long, sharp nails on the body of this unfortunate man. They will name the assassin."

And the old man showed Ordener a number of ugly scratches on the naked, freshly washed corpse.

"What!" said Ordener, "was it some wild beast?"

"No, my young lord."

"But unless it was the Devil—"

"Hush! Beware, lest your guesses come too close to the mark. Did you never hear," added the keeper in a low voice, "of a man or a monster with human face, whose nails are as long as those of Ashtaroth who ruined us all, or of Antichrist who will yet destroy us?"

"Speak more plainly."

"'Woe unto you!' says the Apocalypse—"

"I demand the assassin's name!"

"The assassin—his name? My lord, have pity on me; have pity on yourself!"

"The second of those prayers would destroy the first, even if serious reasons did not compel me to tear that name from your lips. Abuse my patience no longer."

"So be it, if you insist, young man," said Spiagudry, raising himself, and in a loud voice. "The murderer, the profaner, is Hans of Iceland."

This terrible name was not unknown to Ordener.

"What!" he cried, "Hans! that execrable bandit!"

"Do not call him a bandit, for he has no followers."

"Then, wretch, how do you know him? What common crimes have brought you together?"

"Oh, noble master, do not stoop to believe in appearances. Is the oak-tree poisonous because the serpent finds shelter within its trunk?"

"No idle words! A scoundrel has no friend who is not an accomplice."

"I am not his friend, and still less his accomplice; and if all my oaths fail to convince you, sir, let me implore you to observe that this monstrous sacrilege exposes me, twenty-four hours hence, when Gill Stadt's body is to be removed, to the torture allotted to those guilty of profanation, and thus casts me into the most fearful state of anxiety ever endured by innocent man."

These considerations of personal interest moved Ordener more than the suppliant voice of the poor keeper, much of whose pathetic though useless resistance to the little man's sacrilegious act they had doubtless inspired. Ordener reflected a moment, while Spiagudry tried to read in his face whether this pause meant peace or boded a storm.

At last he said, in a severe though quiet tone: "Old man, speak the truth! Did you find any papers upon that officer?"

"None, upon my honor."

"Do you know if Hans of Iceland found any?"

"I swear by Saint Hospitius that I do not know."

"You do not know? Do you know where this Hans of Iceland hides?"

"He never hides; he roams about perpetually."

"Perhaps; but where is his den?"

"That pagan," whispered the old man, "has as many dens as the island of Hitteren has reefs, or the dog-star rays."

"I order you again," broke in Ordener, "to speak in plain terms. Let me set you an example; hearken. You are mysteriously allied with a brigand, whose accomplice you still declare that you are not. If you know him, you must know where he has gone. Do not interrupt me. If you are not his accomplice, you will not hesitate to lead me in search of him!"

Spiagudry could not contain his fright.

"*You*, noble lord! *you*,—great God! full of youth and life,—*you* would provoke, seek out that demon! When four-armed Ingiald fought the giant Nyctolm, at least, he had four arms!"

"Well," said Ordener, with a smile, "if four arms are a requisite, will you not be my guide?"

"I! your guide! How can you jest with an old man who almost needs a guide himself?"

"Listen," replied Ordener; "do not try to jest with me. If this profanation, of which I would fain believe you innocent, exposes you to be punished for sacrilege, you cannot stay here. You must fly. I offer you my protection, but on condition that you lead me to the brigand's lair. Be my guide, I will be your saviour. Nay, more: if I catch Hans of Iceland, I shall bring him here, dead or alive. You can then prove your innocence, and I promise to restore your office. Stay; meantime, here are more coins than your place brings you in a year."

Ordener, by keeping his purse until the last, had observed that gradation in his arguments required by the wholesome laws of logic. They were strong enough in themselves to make Spiagudry consider. He began by taking the money.

"Noble master, you are right," said he; and his eye, hitherto vague and uncertain, was fixed upon Ordener. "If I follow you, I incur the future vengeance of the terrible Hans. If I stay, I fall to-morrow into the hands of Orugix the hangman. What is the penalty of sacrilege? Never mind. In either case, my poor life is in danger; but as, according to the wise remark of Saemond-Sigfusson, otherwise called the Sage, *inter duo pericula æqualia, minus imminens eligendum est*, I will follow you. Yes, sir, I will be your guide. Pray do not forget, however, that I have done all I could to dissuade you from your daring scheme."

"Very good," said Ordener. "Then you will be my guide. Old man," he added, with a meaning glance, "I count upon your fidelity."

"Oh, master!" replied the keeper, "Spiagudry's faith is as pure as the gold which you so graciously gave me."

"Let it remain so, or I will show you that the steel which I bear about me is as sterling as my gold. Where do you think Hans of Iceland is?"

"Why, as the southern part of the province of Throndhjem is full of troops sent thither on some errand of the lord chancellor, Hans must have gone in the direction of Walderhog cave, or toward Lake Miösen. Our road lies through Skongen."

"When can you start?"

"At the close of the day now dawning, when night falls and the Spladgest is closed, your poor servant will begin his duties as your guide, for which he must deprive the dead of his care. We will try to hide the mutilation of the miner from the eyes of the people for this one day."

"Where shall I meet you to-night?"

"In the market-place, if it please my master, near the statue of Justice, which was formerly Freya, and which will doubtless protect me with her shadow, in gratitude for the fine devil which I had carved at her feet."

Spiagudry would probably have repeated the terms of his petition to the governor, had not Ordener interrupted him.

"Enough, old man; it is a bargain."

"A bargain," repeated the keeper.

He had scarcely uttered these words, when a low growl was heard above their heads. The keeper shuddered.

"What is that?" he said.

"Is there not," asked Ordener, equally surprised, "any other living being dwelling here besides yourself?"

"You remind me of my assistant, Oglypiglap," replied Spiagudry, reassured by the thought. "It was probably his snores which we heard. A sleeping Lapp, Bishop Arngrimmsson says, makes as much noise as a waking woman."

As they talked, they approached the door of the Spladgest. Spiagudry opened it softly.

"Good-by, young sir," he said to Ordener; "may Heaven keep you merry. Good-by until to-night. If your road lead you by the cross of Saint Hospitius, deign to utter a prayer for your wretched servant, Benignus Spiagudry."

Then hastily closing the door, as much through fear of being seen as to guard his lamp from the early morning breezes, he returned to Gill's corpse, and did his best so to arrange it that the wound might not be perceived.

Many reasons combined to persuade the timid keeper to accept the stranger's perilous offer. The motives for his bold resolve may be ranked as follows: (1) fear of Ordener here and now; (2) dread of Orugix the hangman; (3) an ancient grudge against Hans of Iceland,—a grudge which he scarcely dared acknowledge even to himself, so strong was the power of fear; (4) a love of science, which would benefit largely by his journey; (5) confidence in his own cunning, which would enable him to evade Hans; (6) a wholly speculative attraction for certain metal contained in the young adventurer's purse, and probably also in the iron casket stolen from the captain and intended for Widow Stadt, a message which now ran a great risk of never leaving the messenger's hands.

Still another and a final reason was the well or ill founded hope of returning sooner or later to the post which he was about to desert. Besides, what did it matter to him whether the robber killed the traveller, or the traveller the robber? At this point in his meditations he could not help saying aloud: "It will be one more corpse for me, anyhow."

Another growl was heard, and the unhappy keeper shivered.

"Indeed, that is not Oglypiglap's snore," said he; "that noise comes from without."

Then, after a moment's thought, he added: "How silly I am to be so frightened! The dog on the wharf probably waked and barked."

Then he finished his arrangement of Gill's disfigured remains, and closing all the doors, threw himself upon his mattress to sleep off the fatigue of the past night and gain strength for the coming one.

IX

Juliet. Oh, think'st thou we shall ever meet again?
Romeo. I doubt it not: and all these woes shall serve
For sweet discourses in our time to come.
Shakespeare: *Romeo and Juliet.*

THE signal-light at Munkholm castle had just been extinguished, and in its place the sailor entering Throndhjem fjord saw the helmet of the soldier on guard gleam from afar in the beams of the rising sun like a planet moving in its orbit, when Schumacker, leaning on his daughter's arm, came down as usual into the garden which surrounded his prison. Both had spent a restless night,—the old man unable to sleep, the maiden kept awake by happy thoughts. They walked in silence for a time; then the aged prisoner said, fixing a sad and serious gaze upon the lovely girl:—

"You blush and smile at your own thoughts, Ethel; you are happy, for you have no cause to blush for the past, and you smile at the future."

Ethel blushed still deeper, and her smile faded.

"My lord and father," she stammered in confusion, "I brought the volume containing the Edda."

"Very well; read, my daughter," said Schumacker; and he resumed his meditations.

Then the melancholy captive, seated on a black rock shaded by a dark fir, listened to his daughter's sweet voice without heeding the words which she read, as a thirsty traveller delights in the murmur of the stream that quenches his fever.

Ethel read him the story of the shepherdess Allanga, who refused a king until he proved himself a warrior. Prince Ragnar-Lodbrok could not win the maid until he returned triumphant over the robber of Klipstadur, Ingulf the Destroyer.

Suddenly a sound of footsteps and the rustling of the foliage interrupted the reading and roused Schumacker from his revery. Lieutenant d'Ahlefeld appeared from behind the rock upon which they sat. Ethel's head drooped as she recognized their tormentor, and the officer exclaimed:—

"I' faith, fair lady, your lovely lips just uttered the name of Ingulf the Destroyer. I heard you, and I presume that you were talking of his grandson, Hans of Iceland, and that reminded you of him. Ladies love to talk of robbers. By the way, there are tales of Ingulf and his descendants which are both fearful and interesting. Ingulf the Destroyer had but one son, born of the witch Thoarka; that son also had but one son, whose mother was likewise a witch. For four centuries the race has been perpetuated thus for the desolation of Iceland, there being always a single scion, who never produces more than one offshoot. By this series of solitary heirs the infernal spirit of Ingulf has been handed down to the present day, and flourishes in the famous Hans of Iceland, who was doubtless so happy as to occupy your virgin thoughts just now."

The officer paused for an instant. Ethel was silent from embarrassment, Schumacker from vexation. Delighted to find them willing, if not to answer, at least to listen, he added,—"The Klipstadur outlaw's one passion is a hatred of the human race, his one thought to harm them."

"He is wise," abruptly remarked the old man.

"He always lives alone," resumed the lieutenant.

"He is fortunate," said Schumacker.

The lieutenant was charmed by this double interruption, which seemed to seal a compact for conversation.

"May the god Mithra preserve us," he cried, "from such wise men and such fortunate men! Accursed be the evil-minded zephyr which brought the last demon of Iceland to Norway. I was wrong to say evil-minded, for they say it was a bishop to whom we owe the pleasure of possessing Hans of Klipstadur. If we may believe the story, certain Iceland peasants, having captured little Hans among the Bessestad mountains in his infancy, were about to kill him, as Astyages slew the Bactrian lion's whelp; but the bishop of Sealholt interfered, and took the cub under his own protection, hoping to make a Christian of the devil. The good bishop tried in a thousand ways to develop his infernal intellect, forgetting that the hemlock cannot be changed into a lily even in the hot-houses of Babylon. So when the young devil grew up, he repaid all this care by escaping one fine night upon the trunk of a tree, across the seas, lighting his flight by setting the bishop's house on fire. That's the old women's account of the way this Icelander came to Norway, and now, thanks to his education, he affords us a perfect type of the monster. Since then the destruction of the Färöe mines, the death of three hundred men crushed beneath the ruins, the overthrow of the hanging rock at Golyn at midnight upon the village below, the fall of Half-Broer bridge from the rocks upon the high-road, the burning of Throndhjem cathedral, the extinction of beacon-lights upon the coast on stormy nights, and countless crimes and murders hidden in Lakes Sparbo or Miösen, or concealed in the caves of Walderhog and Rylass, and in the gorges of the Dovrefjeld, bear witness to the presence of this Ahriman[7] incarnate in the province of Throndhjem. The old women declare that a new hair grows in his beard with every fresh crime; in that case his beard must be as luxuriant as that of the most venerable Assyrian magi. Yet you must have heard, fair lady, how often the governor has tried to stop the extraordinary growth of that beard."

Schumacker again broke the silence.

"And has every effort to capture this fellow," he asked with a look of triumph and an ironical smile, "been unsuccessful? I congratulate the chancellor."

The officer did not understand the ex-chancellor's sarcasm.

"Hans has hitherto proved as invincible as Horatius Cocles. Old soldiers, young militiamen, country boors, mountaineers, all fly or die before him. He is a demon who can neither be avoided nor caught; the best luck that can befall those who go in search of him is not to find him. You may be surprised, gracious lady," he went on, seating himself familiarly beside Ethel, who drew nearer to her father, "at all my curious anecdotes concerning this supernatural being. It was not without a purpose that I collected these strange traditions. It seems to me—and I shall be pleased if you, fair lady, share my opinion—that the adventures of Hans would make a delicious romance, after the style of Mademoiselle de Scudéry's sublime stories, 'Artamenes,' or 'Clelia,' only six volumes of which latter I have yet read, but it is none the less a masterpiece in my eyes. Of course we should have to soften our climate, dress up our traditions, and modify our barbarous names. For instance, Throndhjem, which I should call 'Durtinianum,' should see its forests converted, by a touch of my magic wand, into delightful groves watered by a thousand streamlets far more poetic than our hideous torrents. Our dark, deep caves should give place to charming grottos carpeted with gilded pebbles and azure shells. In one of these grottos should live a famous magician, Hannus of Thule. For you must own that the name Hans of Iceland is by no means agreeable. This giant,—you must feel that it would be absurd not to make the hero of such a work a giant,—this giant should descend in a direct line from the god Mars (Ingulf the Destroyer affords no food for imagination) and the enchantress Theona,—don't you think I have made a happy change in the name Thoarka?—daughter of the Cumean sibyl. Hannus, after being educated by the great Magian of Thule, should finally escape from the pontiff's palace in a car drawn by two dragons,—it would be very narrow-minded to cling to the shabby old legend of the trunk of a tree. Reaching the land of Durtinianum, and ravished by that enchanting region, he should choose it as the place of his abode and the scene of his crimes. It would be no easy matter to draw an agreeable picture of the robberies of Hans. However, we might soften their horror by an ingeniously planned love-affair. The shepherdess Alcyppe, walking one day with her lamb in a grove of myrtles and olives, should be noticed by the giant, who should suddenly yield to the magic of her eyes. But Alcyppe should love the handsome Lycidas, an officer of the militia, garrisoned in her village. The giant should be annoyed by the centurion's happiness, and the centurion by the giant's attentions. You can fancy, dear lady, how charming such imaginative powers might make the adventures of Hannus. I will wager my Polish boots against a pair of slippers that such a subject, treated by Mademoiselle de Scudéry, would set all the women in Copenhagen wild with delight."

The last words roused Schumacker from the melancholy thoughts in which he had been buried during the lieutenant's fruitless display of brains.

"Copenhagen!" he exclaimed. "What news is there from Copenhagen, sir officer?"

"None, i' faith, that I know of," replied the lieutenant, "save that the king has given his consent to the great marriage which is just now occupying the thoughts of both kingdoms."

"What!" rejoined Schumacker; "what marriage?"

The appearance of a fourth speaker arrested the words on the lieutenant's lips.

All three looked up. The prisoner's moody features brightened, the lieutenant's frivolous face grew grave, and Ethel's sweet countenance, which had been pale and confused during the officer's long soliloquy, again beamed with life and joy. She sighed heavily, as if her heart were eased of an intolerable weight, and her sad smile rested upon the new-comer. It was Ordener.

The old man, the girl, and the officer were placed in a singular position toward Ordener; they had each a secret in common with him, therefore each felt embarrassed by the presence of the other. Ordener's return to the donjon was no surprise to Schumacker or Ethel, who were expecting him; but it amazed the lieutenant as much as the sight of the lieutenant astonished Ordener, who might have feared some indiscretion on the part of the officer in regard to the scene of the previous night, if the silence ordained by the etiquette of duelling had not reassured him. He could therefore only be surprised at seeing him quietly seated between his two prisoners.

These four persons could say nothing while together, for the very reason that they would have had much to say had they been alone. Therefore, aside from glances of intelligence and embarrassment, Ordener met with an absolutely silent reception.

The lieutenant burst out laughing.

"By the train of the royal mantle, my dear new-comer, here's a silence by no means unlike that of the senators of Gaul when Brennus the Roman — Upon my honor, I have forgotten which were the Romans and which the Gauls, — the senators or the general. Never mind. Since you are here, help me to enlighten this worthy old gentleman as to the news. I was just about to tell him, when you made your sudden entry on the stage, about the famous marriage which is now absorbing both Medes and Persians."

"What marriage?" asked Ordener and Schumacker with a single voice.

"By the cut of your clothes, sir stranger," cried the lieutenant, clapping his hands, "I guessed that you came from some other world. Your present question turns my doubt to certainty. You must have landed only yesterday on the banks of the Nidder in a fairy-car drawn by two winged dragons; for you could not have travelled through Norway without hearing of the wonderful marriage of the viceroy's son and the lord chancellor's daughter."

Schumacker turned to the lieutenant.

"What! Is Ordener Guldenlew to marry Ulrica d'Ahlefeld?"

"As you say," replied the officer; "and it will all be settled before the fashion of French farthingales reaches Copenhagen."

"Frederic's son must be about twenty-two years old, for I had been in Copenhagen fortress a year when the news of his birth reached me. Let him marry young," added Schumacker with a bitter smile. "When disgrace comes upon him, at least no one can accuse him of having aspired to a cardinal's hat."

The old favorite alluded to one of his own misfortunes, of which the lieutenant knew nothing.

"No, indeed," said he, laughing heartily. "Baron Ordener will receive the title of count, the collar of the Order of the Elephant, and a colonel's epaulettes, which would scarcely match with the cardinal's hat."

"So much the better," answered Schumacker. Then after a pause he added, shaking his head as if he saw his revenge before him, "Some day they may make an iron collar of his fine order; they may break his count's coronet over his head; they may strike him in the face with his colonel's epaulettes."

Ordener seized the old man's hand.

"For the sake of your hatred, sir, do not curse an enemy's good fortune before you know whether it be good fortune in his eyes."

"Pooh!" said the lieutenant. "What are the old fellow's railings to Baron Thorwick?"

"Lieutenant," cried Ordener, "they may be more to him than you think. And," he added, after a brief silence, "your grand marriage is not so certain as you suppose."

"*Fiat quod vis,*" rejoined the lieutenant, with an ironical bow; "the king, the viceroy, and the chancellor have, it is true, made every arrangement for the wedding; but if it displeases you, Sir Stranger, what matter the lord chancellor, the viceroy, and the king!"

"You may be right," said Ordener, seriously.

"Oh, by my faith!"—and the lieutenant threw himself back in a fit of laughter,—"this is too good! How I wish Baron Thorwick could hear a fortune-teller so well instructed in regard to the things of this world decide his fate. Believe me, my learned prophet, your beard is not long enough for a good sorcerer."

"Sir Lieutenant," coldly answered Ordener, "I do not think that Ordener Guldenlew will ever marry a woman whom he does not love."

"Ha, ha! here we have the Book of Proverbs. And who tells you, Sir Greenmantle, that the baron does not love Ulrica d'Ahlefeld?"

"And, if it please you, in your turn, who tells you that he does?"

Here the lieutenant, as often happens, was led by the heat of the conversation into stating a fact of which he was by no means certain.

"Who tells me that he loves her? The question is absurd. I am sorry for your powers of divination; but everybody knows that this match is no less a marriage of inclination than of convenience."

"At least, everybody but me," said Ordener, gravely.

"Except you? So be it. But what difference does that make? You cannot prevent the viceroy's son from being in love with the chancellor's daughter."

"In love?"

"Madly in love!"

"He must indeed be mad to be in love with her."

"Hullo! don't forget of whom and to whom you speak. Would not one say that the son of the viceroy could not take a fancy to a lady without consulting this clown?"

As he spoke, the officer rose. Ethel, who saw Ordener's face flush, hurried toward him.

"Oh!" said she, "pray be calm; do not heed these insults. What does it matter to us whether the viceroy's son loves the chancellor's daughter or not?"

The gentle hand laid on the young man's heart stilled the tempest raging within. He cast an enraptured glance at his Ethel, and did not hear the lieutenant, who, recovering his good-humor, exclaimed: "The lady acts with infinite grace the part of the Sabine woman interceding between her father and her husband. My words were rather heedless; I forgot," he added, turning to Ordener, "that there is a bond of brotherhood between us, and that we can no longer provoke each other. Chevalier, give me your hand. Confess, you too forgot that you were speaking of the viceroy's son to his future brother-in-law, Lieutenant d'Ahlefeld."

At this name Schumacker, who had hitherto looked on with an indifferent or merely an impatient eye, sprang from his stone seat with a terrible cry: "D'Ahlefeld! A D'Ahlefeld here! Serpent! How could I fail to recognize the abominable father in his son? Leave me in peace in my cell! I was not condemned to the punishment of seeing you. It only needs, as he desired just now, that the son of Guldenlew should join the son of d'Ahlefeld! Traitors! cowards! why do they not come themselves to enjoy my tears of madness and rage? Abhorred, abhorred race! Son of d'Ahlefeld leave me!"

The officer, at first bewildered by the sharpness of these invectives soon lost his temper and found his speech.

"Silence, lunatic! Cease your devilish litanies!"

"Leave me! leave me!" repeated the old man; "and take my curse, my curse upon you and the miserable race of Guldenlew, which is to be allied to you!"

"By Heaven!" exclaimed the enraged officer, "you insult me doubly!"

Ordener restrained the lieutenant, who was beside himself with passion.

"Respect an old man, even if he be your enemy, Lieutenant; we have already one question to settle together, and I will answer to you for the prisoner's offences."

"So be it," said the lieutenant; "you contract a double debt. The fight will be to the death, for I have both my brother-in-law and myself to avenge. Think that with my gauntlet you pick up that of Ordener Guldenlew."

"Lieutenant d'Ahlefeld," replied Ordener, "you espouse the cause of the absent with a warmth which proves your generosity. Would there not be as much in showing pity for an unfortunate old man to whom adversity gives some right to be unjust?"

D'Ahlefeld was one of those souls in whom virtue is kindled by praise. He pressed Ordener's hand, and approached Schumacker, who, exhausted by his emotion, had sunk back upon the rock, in the tearful Ethel's arms.

"Lord Schumacker," said the officer, "you abused the privileges of your age, and I might have abused the privileges of my youth, if you had not found a champion. I enter your prison this morning for the last time, for I come to tell you that you may henceforth remain, by special order of the viceroy, free and unguarded in this donjon. Receive this good news from the lips of an enemy."

"Go!" said the old prisoner, in a hollow voice.

The lieutenant bowed and obeyed, inwardly pleased that he had won the approving glance of Ordener.

Schumacker sat for some time with folded arms and bent head, buried in thought. Suddenly he looked up at Ordener, who stood before him in silence.

"Well?" said he.

"My lord Count, Dispolsen was murdered."

The old man's head again drooped upon his breast. Ordener went on: His assassin is a noted robber,—Hans of Iceland."

"Hans of Iceland!" said Schumacker.

"Hans of Iceland!" repeated Ethel.

"He robbed the captain," added Ordener.

"And so," said the old man, "you heard nothing of an iron casket, sealed with the arms of Griffenfeld?"

"No, my lord."

Schumacker hid his face in his hands.

"I will restore it to you, my lord Count; trust me. The murder was committed yesterday morning. Hans fled toward the north. I have a guide who knows all his haunts. I have often roamed through the mountains of Throndhjem. I shall overtake the thief."

Ethel turned pale. Schumacker rose; his expression was almost joyful, as if he believed that virtue still existed in men.

"Noble Ordener," he said, "farewell." And raising his hand to heaven, he disappeared among the bushes.

As Ordener turned, he saw Ethel upon the moss-grown rock, pale as an alabaster image on a black pedestal.

"Good God, Ethel!" he cried, rushing to her and supporting her in his arms, "what is the matter?"

"Oh!" replied the trembling girl in scarcely audible tones. "Oh, if you have, I do not say a spark of love, but of pity for me, sir, if you did not speak yesterday only to deceive me, if it be not to cause my death that you have deigned to enter this prison, Lord Ordener, my Ordener, give up, in Heaven's name, in the name of all the angels,—give up your mad scheme! Ordener, my beloved Ordener!" she continued,—and her tears flowed freely, her head rested on the young man's breast,—"make this sacrifice for me. Do not follow this robber, this frightful demon, with whom you would fight. In whose interest do you go, Ordener? Tell me, what interest can be dearer to you than that of the wretched woman whom but yesterday you called your beloved wife?"

She stopped, choked by sobs. Both arms were thrown around Ordener's neck, and her pleading eyes were fixed upon his.

"My adored Ethel, you are needlessly alarmed. God helps the righteous cause, and the interest in which I expose myself is no other than your own. That iron casket contains—"

Ethel interrupted him: "My interest! Have I any other interest than your life? Ordener, what will become of me?"

"Why do you think that I shall die, Ethel?"

"Ah! Then you do not know this Hans,—this infernal thief? Do you know what a monster you pursue? Do you know that he is lord of all the powers of darkness; that he overthrows mountains upon towns; that subterranean caverns crumble beneath his tread; that his breath extinguishes the beacons on every rocky coast? And how can you suppose, Ordener, that you can resist this giant aided by the demon, with your white arms and feeble sword?"

"And your prayers, Ethel, and the thought that I am fighting for you? Be assured, Ethel, the bandit's strength and power have been greatly exaggerated. He is a man like ourselves, who deals out death until he himself be slain."

"Then you will not heed me? My words are nothing to you? Tell me, what is to become of me if you go; if you roam from danger to danger, exposing—for I know not what earthly interest—your life, which is mine, by yielding it to a monster?"

Here the lieutenant's tales recurred anew to Ethel's fancy, exaggerated by her love and terror. She went on in a voice broken by sobs: "I assure you, dear Ordener, they deceived you who told you that he was only a man. You should believe me rather than others, Ordener; you know that I would not mislead you. Thousands have tried to do battle with him; he has destroyed whole regiments. I only wish others would tell you the same; you might believe them and not go."

Poor Ethel's prayers would doubtless have shaken Ordener's bold resolve, if he had not gone so far. The words uttered by Schumacker in his despair on the previous evening came back to him and strengthened him in his purpose.

"I might, my dear Ethel, tell you that I would not go, and yet carry out my plan; but I will never deceive you, even to console you. I ought not, I repeat, to hesitate between your tears and your true interests. Your fortune, your happiness, perhaps your life,—your very life, my Ethel,—are at stake." And he clasped her affectionately in his arms.

"And what do I care?" she returned, weeping. "My friend, my Ordener, my delight,—for you know that you are my sole delight,—do not give me a fearful and certain misery in exchange for a slight and doubtful misfortune. What is fortune or life to me?"

"Your father's life, Ethel, is also at stake."

She tore herself from his arms.

"My father's life?" she repeated in a low voice, turning pale.

"Yes, Ethel. This brigand, doubtless bribed by Count Griffenfeld's enemies, has in his possession papers whose loss imperils the life of your father, already the object of so many attacks. I would die to win back those papers."

Ethel was pale and dumb for some moments. Her tears were dried, her heaving breast labored painfully; she looked on the ground with a dull and indifferent gaze,—the gaze of the condemned man as the axe is lifted over his head.

"My father's life!" she sighed.

Then she slowly turned her eyes toward Ordener.

"What you do is useless; but do it."

Ordener pressed her to his bosom. "Oh, noble girl, let me feel your heart beat against mine! Generous friend! I will soon return. Nay, you shall soon be mine; I would save your father, that I may better deserve to be his son. My Ethel, my beloved Ethel!"

Ordener bidding Ethel farewell.
Photo-Etching.—From drawing by Démarest.

Who can describe the emotions of a true heart which feels that it is appreciated by another noble heart? And if the love uniting these two similar souls be an indissoluble bond, who can paint their indescribable raptures? It seems as if they must feel, crowded into one brief instant, all the joy and all the glory of life, embellished by the charm of generous sacrifice.

"Oh, my Ordener, go; and if you never return, grief will kill me. I shall have that tardy consolation."

Both rose, and Ordener placed Ethel's arm within his own, and took that adored hand in his. They silently traversed the winding alleys of the gloomy garden, and reluctantly reached the gate which led into the world.

There, Ethel, drawing a pair of tiny gold scissors from her bosom, cut off a curl of her beautiful black hair.

"Take it, Ordener; let it go with you; let it be happier than I am."

Ordener devotedly pressed to his lips this gift from his beloved.

She added: "Ordener, think of me; I will pray for you. My prayers may be as potent with God as your arms with the demon."

Ordener bowed before this angel. His soul was too full for words. They remained clasped in each other's arms for some time. As they were about to part, perhaps forever, Ordener, with a sad thrill, enjoyed the happiness of holding Ethel to his heart once more. At last, placing a long, pure kiss upon the sweet girl's clouded brow, he rushed violently down the winding stairs, which a moment later echoed with the sweet and painful word, "Farewell!"

X

You would never think her unhappy. Everything about her
speaks of happiness. She wears necklaces of gold, and purple
robes. When she goes out, a throng of vassals lie prostrate
in her path, and obedient pages spread carpets before her
feet. But none see her in the solitude that she loves; for then
she weeps, and her husband does not see her tears. — I am
that miserable being, the spouse of an honorable man, of a
noble count, the mother of a child whose smiles stab me to
the heart. — Maturin: *Bertram*.

THE Countess d'Ahlefeld rose after a sleepless night to face a restless
day. Half-reclining on a sofa, she pondered the bitter after-taste of corrupt
pleasures, and the crime which wastes life in ecstasy without enjoyment
and grief without alleviation. She thought of Musdœmon, whom guilty
illusions had once painted in such seductive colors, so frightful now that she
had penetrated his mask and seen his soul through his body. The wretched
woman wept, not because she had been deceived, but because her eyes were
no longer blinded, — tears of regret, but not of repentance; therefore her
tears afforded her no relief. At this moment her door was opened. She dried
her eyes quickly, and turned away, annoyed at being surprised, for she had
given orders that she was not to be disturbed. On seeing Musdœmon her
vexation changed to fright, which was dispelled when she found that her
son Frederic was with him.

"Mother," cried the lieutenant, "how does it happen that you are here?
I thought you were at Bergen. Have our fine ladies taken to running about
the country?"

The countess received Frederic with kisses, to which, like all spoiled
children, he responded very coldly. This was possibly the worst of
punishments to the unhappy woman. Frederic was her beloved son, the
only creature in the world for whom she felt an unselfish affection; for a
degraded woman often, even when all sense of wifely duty has vanished,
retains some trace of the mother.

"I see, my son, that when you heard I was in Throndhjem you hastened
to me at once."

"Oh, no; not I. I was bored to death at the fort; so I came to town, where I met Musdœmon, who brought me here."

The poor mother sighed heavily.

"By the way, mother," continued Frederic, "I am very glad to see you, for you can tell me whether knots of pink ribbon on the hem of the doublet are still worn in Copenhagen. Did you think to bring me a flask of that Oil of Youth to whiten the skin? You did not forget, I hope, the last French novel, or the pure gold lace which I asked you to get for my scarlet cloak, or those little combs which are so much used just now to hold the curls in place, or—"

The poor woman had brought nothing to her son, the only love she had on earth.

"My dear boy, I have been ill, and my sufferings prevented my thinking of your pleasures."

"Have you been ill, mother? Well, are you better now? By the bye, how is my pack of Norman hounds? I'll wager that they have neglected to bathe my monkey in rose-water every night. You'll see that I shall find my parrot Bilboa dead on my return. When I am away no one thinks of my pets."

"At least your mother thinks of you, my son," said his mother in a faltering voice.

Had this been the inexorable hour when the destroying angel hurls sinful souls into everlasting torments, he would have felt pity for the torture which at this instant wrung the heart of the unfortunate countess. Musdœmon laughed in his sleeve.

"Sir Frederic," said he, "I see that the steel sword has no desire to rust in its iron scabbard. You do not care to lose the wholesome traditions of Copenhagen drawingrooms within the walls of Munkholm. But yet, allow me to ask you, what is the use of all this Oil of Youth, these pink ribbons, and little combs? What is the use of all these preparations for a siege, if the only feminine fortress within the walls of Munkholm is impregnable?"

"Upon my honor, she is," laughingly responded Frederic. "Certainly, if I have failed, General Schack himself would fail. But how can you surprise a fortress where nothing is exposed,—where every post is unremittingly guarded? How can you contend against chemisettes which cover all but the neck, against sleeves that hide the whole arm, so that only the face and hands remain to prove that the young woman is not as black as the Emperor of Mauritania? My dear tutor, you yourself would have to go to school again. Believe me, that fort is not to be taken where Modesty is garrisoned."

"Indeed!" said Musdœmon. "But may not Modesty be forced to surrender, if Love lay siege to it, instead of confining himself to a blockade of delicate attentions?"

"Labor in vain, my dear friend. Love is already in possession of the place, but he serves to reinforce Modesty."

"Ah, Sir Frederic, this is news indeed, — with Love on your side — "

"And who tells you, Musdœmon, that he is on my side?"

"On whose, then?" exclaimed Musdœmon and the countess, who had listened in silence until now, but who was reminded of Ordener by the lieutenant's last words.

Frederic was about to answer, and was already preparing a spicy account of the scene of the previous night, when he remembered the silence prescribed by the etiquette of duelling, which changed his gayety to confusion.

"I' faith," said he, "I don't know, — that of some clown perhaps, some retainer."

"Some soldier of the garrison?" said Musdœmon, laughing heartily.

"What, my son!" exclaimed the countess in her turn. "Are you sure that she loves a rustic, a serf? What luck, if you are sure of it!"

"Oh, of course I am sure. But it's not one of the soldiers of the garrison," added the lieutenant, with an offended air. "I am sure enough of what I say, however, to beg you, mother, to cut short my very unnecessary exile at that confounded castle."

The countess's face brightened on hearing of the young girl's fall. Ordener Guldenlew's eagerness to visit Munkholm now appeared to her in very different colors. She gave her son the benefit of them.

"You must give us an account, Frederic, of Ethel Schumacker's loves. I am not surprised; the daughter of a boor can only love a boor. Meantime, do not curse that castle which yesterday afforded you the honor of the first advances towards an acquaintance, from a certain distinguished personage."

"What, mother!" said the lieutenant, staring at her, — "what distinguished personage?"

"A truce to jests, my son. Did no one visit you yesterday? You see that I know all about it."

"I' faith, more than I do, Mother. Deuce take me if I saw a face yesterday, except those of the masks carved beneath the cornices of those old towers."

"What, Frederic! You saw nobody?"

"No one, mother!"

In omitting to mention his antagonist of the donjon, Frederic obeyed the law which bound him to silence; besides, could that clodhopper be counted as any one?

"What!" said his mother. "Did not the viceroy's son visit Munkholm last night?"

The lieutenant laughed.

"The viceroy's son! Indeed, mother, you must be dreaming, or else you are joking."

"Neither, my son. Who was on guard yesterday?"

"I myself, mother."

"And you did not see Baron Ordener?"

"Not a bit of it," repeated the lieutenant.

"But consider, my boy, he may have entered in disguise. You never saw him, having been brought up at Copenhagen, while he was educated at Throndhjem. Remember all the stories about his caprices and whims, and his eccentric ideas. Are you sure, my son, that you did not see any one?"

Frederic hesitated an instant.

"No," he cried, "no one. I can say no more."

"Then," replied the countess, "I suppose the baron did not go to Munkholm."

Musdœmon, at first surprised like Frederic, had listened attentively. He interrupted the countess.

"Allow me, noble lady. Master Frederic, pray tell me the name of the dependent loved by Schumacker's daughter."

He repeated his question; for Frederic, who for some moments had been lost in thought, did not hear him.

"I do not know; or rather—no, I do not know."

"And how, sir, do you know that she loves a dependent?"

"Did I say so? A dependent?—well, yes; he is a dependent."

The awkwardness of the lieutenant's position increased momentarily. This series of questions, the ideas to which they gave rise, his enforced silence, threw him into a confusion which he feared he could not much longer control.

"Upon my word, Mr. Musdœmon, and you, my lady mother, if a mania for asking questions be the latest fashion, you may amuse yourselves by questioning each other. For my part, I'll have nothing more to say to you."

And flinging open the door, he disappeared, leaving them plunged in an abyss of doubt. He hastened down into the courtyard, for he heard Musdœmon's voice calling him back.

He mounted his horse and rode toward the harbor, where he intended to take a boat for Munkholm, thinking that there he might find the stranger who had given rise to such serious thoughts in the greatest feather-brain of a feather-brained capital.

"If that was Ordener Guldenlew," he reflected, "then my poor Ulrica — But no; it is impossible that he could be such a fool as to prefer the penniless daughter of a prisoner of State to the wealthy daughter of an all-powerful minister. At any rate, Schumacker's daughter can be no more than a caprice; and there is nothing to hinder a man who has a wife from having a mistress too; in fact, it is quite the stylish thing. But no, it was not Ordener. The viceroy's son would never wear such a shabby jacket. And that old black plume without a buckle, beaten by the wind and rain! And that great cloak, big enough for a tent! And that disordered hair, with no combs and no frizzes! And those boots with iron spurs, covered with mud and dust! Indeed, it could never be he. Baron Thorwick is a knight of the Dannebrog. That fellow wore no decoration. If I were a knight of the Dannebrog, I believe I should wear the collar of the order to bed. Oh, no! He had never even read 'Clelia.' No, it was not the viceroy's son."

XI

If man could still retain his warmth of soul when experience has taught him, if he could inherit the legacies of time without bending beneath the weight, he would never attack those exalted virtues whose first lesson is ever self-sacrifice.—Madame de Staël: *Germany.*

"WELL, what is it? You, Poël! what brings you here?"

"Your Excellency forgets that you yourself summoned me."

"Did I?" said the general. "Oh, I wanted you to hand me that portfolio."

Poël handed the governor the portfolio, which he could have reached himself by stretching out his arm.

His Excellency mechanically replaced it without opening it; then he turned over some papers in an absentminded way.

"Poël, I was going to ask you—What time is it?"

"Six o'clock in the morning," replied the general's servant, who was facing the clock.

"I was going to tell you, Poël—What is the news to-day at the palace?"

The general went on shuffling his papers, writing a few words on each with a preoccupied air.

"Nothing, your Excellency, except that we are still expecting my noble master, about whom I see the general is anxious."

The general rose from his big writing-table, and looked at Poël somewhat angrily.

"Your eyes are very poor, Poël. I, anxious about Ordener, indeed! I know the reason for his absence; I do not expect him yet."

General Levin de Knud was so jealous of his authority that he would have considered it compromised had a subaltern been able to guess his secret thoughts, and learn that Ordener had acted without his orders.

"Poël," he added, "you may go."

The servant left the room.

"Really," exclaimed the general when he was left alone, "Ordener uses and abuses his privileges. A blade too often bent will break. To make me spend a night in sleepless impatience! To expose General Levin to the sarcasms of a chancellor's wife and the conjectures of a servant! And all this that an aged enemy may have those first greetings which are due to an old friend! Ordener! Ordener! whims are destructive of liberty! Let him come, only let him come now, deuce take me if I don't receive him as gunpowder does fire,—I'll blow him up! To expose the governor of Throndhjem to a servant's conjectures and a she-chancellor's sarcasms! Let him come!"

The general went on making marginal notes on his papers without reading them, so all-absorbing was his ill-temper.

"General! my noble father!" cried a familiar voice; and Ordener clasped in his arms the old man, who did not even try to repress a cry of joy.

"Ordener, my good Ordener! Zounds! how glad I am!" He collected his thoughts in the middle of his phrase. "I am glad, Baron, that you have learned to control your feelings. You seem pleased to see me again. It was probably to mortify your flesh, that you deprived yourself of that pleasure for a whole day and night."

"Father, you have often told me that an unfortunate enemy should be put before a fortunate friend. I come from Munkholm."

"Of course," said the general, "when the enemy's misfortune is imminent. But Schumacker's future—"

"Looks more threatening than ever. Noble General, there is an odious plot on foot against that unlucky man. Men born his friends, would ruin him; a man born his foe, must serve him."

The general, whose face had gradually cleared, interrupted Ordener.

"Very good, my dear Ordener. But what are you talking about? Schumacker is under my protection. What men? What plots?"

Ordener could scarcely have replied plainly to this question. He had but very vague gleams of light, very uncertain suspicions as to the position of the man for whom he was about to expose his life. Many will think that he acted foolishly; but young hearts do what they think right by instinct, and not from calculation; and besides, in this world, where prudence is so barren and wisdom so caustic, who denies that generosity is folly? All is relative on earth, where all is limited; and virtue would be the greatest madness if there were no God behind man. Ordener was at the age to believe and to be believed. He risked his life trustingly. Even the general accepted reasons which would not have borne calm discussion.

"What plots? What men? Good father, in a few days I shall have solved the mystery; then you shall know all that I know. I must start off again to-night."

"What!" cried the old man, "can you spare me but a few hours? Where are you going? Why are you going, my dear son?"

"You have sometimes allowed me, my noble father, to perform a praiseworthy act in secret."

"Yes, my brave boy; but you are going without knowing why, and you know what an important affair requires your presence here."

"My father has given me a month to consider the matter, and I shall devote that time to the interests of another. A good deed is often fruitful in good advice. Besides, we will see about it on my return."

"How!" anxiously asked the general; "don't you like this match? They say that Ulrica d'Ahlefeld is very beautiful. Tell me, have you seen her?"

"I believe I have," said Ordener. "Yes, I believe that she is handsome."

"Well?" rejoined the governor.

"Well," said Ordener, "she will never be my wife."

These cold, decisive words startled the general as if he had received a violent blow. He recalled the suspicions of the haughty countess.

"Ordener," said he, shaking his head, "I ought to be wise, for I have sinned. Well, I am nothing but an old fool! Ordener, the prisoner has a daughter—"

"Oh," cried the young man, "General, I wanted to speak to you of her. I ask your protection, father, for that helpless and oppressed young girl."

"Indeed," said the governor, gravely, "your request is urgent."

Ordener recovered himself.

"And why should it not be urgent for a poor captive whose life, and, what is far more precious, her honor, is in danger?"

"Life! honor! Why, I still govern here, and I know nothing of all these horrors! Explain yourself."

"Noble father, the lives of the prisoner and his defenceless daughter are threatened by an infernal plot."

"What you say is serious. What proofs have you?"

"The oldest son of a powerful family is even now at Munkholm. He is there to seduce Countess Ethel; he told me so himself."

The general started back.

"Good God! Poor, forlorn creature! Ordener, Ordener, Ethel and Schumacker are under my protection. Who is this wretch? What is the name of the family?"

Ordener approached the general and wrung his hand.

"It is the D'Ahlefeld family."

"D'Ahlefeld!" said the governor. "Yes, it is all clear. Lieutenant Frederic is at Munkholm now. My noble Ordener, would they marry you to such a brood! I understand your aversion, Ordener."

The old man, folding his arms, thought for some moments, then clasped Ordener in his embrace.

"Ordener, you may go. Your friends shall not lack protection; I will guard them. Yes, go; you are perfectly right. That infernal Countess d'Ahlefeld is here; did you know it?"

"The noble lady, Countess d'Ahlefeld," said the usher, opening the door.

At that name, Ordener mechanically withdrew to the back of the room; and the countess, entering without seeing him, exclaimed, —

"General, your pupil is deceiving you. He never went to Munkholm."

"Indeed?" said the general.

"Good gracious, no! My son Frederic, who has just left the palace, was on duty yesterday in the donjon, and he saw no one."

"Really, noble lady?" repeated the general.

"So," added the countess, with a triumphant smile, "you need not wait for your Ordener any longer, General."

The governor was cold and calm.

"I am no longer expecting him, Countess, it is true."

"General," said the countess, turning, "I thought we were alone. Who is this?"

The countess looked searchingly at Ordener, who bowed.

"Really," she continued, "I never saw him but once; still, if it were not for that dress, I should say — General, is this the viceroy's son?"

"Himself, noble lady," said Ordener, with another bow.

The countess smiled.

"In that case, permit a lady who will soon be more closely allied to you, to ask where you were yesterday, Count?"

"Count! I do not think that I am so unfortunate as to have lost my noble father yet, my lady countess."

"Certainly not; that was not my meaning. It is better to become a count by taking a wife than by losing a father."

"One is no better than the other, noble lady."

The countess, although slightly confused, made up her mind to laugh heartily.

"Come, the stories that I have heard are true. Your manners are somewhat boorish; but you will grow more used to accepting gifts from fair hands when Ulrica d'Ahlefeld has put the chain of the Order of the Elephant about your neck."

"A chain indeed!" said Ordener.

"You will see, General Levin," resumed the countess, whose laugh was somewhat forced, "that your intractable pupil will not consent to receive his colonel's brevet from a lady's hand either."

"You are right, Countess," replied Ordener; "a man who wears a sword ought not to owe his epaulettes to a petticoat."

The great lady's face darkened.

"Ho! ho! whence comes the baron? Is it really true that your Highness was not at Munkholm yesterday?"

"Noble lady, I do not always satisfy all questions. But, General, you and I will meet again."

Then, pressing the old man's hand and bowing to the countess, he quitted the room, leaving the lady, amazed at the extent of her own ignorance, alone with the governor, who was furious at the amount of his knowledge.

XII

The fellow that sits next him now, parts bread with him, and pledges the breath of him in a divided draught, is the readiest man to kill him.—Shakespeare: *Timon of Athens.*

IF the reader will transport himself to the highway leading from Throndhjem to Skongen, a narrow, stony road which skirts Throndhjem Fjord until it reaches the village of Vygla, he will not fail to hear the footsteps of two travellers, who left the city by what is known as Skongen Gate, at nightfall, and are rapidly climbing the range of hills up which the path to Vygla winds. Both are wrapped in cloaks. One walks with a firm, youthful step, his body erect and his head well up; the point of his sword hangs below the hem of his cloak, and in spite of the darkness, we see the plume in his cap waving in the breeze. The other is rather taller than his companion, but slightly bent; upon his back is a hump, doubtless formed by a wallet which is hidden by his large black mantle, whose ragged edges bear witness to its long and faithful service. His only weapon is a stick, with which he supports his rapid and uneven steps.

If darkness prevent our reader from distinguishing the features of the two travellers, he may perhaps recognize them by the conversation which one of them opens after an hour of silent, consequently tedious travel.

"Master, my young master! we have reached the point from which Vygla tower and Throndhjem spires may both be seen at the same time. Before us, on the horizon, that black mass is the tower; behind us lies the cathedral; its flying buttresses, darker still against the sky, stand out like the skeleton ribs of a mammoth."

"Is Vygla far from Skongen?" asked the other wayfarer.

"We have to cross the Ordals, sir; we shall not reach Skongen before three o'clock in the morning."

"What hour is that striking now?"

"Good heavens, master! you make me shiver. Yes, that is Throndhjem clock; the wind brings the sound to us. That's a sign of storm. The northwest wind brings clouds."

"In truth, the stars have all disappeared behind us."

"Pray let us make haste, my noble lord, the storm is close at hand, and Gill's corpse and my escape may already have been discovered in the city. Let us make haste!"

"Willingly. Old man, your load seems heavy; give it to me, I am younger and stronger than you."

"No, indeed, noble master; it is not for the eagle to carry the shell of the tortoise. I am too far beneath you for you to burden yourself with my wallet."

"But, old man, if it tires you? It seems heavy. What have you in it? Just now you stumbled, and it clinked as if there were iron in it."

The old man sprang away from the young man.

"It clinked, master? Oh, no! you are mistaken. It contains nothing—but food, clothes. No, it does not tire me, sir."

The young man's friendly offer seemed to give his old comrade a fright which he tried to disguise.

"Well," replied the young man, without noticing it, "if your bundle does not tire you, keep it."

The old man, although his fears were set at rest, made haste to change the conversation.

"It is hard to travel by night as fugitives, over a road which it would be so agreeable, sir, to take by day as observers of Nature. On the shores of the fjord, to our left, are a quantity of Runic stones, upon which may be studied inscriptions traced, they say, by gods and giants. On our right, behind the rocks at the edge of the road, lies the salt-marsh of Sciold, which undoubtedly communicates with the sea by some subterranean passage; for the sea lobworm is caught there, that strange fish, which, as your servant and guide discovered, eats sand. It was in the Vygla tower, which we are now approaching, that the pagan king Vermond roasted the breasts of Saint Etheldreda, that glorious martyr, with wood from the true cross, brought to Copenhagen by Olaf III., and conquered from him by the Norwegian king. They say that since then repeated attempts have been made to turn that cursed tower into a chapel; every cross placed there, is consumed in its turn by fire from heaven."

At this instant a tremendous flash of lightning covered the fjord, the hill, the rocks, the tower, and faded before the two travellers could distinguish any of these objects. They instinctively paused, and the lightning was almost immediately followed by a violent peal of thunder, which echoed from cloud to cloud across the sky, and from rock to rock along the earth.

They raised their eyes. All the stars were hidden, huge clouds rolled rapidly over one another, and the tempest hung like an avalanche above their heads. The tremendous blast, before which all these masses fled, had not yet descended to the trees, which no breath stirred, and upon which no drop of rain had as yet fallen. The roar of the storm was heard aloft, and this, with the noise of the fjord, was the only sound to be heard in the darkness of the night, made doubly dark by the blackness of the tempest.

This tumultuous silence was suddenly interrupted, close beside the travellers, by a growl which made the old man tremble.

"Omnipotent God!" he cried, grasping the young man's arm, "that is either the laugh of the Devil in the storm, or the voice of—"

A fresh flash, a fresh peal, cut short his words. The tempest then burst with fury, as if it had only waited this signal. The travellers drew their cloaks closer, to protect themselves alike from the rain falling in torrents from the clouds, and from the thick dust swept in whirlwinds from the dry earth by a howling blast.

"Old man," said the youth, "a flash of lightning just now showed me Vygla tower on our right; let us leave the path and seek shelter there."

"Shelter in the Cursed Tower!" exclaimed the old man; "may Saint Hospitius protect us! Think, young master; that tower is deserted."

"So much the better, old man! We shall not be kept waiting at the door."

"Think of the abominable act which polluted it!"

"Well, let it purify itself by sheltering us. Come, old man, follow me. I tell you that on such a night I would test the hospitality of a den of thieves."

Then, in spite of the old man's remonstrances, he grasped his arm and hastened toward the building, which, as the frequent flashes showed him, was close at hand. As they approached, they saw a light in one of the loopholes of the tower.

"You see," said the young man, "that this tower is not deserted. You feel easier now, no doubt."

"Oh, my God! my God!" cried the old man, "where are you taking me, master? Saint Hospitius forbid that I should enter that oratory of the Devil!"

They had now reached the foot of the tower. The young traveller knocked loudly at the new door of this much dreaded ruin.

"Calm yourself, old man. Some pious hermit has come hither to sanctify this profane abode by dwelling in it."

"No," said his comrade, "I will not enter. I'll answer for it that no monk can live here, unless he has one of Beelzebub's seven chains for a chaplet."

However, a light had descended from one narrow window to another, and now shone through the key-hole.

"You are very late, Nychol!" cried a sharp voice; "the gallows was erected at noon, and it takes but six hours to come from Skongen to Vygla. Did you have an extra job?"

These questions were asked just as the door was opened. The woman who opened it, seeing two strange faces instead of the one which she expected, uttered a frightened, threatening shriek, and started back.

Her appearance was by no means reassuring. She was tall; she held above her head an iron lamp, which threw a bright light upon her face. Her livid features, her bony, angular figure, were corpse-like, and her hollow eyes emitted ominous flashes like those of a funeral torch. She wore a red serge petticoat, reaching to her bare feet, and apparently stained in spots with deeper red. Her fleshless breast was half covered by a man's jacket of the same color, the sleeves of which were cut off at the elbow. The wind, coming in at the open door, blew about her head her long gray hair, which was insecurely fastened with a strip of bark, and lent an added ferocity to her savage face.

"Good lady," said the younger of the new-comers, "the rain falls in floods; you have a roof, and we have gold."

His aged comrade plucked him by the cloak, whispering, "Oh, master, what are you saying? If this be not the abode of the Devil, it is the habitation of some robber. Our money, instead of protecting us, will be our ruin."

"Hush!" said the young man; and drawing a purse from his bosom, he displayed it to his hostess, repeating his request as he did so.

The woman, recovering from her surprise, studied them in turn with fixed and haggard eyes.

"Strangers," she cried at last, as if she had not heard their voices, "have your guardian angels forsaken you? What would you with the cursed inhabitants of the Cursed Tower? Strangers, they were no mortals who sent you here for shelter, or they would have told you: Better are the lightning and the storm than the hearth within Vygla tower. The only living man who may enter here, enters the abode of no other human being; he only leaves solitude for a crowd; he lives only by death; he has no place save in the curses of men; he serves their vengeance only; he exists by their crimes alone; and the vilest criminal, in the hour of his doom, vents on him the universal scorn, and feels that he has a right to add to it his own contempt. Strangers! You must indeed be strangers, for your foot does not yet shrink with horror from the threshold of this tower. Disturb no longer the she-wolf and her cubs; return to the road travelled by the rest of mankind, and if you would not be shunned by your fellows, do not tell them that your face ever caught the rays of the lamp of the dwellers in Vygla tower." With these words, pointing to the door, she advanced toward the two travellers. The old man trembled in every limb, and looked imploringly at the young man, who, understanding nothing of the tall woman's words because of the great rapidity of her speech, thought her crazy, and was in no wise disposed to go out again into the rain, which still fell heavily.

"Faith, good hostess, you describe a strange character, whose acquaintance I would not lose this chance of making."

"His acquaintance, young man, is soon made, sooner ended. If your evil spirit urge you to seek it, go kill some living man, or profane the dead."

"Profane the dead!" repeated the old man, in a faltering voice, hiding himself in his companion's shadow.

"I scarcely comprehend," the latter said, "your suggestions, which seem somewhat indirect; it is shorter to stay here. No one but a madman would continue his journey in such weather."

"Unhappy man!" exclaimed the woman, "do not knock at the door of one who can open no door save that of the tomb."

"And if the door of the tomb should indeed open for me with that of your abode, woman, it shall not be said that I shrank from an ill-omened word. My sword is my safeguard. Come, close the door, for the wind is cold, and take this money."

"Bah! what is your money to me!" rejoined their hostess; "precious in your hands, in mine it would become more vile than pewter. Well, stay if you will, and give me the gold. It may protect you from the storms of Heaven; it cannot save me from the scorn of men. Nay; you pay a higher price for hospitality than others pay for murder. Wait here an instant, and give me your gold. Yes, it is the first time that a man's hands have entered here filled with gold, without being stained with blood."

So saying, after putting down her lamp and barricading the door, she disappeared beneath the arch of a dark staircase built at the back of the room.

While the old man shuddered, and, invoking the glorious Saint Hospitius under every name, cordially, but in an undertone, cursed his young companion's imprudence, the latter took the light and surveyed the large circular apartment in which they had been left. What he saw as he approached the wall, startled him; and the old man, who had watched him closely, exclaimed, —

"Good God, master! a gallows?"

A tall gallows, in fact, rested against the wall, reaching to the keystone of the damp, high, arched roof.

"Yes," said the young man, "and here are saws of wood and iron, chains and iron collars; here is a rack, and huge pincers hanging over it."

"Holy saints of Paradise!" cried the old man; "where are we?"

The young man calmly went on with his inspection.

"This is a roll of hempen cord; here are furnaces and caldrons; this part of the wall is covered with tongs and scalpels; here are leathern whips with steel tips, an axe and a mace."

"This must be the wardrobe of hell!" interrupted the old man, terrified by this dreadful catalogue.

"Here," continued the other, "are copper screws, wheels with teeth of bronze, a box of huge nails, and a lever. In truth, these are sorry furnishings. It may seem to you hard that my impatience should have brought you hither with me."

"Really, you agree to that!"

The old man was more dead than alive.

"Do not be frightened. What matters it where you are? I am with you."

"A fine protection!" muttered the old man, whose increasing terror modified his fear and respect for his young companion; "a sword three feet long against a gibbet nine feet high!"

The big, red woman returned, and again taking up the iron lamp, beckoned to the travellers to follow her. They cautiously climbed a narrow, rickety flight of stairs built in the thickness of the tower wall. At each loop-hole a blast of wind and rain threatened to extinguish the quivering flame of the lamp, which their hostess shielded with her long, transparent hands. After stumbling more than once upon a rolling stone, in which the old man's alarmed fancy saw human bones scattered over the stairs, they reached the next floor, and found themselves in a circular hall like the one below. In the centre, according to Gothic custom, burned a huge fire, the smoke of which escaped through a hole in the roof, but not without perceptibly obscuring the atmosphere of the hall. It was the light from this fire, combined with that of the iron lamp, which had caught the notice of the two wayfarers. A spit, loaded with fresh-killed meat, revolved before the flames. The old man turned from it in disgust.

"It was upon that execrable hearth," said he to his comrade, "that the embers of the true cross consumed the limbs of a saint." A rude table stood some distance away from the fire. The woman invited the travellers to be seated at it.

"Strangers," said she, placing the lamp before them, "supper will soon be ready, and my husband will probably make haste to get here, for fear the midnight ghost should carry him off as it passes the Cursed Tower."

Ordener—for the reader has doubtless already guessed that he and his guide, Benignus Spiagudry, were the two travellers—could now examine at his leisure the strange disguise, in the concoction of which Benignus had exhausted all the resources of his fertile fancy, spurred on by a dread of recognition and capture. The poor fugitive had exchanged his reindeer-skin garments for a full suit of black, left at the Spladgest by a famous Throndhjem grammarian, who drowned himself in despair because he could not find out why "Jupiter" changed to "Jovis" in the genitive. His wooden shoes gave place to a stout pair of postilion boots, whose owner had been killed by his horses, in which his slender shanks had so much spare room that he could not have walked without the aid of half a truss of hay. The huge wig of an elegant young Frenchman, slain by thieves just outside the city gates, concealed his bald pate and floated over his sharp, crooked shoulders. One of his eyes was covered with a plaster, and, thanks to a pot of paint which he had found in the pocket of an old maid who died of disappointed love, his pale, hollow cheeks were tinged with an unwonted crimson, an ornament which the rain had now divided with his chin. Before seating himself, he carefully placed beneath him the pack which he carried on his back, first wrapping it in his old mantle, and while he absorbed his comrade's entire attention, all his thoughts seemed centred in the roast which his hostess was watching, toward which he cast ever and anon a glance of anxiety and alarm. Broken ejaculations fell from his lips at intervals:

"Human flesh! *Horridas epulas!* Cannibals! A feast for Moloch! *Ne pueros coram populo Medea trucidet!* Where are we?—Atreus—Druidess—Irmensul—The Devil struck Lycaon with lightning—" Finally he exclaimed: "Good Heavens! God be thanked! I see a tail!"

Ordener, who, having watched and listened attentively, had closely followed the train of his thoughts, could not help smiling.

"That tail need not comfort you. It may be the Devil's hind quarter."

Spiagudry did not hear this pleasantry. His eyes were riveted on the back of the room. He trembled, and whispered in Ordener's ear,—

"Master, look yonder, on that heap of straw, in the shadow!"

"Well, what is it?" said Ordener.

"Three naked bodies,—the corpses of three children!"

"Some one is knocking at the door," cried the red woman, who was squatting by the fire.

In fact, a knock, followed by two louder raps, was heard above the ever-increasing din of the storm.

"It is he at last! It is Nychol!"

And seizing the lamp, their hostess hurried downstairs.

The two travellers had not had time to resume their conversation, when they heard a confused murmur of voices below, in the midst of which they caught these words, uttered in a voice which made Spiagudry start and shiver:

"Be quiet, woman; we shall stay. The thunderbolt enters without waiting for the door to be opened."

Spiagudry pressed closer to Ordener.

"Master, master," he quavered, "we are lost!"

The sound of footsteps was heard on the stairs, and two men in ecclesiastic dress entered the room, followed by the startled hostess.

One of these men was tall, and wore the black gown and close-clipped hair of a Lutheran minister; the other was shorter, and wore a hermit's robe tied with a girdle of rope. The hood drawn over his face concealed all but his long black beard, and his hands were entirely hidden by his flowing sleeves.

When he saw these two peaceful strangers, Spiagudry recovered from the terror which the peculiar voice of one of them had caused.

"Don't be alarmed, my good lady," said the minister. "Christian ministers do good even to those who injure them; why should they harm those who help them? We humbly beg for shelter. If the reverend gentleman with me spoke harshly to you just now, he was wrong to forget the gentle voice recommended to us in our ordination vows. Alas! the most saintly may err. I lost my way on the road from Skongen to Throndhjem, and could find no guide through the darkness, no shelter from the storm. This reverend brother, whom I encountered, being like myself far from home, deigned to allow me to accompany him hither. He praised your kind hospitality, dear lady; doubtless he was not mistaken. Do not say to us, like the wicked shepherd, '*Advene, cur intras?*' Take us in, worthy hostess, and God will save your crops from the storm, God will protect your flocks from the tempest, as you give a refuge to travellers who have gone astray!"

"Old man," broke in the woman in a fierce voice, "I have neither crops nor flocks."

"Well, if you are poor, God blesses the poor more than the rich. You and your husband shall live to a good old age, respected, not for your wealth, but for your virtues; your children shall grow up blessed in the esteem of all men, and be what their father was before them."

"Silence!" cried the hostess. "If they continue to be what we are, our children must grow old as we have, scorned by all,—a scorn handed down from generation to generation. Silence, old man! Your blessing turns to curses on our heads."

"Heavens!" returned the minister, "who then are you? Amid what crimes do you pass your life?"

"What do you call crime? What do you call virtue? We enjoy one privilege,—we can possess no virtue and commit no crime."

"The woman's reason wanders," said the minister, turning to the little hermit, who was drying his coarse robe before the fire.

"No, priest!" replied the woman. "Learn where you are. I would rather inspire horror than pity. I am not mad, but the wife of—"

A prolonged and violent knocking at the door drowned her words, to the great disappointment of Spiagudry and Ordener, who had silently listened to the dialogue.

"Cursed," muttered the red woman, "be the mayor and council of Skongen, who gave us this tower so near the high-road for our dwelling! Perhaps that is not Nychol, now."

Still, she took up the lamp.

"After all, if it be another traveller, what matters it? The brook can flow where the torrent has passed."

The four travellers, left alone, examined each other by the firelight. Spiagudry, terrified at first by the hermit's voice, and then reassured by his black beard, might have trembled afresh if he had seen the piercing eye with which the monk observed him from beneath his cowl.

In the general silence the minister ventured a question: "Brother monk, I presume that you are one of the Catholic priests who escaped from the last persecution, and that you were returning to your retreat when I was fortunate enough to meet you. Can you tell me where we are?"

The broken door of the ruined staircase opened before the hermit could answer.

"Woman, let a storm but burst, and there is always a crowd to sit at our hated board and take shelter beneath our accursed roof."

"Nychol," replied the wife, "I could not help it!"

"What do I care how many guests you have, provided they pay? Money is as well earned by lodging a traveller as by strangling a thief."

The speaker paused at the door, and the four strangers had ample opportunity to examine him. He was a man of colossal size, dressed, like their hostess, in red serge. His enormous head seemed to rest directly upon his broad shoulders, in strong contrast with his gracious lady's long, bony neck. He had a low forehead, flat nose, and thick eyebrows; his eyes, rimmed with red, shone like burning coals in a pool of blood. The lower part of his face was shaved smooth, exposing his big mouth, whose black lips were parted in a hideous grin, like the gaping edges of a never-healing wound. Two wisps of frizzled beard, extending from his cheeks to his chin, made his face seem square when seen from the front. He wore a gray felt hat, which dripped with rain, and which he did not deign to remove in the presence of the four travellers.

As he looked at him, Benignus Spiagudry uttered a cry of fright, and the Lutheran minister turned away, struck with horror and surprise; while the master of the house, recognizing, addressed him thus: "What, are you here, minister! Indeed, I did not expect to have the pleasure of seeing your scared and woebegone face again to-day."

The priest mastered his first feeling of repulsion. His face became serious and serene.

"And I, my son, rejoice at the chance which has brought together the shepherd and the lost sheep, to the end, no doubt, that the sheep may return to the fold."

"Ah, by Haman's gibbet," rejoined the other with a loud laugh, "this is the first time that ever I was compared to a sheep! Believe me, Father, if you would flatter the vulture, you must not call him a dove."

"He who can change the vulture to a dove, consoles, my son, and does not flatter. You think that I fear you, and I only pity you!"

"You must indeed have a goodly store of pity. I should have fancied that you had exhausted it all on that poor devil to whom you displayed your cross this morning in the hope of hiding my gallows from his eyes."

"That unfortunate man," replied the priest, "was less to be pitied than you; for he wept, and you laugh. Happy is he who learns in the moment of atonement how much less powerful is man's arm than the word of God!"

"Well said, Father!" replied the host, with a horrid and ironical mirth. "Happy is he who weeps! That fellow to-day, moreover, had no other fault than that of loving the king so much that he could not live without making his Majesty's picture upon little copper medals, which he then gilded artistically to render them more worthy of the royal effigy. Our gracious sovereign was not ungrateful, and rewarded him for such a display of affection with a fine hempen decoration, which, let me inform my worthy guests, was conferred upon him this very day, in Skongen market-place, by me, lord chancellor of the Order of the Gibbet, assisted by this gentleman here present, grand chaplain of the said order."

"Stop, wretched man!" broke in the priest. "How can he who punishes forget that punishment awaits us all? Listen to the thunder—"

"Well, what is thunder? Satan's laughter."

"Good God, he has just looked on death, and he blasphemes!"

"A truce to your sermons, old fool!" cried the host, in a loud, angry tone, "unless you would curse the angel of darkness who has brought us together twice in one day, in the same carriage and under the same roof. Imitate your friend the hermit, who is silent, for he longs to be back again in his cave at Lynrass. I thank you, brother monk, for the blessing which I see you bestow upon the Cursed Tower every morning as you cross the hill; but the fact is that you always seemed tall to me until now, and that black beard of yours looked white. Are you sure that you are the hermit of Lynrass,—the only hermit in the province of Throndhjem?"

"I am the only one," said the hermit in a hollow voice.

"We are, then," rejoined his host, "the two recluses of the district— Hollo, Becky, make haste with that roast lamb, for I am hungry. I was detained at Burlock village by that confounded Dr. Manryll, who would only give me twelve escalins for the corpse. That miserable fellow who keeps the Throndhjem Spladgest gets forty. Ha, Master Periwig, what's the matter with you? Are you going to tumble over? By the way, Becky, have you finished the skeleton of that famous magician, Orgivius the poisoner? It is high time it was delivered to the Bergen Museum. Did you send one of your little pigs to the mayor of Loevig to get what he owes me,—four double crowns for boiling a witch and two alchemists, and for removing several chains from the cross-beams of his tribunal, which they disfigured; twenty escalins for hanging Ishmael Typhaine, a Jew against whom the good bishop entered a complaint; and a crown for putting a new wooden arm to the stone gallows of the tower."

"Your wages," replied his wife in sour tones, "remain in the mayor's hands, because your son forgot to take a wooden spoon to receive the money, and none of the judge's servants were willing to put it into his hand."

The husband frowned.

"Only let their necks fall into my hands, and they shall see whether I need a wooden spoon to touch them. But we must manage the mayor carefully, for it is to him that robber Ivar complained that he was put to the rack by me, and not by a regular executioner, alleging that, as he had not yet been tried, he was not upon my level. By the way, wife, do keep the children from playing with my nippers and pincers; they have spoiled all my tools, so that I really could not use them to-day. Where are they, the little monsters?" added the man, going up to the heap of straw where Spiagudry had fancied that he saw three dead bodies. "Here they are in bed; they sleep through all our noise as soundly as if they had been hanged."

From these words, whose grim horror was in strong contrast with the speaker's mirth and fierce, frightful composure, the reader will have guessed who was the inhabitant of the Vygla tower. Spiagudry, who upon his first appearance recognized him from having often seen him act in his official capacity in the Throndhjem market-place, felt ready to faint, particularly when he considered his own powerful personal motive for dreading this awful personage. He leaned over to Ordener, and said in scarcely articulate tones, "It is Nychol Orugix, the hangman of the province of Throndhjem!"

Ordener, at first struck with horror, shuddered, and regretted both his journey and the storm. But soon a peculiar feeling of curiosity took possession of him, and although he pitied his old guide's distress and terror, he devoted his entire attention to observing the speech and manners of the singular being before him,—just as a man might listen eagerly to the growl of a hyena or the roar of a tiger, brought from the desert to one of our great cities. Poor Benignus was far from being sufficiently easy in his mind to make psychological observations. Hidden behind Ordener, he drew his mantle closely about him, raised a restless hand to his plaster, pulled the back of his loose periwig over his face, and sighed heavily.

Meantime the hostess had dished up the joint of roast lamb, with its reassuring tail, on a large earthen platter. The hangman seated himself opposite Ordener and Spiagudry, between the two clergymen; and his wife, after putting upon the table a jug of sweetened beer, a piece of *rindebrod*,[8] and five wooden plates, sat down by the fire and busied herself in sharpening her husband's dull tools.

"There, reverend sir," said Orugix, laughing; "the sheep offers you a piece of lamb. And you, Sir Periwig, was it the wind that blew your hair over your face?"

"The wind, sir, — the storm —" stammered the trembling Spiagudry.

"Come, pluck up a spirit, old boy! You see that these reverend gentlemen and I are good fellows. Tell us who you are, and who your silent young friend is, and talk a bit. If your conversation is as amusing as your person, it must be funny indeed."

"Your worship jests," said the keeper, pursing his lips, showing his teeth and winking, to make himself look merry. "I am but a poor old man."

"Yes," interrupted the jovial hangman, "some old scientist, some old sorcerer."

"Oh, my lord and master, a scientist, but no sorcerer!"

"So much the worse; a sorcerer would complete our joyful Sanhedrim. Gentlemen and guests, let us drink to restore this old sage's speech, so that he may enliven us at supper; the health of the man we hanged to-day, brother preacher! Well, father monk, do you refuse my beer?"

The hermit had, indeed, drawn from under his gown a large gourd of clear water, from which he filled his glass.

"Zounds, hermit of Lynrass!" cried the hangman, "if you will not taste my beer, I will taste the water which you prefer to it."

"So be it," answered the hermit.

"First take off your glove, worthy brother," answered the hangman. "Water should always be poured with the bare hand."

The hermit shook his head, saying, "It is a vow."

"Well, then, pour," said the hangman.

Hardly had Orugix raised the glass to his lips when he set it down hastily, while the hermit drained his at a draught.

"By the Holy Grail! good hermit, what is that infernal stuff? I have not drank its like since the day that I came near drowning in my voyage from Copenhagen to Throndhjem. Truly, hermit, that is no water from Lynrass spring; it is salt water."

"Salt water," repeated Spiagudry, his terror increasing as he looked at the hermit's glove.

"Well, well!" said the hangman, turning toward him with a loud laugh; "so everything alarms you, old Absalom,—even to the drink of a holy monk who chooses to mortify his flesh!"

"Alas, no, master! But salt water—There is but one man—"

"Come, come, you don't know what you are talking about, sir doctor; your distress must be caused by your bad conscience, or else you despise our company."

These words, uttered in a humorous tone, reminded Spiagudry that he must needs hide his fears. To mollify his much-dreaded host, he called his vast memory to his aid, and summoned up all the presence of mind which was left to him.

"I despise you,—you, my lord and master! You, whose presence in a province gives that province the *merum imperium*![9] You, mighty hangman, the executioner of secular vengeance, the sword of justice, the shield of innocence! You, whom Aristotle in the sixth book and last chapter of his 'Politics' ranks with magistrates, and whose salary Paris de Puteo, in his treatise 'De Syndico,' fixes at five gold crowns, as this passage proves: *Quinque aureos manivolto!* You, sir, whose Cronstadt colleagues were ennobled when they had cut off three hundred heads,—you, whose terrible but most honorable functions are performed with pride in Franconia by the most recent bridegroom, in Reutlingen by the youngest of the city councillors, in Stedien by the last-made citizen! And do I not also know, good master, that your colleagues in France have the right of *havadium* upon every leper, upon pigs, and upon cake on Epiphany eve? How could I fail to feel the deepest respect for you when the abbot of Saint Germain des Prés gives you a boar's head every year, on Saint Vincent's Day, and puts you at the head of his procession!"

Here the keeper's erudite flow of fancy was abruptly cut short by the hangman.

"Upon my word, this is the first that I have heard of it. The learned abbot of whom you speak, my worthy friend, has hitherto defrauded me of all these fine privileges which you describe in such attractive fashion.— Strangers," continued Orugix, "aside from all this old fool's extravagant nonsense, it is quite true that I have missed my career. I am only the poor hangman of a poor province. Well, I certainly ought to have done better than Stillison Dickoy, the famous hangman of Moscow. Would you believe that I am the same man who was chosen twenty-four years ago to behead Schumacker?"

"Schumacker, Count of Griffenfeld!" exclaimed Ordener.

"Does that surprise you, Sir Silent? Yes, that selfsame Schumacker who, strange to say, would again fall into my hands should it please the king to recall his reprieve. Let us empty this jug, gentlemen, and I will tell you how it happens that after so brilliant a beginning I end my career so miserably.

"In 1676, I was assistant to Rhum Stuald, the royal hangman at Copenhagen. At the time of Count Griffenfeld's sentence, my master falling ill, I was, thanks to my powerful patrons, selected to act in his place. On June 5,—I shall never forget that day,—at five o'clock in the morning, assisted by the carpenter, I erected in the public square a huge gallows, which we hung with black, out of respect for the prisoner. At eight, the king's guards surrounded the scaffold, and the Schleswig Uhlans kept back the crowd that thronged the square. Who would not have been dazzled in my place? Erect, and sword in hand, I stood waiting on the platform. All eyes were upon me; at that moment I was the most important personage in the two kingdoms. My fortune, thought I, is made; for what could all these great lords, who have sworn the chancellor's ruin, do without me? I already regarded myself as the royal hangman of the town, by letters-patent; I had servants and privileges of every sort. Just listen! The clock on the fortress struck ten. The prisoner left his cell, crossed the square, and ascended the scaffold with a firm step and calm face. I wanted to tie his hair; he refused, and himself performed this last office. 'It's a long time,' he said smilingly to the prior of St. Andrew's, since I dressed my own hair.' I offered him the black bandage; he declined it scornfully, but without showing any contempt for me. 'My friend,' said he, 'this is perhaps the first time on record, that the space of a few feet ever held the two officers representing the extremes of the law,—the chancellor and the executioner!' Those words have remained graven on my memory. He also refused the black cushion which I would have given him for his knees, embraced the priest, and knelt, after declaring his innocence in a loud voice. Then I broke his escutcheon with a single blow of my mace, crying aloud, as is the custom, 'This is not done without just cause!' This affront shook the count's firm bearing; he turned pale, but soon mastered himself and said, 'The king gave me my arms; the king can take them from me!' He placed his head on the block, turned his eyes toward the east, and I raised my sword in both hands. Now listen! At that instant a shout fell upon my ears,—'Pardon, in the king's name! Pardon for Schumacker!' I turned; I saw a royal aide-de-camp galloping toward the gallows waving a parchment. The count rose, with a look not of pleasure, but of satisfaction. The parchment was handed to him. 'Good God!' cried he, 'imprisonment for life! Their mercy is more cruel than death.' He stepped, looking like a thief, from the scaffold which he had mounted so serenely. It was nothing to me. I had no idea that this man's salvation meant my ruin. After removing the scaffold, I returned to my master still full of hope, although slightly disappointed at losing the golden crown, my fee for removing a head. That was not all. Next day I received an order to leave the city, and an appointment as executioner for the province of Throndhjem. A provincial hangman, and that in the most miserable province of Norway! Now you shall see, gentlemen, how small causes sometimes bring about great results. The count's enemies, by way of displaying their generosity, had done all in their power to keep back the pardon until the execution was over. It lacked but one minute; they blamed me for being so slow, as if it would have been decent to prevent an illustrious man from amusing himself for a few moments, before he breathed his last! As if a royal executioner beheading a lord high chancellor could act with no more dignity and sense of proportion than a country hangman turning off a Jew! Ill-will was added to this. I had a brother; indeed, I think I have one still. He had changed his name, and succeeded in finding employment in the house of the new chancellor, Count d'Ahlefeld. My presence in Copenhagen disturbed the scoundrel. My brother despised me, because it might some time fall to my lot to hang him."

Here the fluent narrator stopped to give vent to his mirth; then he went on: —

"You see, my dear guests, that I made the best of it. The deuce take ambition! I ply my calling honestly. I sell my dead bodies, or Becky turns them into skeletons, which the Bergen anatomical museum buys. I laugh at everything, even at that poor woman who was a gypsy, and whom solitude has driven mad. My three heirs are growing up in the fear of the Devil and the gallows. My name is the terror of all the children in Throndhjem. The city council furnish me with a cart and red clothes. The Cursed Tower protects me from rain as well as the bishop's palace could do. Old priests, driven hither by a storm, preach to me; learned men fawn upon me. In fine, I am as happy as most people; I drink, eat, hang, and sleep."

The hangman did not close this long speech without frequent interludes of beer and noisy bursts of laughter.

"He kills, and he sleeps!" murmured the minister; "poor wretch!"

"What a lucky fellow the rascal is!" exclaimed the hermit.

"Yes, brother monk," said the hangman; "just as much of a rascal as you are, but assuredly much luckier. You see, the business would be a capital one if people did not seem to take pleasure in cutting down my profits. Would you believe it, some great wedding has just afforded the chaplain newly appointed to Throndhjem a pretext for asking the pardon of twelve criminals who really belonged to me?"

"Belonged to you!" cried the minister.

"Yes, to be sure, Father. Seven of them were sentenced to be whipped, two to be branded on the left cheek, and three to be hanged, which makes twelve in all. Yes, I shall lose twelve crowns and thirteen escalins if the pardon is granted. What do you think, strangers, of such a chaplain, who disposes so easily of my property? That confounded priest's name is Athanasius Munder. Oh, if I could only get hold of him!"

The minister rose, and said in a quiet voice, with a calm manner, "My son, I am Athanasius Munder."

At these words Orugix's face became inflamed with fury; he started from his seat. Then his angry eye met the friendly gaze of the chaplain, and he sat down again slowly, in mute confusion.

There was a momentary silence. Ordener, who had risen from the table ready to defend the priest, was first to break it.

"Nychol Orugix," said he, "here are thirteen crowns to pay for the pardon of those prisoners."

"Alas!" interrupted the minister, "who knows whether I can obtain their pardon? I must first manage to get a word with the viceroy's son, for it all depends upon his marrying the chancellor's daughter."

"Sir chaplain," answered the young man in a firm voice, "your wish shall be granted. Even if Ordener Guldenlew never wears the marriage ring, the chains of your *protégés* shall be loosed."

"Young stranger, you can do nothing in the matter; but God hears, and will reward you!"

Meantime, Ordener's thirteen crowns had finished the work which the priest's mild gaze began. Nychol's anger being allayed, he recovered his good-humor.

"Come, reverend sir, you are a good man, worthy to serve in St. Hilary's chapel; I spoke more harshly than I intended. You do but follow your own path; it is not your fault if it crosses mine. But there is one man to whom I do bear a grudge, and that's the guardian of the dead at Throndhjem,—that old sorcerer, the keeper of the Spladgest. What's his name now,—Spliugry? Spadugry? Tell me, you old philosopher, who seem to be a perfect Babel of learning,—you who know everything, can't you help me to remember the name of that magician, your brother? You must have met him sometimes of a Sabbath, riding through the air on a broomstick, eh?"

Certainly, if poor Benignus could have escaped at that moment upon some such aerial steed, the narrator of this story doubts not that he would most gladly have trusted his frail and terrified body to its tender mercies. Never before was his love of life so strong as now that he clearly perceived the extreme imminence of his danger. Everything that he saw frightened him,—the legends of the Cursed Tower, the wild eyes of the red woman, the voice, gloves, and beverage of the mysterious monk, the rash courage of his young companion, and especially the hangman,—the hangman, into whose abode he had fallen in his effort to escape from the charge of crime. He trembled so violently that he could scarcely move, particularly when the conversation turned upon himself, and he heard the dreadful Orugix's question. As he had no desire to imitate the heroism of the priest, his faltering tongue found great difficulty in framing a reply.

"Well!" repeated the hangman, "don't you know the name of the keeper of the Spladgest? Does your wig make you deaf?"

"Somewhat, sir; but," he finally stammered out, "I don't know his name, I swear I don't."

"He don't know?" said the hermit's terrible voice. "He does wrong to take oath to it. That man's name is Benignus Spiagudry."

"My name! my name! Great heavens!" exclaimed the affrighted old man.

The hangman burst out laughing.

"And who said that it was your name? We are talking of that dog of a keeper. In good sooth, this learned fellow is scared at nothing. How would it be if his ridiculous grimaces had a genuine cause? It would be fun to hang the old fool. So then, venerable doctor," added the hangman, whom Spiagudry's fears entertained, "you do not know this Benignus Spiagudry?"

"No, master," said the keeper, somewhat reassured by his disguise; "I assure you I don't know him. And since he is so unfortunate as to displease you, I should be very sorry, master, indeed I should, if I did know the fellow."

"And you, hermit," said Orugix,—"you seem to know him?"

"Yes, truly," replied the hermit; "he is a tall, dried-up, bald old fellow—"

Spiagudry, justly alarmed at this minute description, hastily adjusted his wig.

"He has," added the hermit, "long hands like those of a thief who has not seen a traveller for a week, a bent back—"

Spiagudry sat up as straight as he could.

"Moreover, he might easily be taken for one of the corpses in his charge if he had not such sharp eyes."

Spiagudry clapped his hand to his plaster.

"Many thanks, Father," said the hangman; "I shall know the old Jew now, wherever I may run across him."

Spiagudry, who was an excellent Christian, indignant at this intolerable insult, could not help exclaiming, "Jew, master!"

Then he stopped short, trembling lest he had said too much.

"Well, Jew or Pagan, what does it matter which, if he have dealings with the Devil, as they say he has?"

"I should readily believe it," rejoined the hermit, with a sarcastic smile, not quite hidden by his cowl, "if he were not such a coward. But how could he covenant with Satan? He is as cowardly as he is wicked. When fear takes possession of him, he actually forgets his own identity."

The hermit spoke slowly, as if with intention, the very deliberation of his words lending them peculiar force.

"He forgets his own identity!" mentally repeated Spiagudry.

"It's a pity for a bad man to be a coward," said the hangman; "for he's not worth hating. We fight a serpent, but we can only crush a lizard."

Spiagudry ventured a few words in his own defence.

"But, gentlemen, are you sure that the official of whom you speak is really what you say? Is his reputation so bad?"

"His reputation!" repeated the hermit; "he has the worst reputation of any man in the district!"

Benignus, in his disappointment, turned to the hangman.

"Master, what fault have you to find with him? For I do not doubt that your dislike is just."

"You are right, old man, not to doubt it. As his trade resembles mine, Spiagudry does all he can to injure me."

"Oh, master, never believe it! Or, if it be so, it is because he never saw you, as I have, surrounded by your good wife and lovely children, admitting strangers to the delights of your domestic circle. Had he enjoyed your kind hospitality as I have, sir, the unfortunate man could never be your enemy."

Spiagudry had scarcely ended this wily speech, when the tall woman, who had been silent until then, rose, and said in a sharp, stern voice, "The viper's tongue is never more venomous than when it is smeared with honey." Then she sat down again, and went on polishing her pincers,—a task whose hoarse, grating sound, filling up the spaces in the conversation, performed the office of the chorus in a Greek tragedy, at the expense of the ears of the four travellers.

"That woman is crazy indeed!" thought the keeper, unable otherwise to explain the ill effect of his flattery.

"Becky is right, my fair-haired sage," exclaimed the hangman. "I shall think you have a viper's tongue, if you defend that Spiagudry much longer."

"God forbid, master!" exclaimed the latter; "I would not defend him for the world."

"Very good. You do not know how far he carries his insolence. Would you believe that the impudent scamp is bold enough to dispute my right to the possession of Hans of Iceland?"

"Hans of Iceland!" exclaimed the hermit.

"Yes, to be sure. Do you know that famous knave?"

"Yes," said the hermit.

"Well, every thief belongs to the hangman, doesn't he? What does that infernal Spiagudry do? He asks to have a price set upon the head of Hans."

"He asks to have a price set upon the head of Hans?" interrupted the hermit.

"He had the audacity to do so, and that, simply that the body might fall to his share, and I might be defrauded of my property."

"What an outrage, Master Orugix, to dare to dispute your right to a thing which so plainly belongs to you!"

These words were accompanied by a malicious smile, which alarmed Spiagudry.

"The trick is all the worse, hermit, because I only need one good hanging, such as that of Hans would be, to remove me from my obscurity, and to make the fortune which I failed to make by beheading Schumacker."

"Indeed, Master Nychol?"

"Yes, brother monk, on the day that Hans is arrested, come and see me, and we will sacrifice a fat pig to my future greatness."

"Gladly; but who knows whether I shall be at liberty upon that day? Besides, you just now sent ambition to the Devil."

"Oh, why not, Father, when I see that to destroy my best founded hopes it only needs a Spiagudry, and a request to set a price upon a man's head?"

"Ah!" repeated the hermit, in a peculiar tone; "so Spiagudry asked that a price be set!"

That voice was to the wretched keeper what the toad's eye is to a bird.

"Gentlemen," he urged, "why judge rashly? It is not at all sure; it may be a false report."

"A false report!" cried Orugix; "the thing is but too certain. The petition of the city council, supported by the signature of the keeper of the Spladgest, is in Throndhjem at this very moment. It only waits the decision of his excellency the governor-general."

The hangman was so well informed, that Spiagudry dared not continue his defence; he contented himself with swearing inwardly, for the hundredth time, at his youthful companion. But what was his horror when he heard the hermit, who for some moments had seemed lost in thought, suddenly exclaim in bantering tones: "Master Nychol, what is the penalty for sacrilege?"

These words produced the same effect on Spiagudry as if his periwig and plaster had been torn off. He anxiously awaited the reply of Orugix, who stopped to empty his glass.

"That depends on the nature of the sacrilege," said the hangman.

"Suppose it was profaning the dead?"

Upon this the shivering Spiagudry expected every instant to hear his name issue from the lips of the unaccountable monk.

"Formerly," coolly remarked Orugix, "they buried the offender alive, with the body he had outraged."

"And now?"

"Now the punishment is milder."

"Is milder!" said Spiagudry, scarcely daring to breathe.

"Yes," rejoined the hangman, with the satisfied and indifferent air of an artist talking of his own art; "they brand him first, with a hot iron, with the letter S, on the calf of the leg."

"And then?" broke in the old keeper, upon whom it would have been difficult to inflict this part of the sentence.

"Then," said the executioner, "they merely hang him."

"Mercy!" said Spiagudry; "hang him!"

"Well, what's the matter with you? You look at me as the victim looks at the gallows."

"I am glad," said the hermit, "to see that people are growing more humane."

At this moment, the storm having ceased, the clear, intermittent sound of a horn was distinctly heard outside.

"Nychol," said his wife, "they are in search of some malefactor; that's the horn of the bowmen."

"The horn of the bowmen!" repeated each of the company, in different accents, but Spiagudry in tones of unmistakable terror.

They had scarcely uttered the words when there was a knock at the door.

XIII

Only a man, a sign, is needed; the elements of revolution are ready. Who will be the first? So soon as there is a fulcrum, everything will move. — Bonaparte.

LOEVIG is a large town, situated on the north side of Throndhjem fjord, and sheltered by a low chain of bare hills, singularly diversified by various sorts of crops, like broad bits of mosaic resting upon the horizon. The appearance of the town is gloomy; the fishermen's cabins, made of twigs and reeds, the conical hut, constructed of earth and stones, in which the invalid miner spends the few days which his scanty savings allow him to devote to sunshine and rest, and the frail ruin which the chamois-hunter in his turn decks with a straw roof and walls hung with skins, line streets longer than the town itself, because they are narrow and crooked. In a square where now exist only the remains of a great tower, once stood the ancient fortress built by Horda the Fine Archer, lord of Loevig, and brother-in-arms of the pagan king Halfdan, occupied in 1698 by the mayor of the town, who would have been the best-lodged citizen in the city, if it had not been for the silvery stork who every summer perched on the tip of the sharp spire of the church, like the white pearl on the top of a mandarin's pointed cap.

On the morning of the same day that Ordener reached Throndhjem, another personage, also incognito, landed at Loevig. His gilded litter, although without armorial bearings, his four tall lackeys, armed to the teeth, instantly became the topic of every conversation, and roused the curiosity of all. The landlord of the Golden Gull, a small tavern at which the great man alighted, himself assumed an air of mystery, and answered every question with an "I don't know," which seemed to imply, "I know all, but you shall know nothing." The tall lackeys were as mute as fishes, and more obscure than the mouth of a mine.

The mayor shut himself up in his tower, waiting with great dignity for the stranger to make the first visit; but the inhabitants were soon surprised to see him call twice at the Golden Gull in vain, and at evening lie in wait for a bow from the stranger, as he sat at the half-open window. From this the gossips inferred that the great man had made his high rank known to the lord mayor. They were mistaken. A messenger sent by the stranger presented himself at the mayor's office to get his passport signed, and the mayor noticed upon the green seal two crossed hands supporting an ermine mantle, surmounted by a count's coronet upon a shield, from which depended the collars of the Orders of the Elephant and the Dannebrog. This was enough for the mayor, who was most desirous of obtaining from the chancellor the lord mayoralty of Throndhjem. But his advances were useless, for the great man would see no one.

The second day of the traveller's stay in Loevig was drawing to its close, when the landlord entered his room, saying with a low bow that the messenger expected by his Grace had arrived.

"Very well," said his Grace; "let him come up."

A moment later the messenger entered, carefully closed the door, then bowing to the ground before the stranger, who had half turned toward him, waited in respectful silence until he should be addressed.

"I expected you this morning," said the stranger; "what detained you?"

"The interests of your Grace, Count; have I another thought?"

"How is Elphega? How is Frederic?"

"They are well."

"Good! good!" broke in the master; "have you nothing more interesting to tell me? What is the news at Throndhjem?"

"Nothing, except that Baron Thorwick arrived there yesterday."

"Yes, I know that he wanted to consult that old Mecklenburger, Levin, about his marriage. Do you know the result of his interview with the governor?"

"To-day at noon, when I left, he had not yet seen the general."

"What! and he arrived last night! You surprise me, Musdœmon. And had he seen the countess?"

"Still less, sir."

"Then you saw him?"

"No, noble master; besides, I do not know him."

"And how, if no one has seen him, do you know that he is in Throndhjem?"

"Through his servant, who was at the governor's palace yesterday."

"But he, —did he go elsewhere?"

"His servant declares that as soon as he arrived, he set off for Munkholm, after first visiting the Spladgest."

The count's eye flashed fire.

"For Munkholm! For Schumacker's prison! Are you positive? I always suspected that honest Levin of being a traitor. For Munkholm! What can be the attraction there? Did he want to ask Schumacker's advice also? Did he—"

"Noble lord," interrupted Musdœmon, "it is by no means certain that he went there."

"What! Then why did you say so? Are you trifling with me?"

"Pardon me, your Grace! I merely repeated what the baron's servant said. But Mr. Frederic, who was on duty yesterday at Munkholm, saw nothing of Baron Ordener."

"That's no proof! My son does not know the viceroy's son. Ordener may have entered the fortress in disguise."

"Yes, sir; but Mr. Frederic asserts that he saw no one."

The count grew calmer.

"That's a different matter. Did my son really say so?"

"He assured me of the fact three separate times; and Mr. Frederic's interests in this case are identical with your own."

This suggestion quite relieved the count.

"Ah!" said he, "I understand. The baron, on his arrival, must have wished to take a short sail on the fjord, and his servant fancied that he went to Munkholm. After all, why should he go there? I was foolish to take alarm. My son-in-law's lack of eagerness to see old Levin proves, on the contrary, that his affection for him is not so strong as I feared. You will hardly believe it, my dear Musdœmon," added the count, "but I actually imagined that Ordener was in love with Ethel Schumacker, and I constructed a romance and an intrigue out of this journey to Munkholm. But, thank God, Ordener is not such a fool as I am. By the way, my friend, how fares it with that young Danaë in Frederic's hands?"

Musdœmon had shared his master's fears regarding Ethel Schumacker, and had struggled against them without overcoming them quite so readily. However, charmed to see his master smile, he took care not to disturb his peace of mind, but rather sought to add to it, that he might increase that serene temper so necessary in the great for the well-being of their favorites.

"Noble Count, your son has failed with Schumacker's daughter; but it seems that another has been more fortunate."

The count interrupted him eagerly.

"Another! What other?"

"Oh, I don't know,—some peasant, serf, or vassal."

"Do you speak the truth?" cried the count, his stern, dark face beaming.

"Mr. Frederic declares that it is so, and he told the countess the same story."

The count rose and paced the room, rubbing his hands.

"Musdœmon, dear Musdœmon, but one more effort, and our end is gained. The young shoot is blasted. We have only to uproot the parent tree. Have you any other good news?"

"Dispolsen has been murdered."

The count's features brightened.

"Ah, you see that we advance from victory to victory. Have we his papers? Above all, have we that iron casket?"

"I regret to inform your Grace that the murder was not committed by our people. He was killed and robbed upon Urchtal Sands, and the deed is attributed to Hans of Iceland."

"Hans of Iceland!" repeated his master, his brow again clouding. "What! that famous brigand whom we meant to put in charge of our rebellion?"

"The same, noble Count; and I fear, from what I can gather, that it will be no easy task to find him. At any rate, I have secured a leader who will take his name, and can replace him if necessary,—a wild mountaineer, tall and strong as an oak, fierce and bold as a wolf in a wilderness of snow, this terrible giant must surely look much like the real Hans of Iceland."

"Then Hans of Iceland is tall?" inquired the count.

"That is the general opinion, your Grace."

"I cannot but admire, my dear Musdœmon, the art with which you lay your plans. When is the insurrection to break out?"

"Oh, very soon, your Grace; perhaps it is on foot even now. The royal protectorate has long been odious to the miners; they all grasped with joy at the idea of revolt. The movement will begin at Guldbrandsdal, extend to Sund-Moer, and reach Kongsberg. Two thousand miners can be raised in three days. The rebellion will be kindled in Schumacker's name; our emissaries use no other. The reserve forces in the South and the garrisons at Throndhjem and Skongen can be called out, and you will be here on the spot most opportunely to put down the rebellion,—a fresh and significant service in the eyes of the king,—and to rid him of this Schumacker, the source of such anxiety to the throne. Upon these firm foundations will rise the structure to be crowned by the marriage of our noble lady Ulrica and Baron Thorwick."

A private interview between two scoundrels is never long, because all that is human in their souls quickly takes alarm at the infernal qualities revealed. When two depraved spirits mutually display their naked vices, each is disgusted by the other's iniquity. Crime itself revolts at crime; and two evil-doers conversing, with all the cynicism of intimacy, of their pleasures and their interests, are like a fearful mirror, each reflecting the other's monstrous features. Their own degradation mortifies them when seen in another, their own pride confounds them, their own nothingness alarms them; and they cannot fly from themselves or disavow their own portrait in their fellowman; for each odious harmony, each frightful coincidence, each hideous parallel finds within them an untiring voice to denounce them in their ever-wearied ear. However secret may be their intercourse, it has always two intolerable witnesses,—God, whom they cannot see, and conscience, which they feel.

His confidential talks with Musdœmon distressed the count the more because the latter always unhesitatingly imputed to his master a good share of the crimes committed or about to be committed. Many courtiers think it wise to save great men from the appearance of wrong-doing; they assume the responsibility of evil, and often spare their patron's blushes by allowing him to feign resistance to advantageous crime. Musdœmon, by a refinement of skill, pursued the contrary course. He wished it to seem that he seldom advised, and always obeyed. He knew his master's soul as familiarly as that master knew his heart; therefore he never compromised himself without compromising the count. There was no head, save that of Schumacker, that the count would have been so glad to see fall; Musdœmon knew this as well as if his master had told him, and his master knew that he knew it.

The count had learned all that he wished to learn; he was satisfied; he was now eager to dismiss Musdœmon.

"Musdœmon," said he, with a gracious smile, "you are the most faithful and most zealous of all my servants. All goes well, and I owe it to your devotion. I make you private secretary to the chancellor's office."

Musdœmon bowed low.

"Nor is that all," added the count; "I will ask for you, for the third time, the Order of the Dannebrog. But I still fear that your birth, your humble relations—"

Musdœmon blushed, turned pale, and hid his change of color by another bow.

"Come," said the count, offering him his hand to kiss, "come, Mr. Private Secretary, draw up your *placeat*! It may chance to find the king in gracious mood."

"Whether his Majesty grant my petition or not, your Grace's kindness overwhelms me."

"Make haste, my dear fellow, for I am anxious to be off. We must try to get some exact information about this Hans."

Musdœmon, with a third bow, opened the door.

"Ah!" said the count, "I forgot. In your new position as private secretary, you may write to the chancellor's office and order them to dismiss this mayor of Loevig, who compromises the dignity of his position in the eyes of the villagers by his servility to strangers whom he does not know."

XIV

The monk at midnight visiting the cross,
The knight taming his fiery steed,
The man who with dread sound of trumpet dies,
And he who dies with peaceful voice of prayer,
Are all the objects of Thy care, lavished alike
On every pious soul, whether he tonsure wear or helm.
Hymn to Saint Anselm.

"YES, master, we really owe a pilgrimage to Lynrass grotto. Who would have thought that the hermit, whom I cursed as if he had been the Devil, would prove to be our guardian angel, and that the sword which seemed to threaten our very lives would serve for a bridge to take us over the abyss?"

It was in these somewhat grotesquely figurative terms that Benignus Spiagudry poured into Ordener's ears his joy, his admiration, and his gratitude for the mysterious monk. As will readily be supposed, our two travellers had left the Cursed Tower; nay, when we again encounter them, they have even left the village of Vygla far behind them, and are painfully pursuing a steep path, interrupted by frequent pools or blocked by huge stones, which transient torrents caused by storms had washed down from the wet, sticky soil. Day had not yet dawned; but the bushes growing above the rocks on either side of the road stood out against the clear sky like dark silhouettes, and various objects, although still colorless, gradually assumed form in the dim, dull light which daybreak in the North filters through the chill fogs of early morning.

Ordener was silent, for he had yielded to that somnolent state sometimes permitted by the mechanical motion of walking. He had not slept since the night before, when he allowed himself to rest in a fishing-boat moored in Throndhjem harbor for the few hours intervening between his departure from the Spladgest and his arrival at Munkholm. Accordingly, while his body moved toward Skongen his spirit had flown back to Throndhjem Fjord, — to that gloomy prison and those melancholy towers which contained the only being on earth to whom he attached any idea of hope and happiness.

Awake, thoughts of his Ethel filled his mind; asleep, her memory became a fanciful image which irradiated all his dreams. In this second life of sleep, where for a time the soul alone exists, and the physical being with all its material ills seems to disappear, he saw the beloved maiden, no more beautiful, no purer, than in reality, but happier, freer, more wholly his own. Only, upon the road to Skongen, the oblivion of his body, the torpor of his senses, could not be complete; for from time to time a bog, a stone, the branch of a tree, impeding his progress, recalled him suddenly from the ideal to the real. He would then raise his head, half open his drowsy eyes, and regret the fall from bright celestial wanderings to his painful earthly journey, where nothing could compensate for his lost illusions, save that he felt close to his heart the ringlet which was his until Ethel herself should be his own. Then this memory revived the charming dream-image, and he gently relapsed, not into slumber, but into a vague, persistent revery.

"Master," repeated Spiagudry, in a louder tone, which, combined with a blow from the trunk of a tree, aroused Ordener, "fear nothing. The bowmen turned to the right with the hermit when they left the tower, and we are far enough away from them to venture to speak. It is true that silence was most prudent until now."

"Indeed," said Ordener, yawning, "you push your prudence to extremes. It is at least three hours since we left the tower and the bowmen behind us."

"That is true, sir; but prudence never does any harm. Only think, if I had declared myself when the chief of that infernal troop asked for Benignus Spiagudry in a voice like that of Saturn calling for his new-born son that he might devour him! Suppose, even, I had not taken refuge in a prudent silence at that awful moment, where should I be now, noble master?"

"Faith, old man, I fancy that at that moment nothing, not even pincers, could have drawn your name from you."

"Was I wrong, master? If I had spoken, the monk,—may Saint Hospitius, and Saint Usbald the Solitary, bless him!—the monk would have had no opportunity to ask the captain of the archers whether his men did not belong to the Munkholm regiment; a trifling question, merely asked in order to gain time. Did you notice, sir, after that stupid archer answered 'Yes,' with what a peculiar smile the monk requested him to follow him, saying that he knew the hiding-place of the fugitive, Benignus Spiagudry?"

Here the keeper paused for a moment, as if to make a fresh start; for he suddenly resumed, in a voice quivering with emotion: "A good priest, a worthy and upright anchorite, practising the principles of Christian virtue and evangelic charity; and I was alarmed at his mere outward appearance, forbidding enough, truly; but what a beautiful soul lies beneath! Did you notice too, noble master, that there was something peculiar in the tone with which he said to me, 'We shall meet again!' as he led away the archers? At any other time that tone would have alarmed me; but it is not the pious and excellent hermit's fault. Solitude undoubtedly gives that strange intonation; for I know, sir," —here the voice of Benignus sank lower, — "I know another hermit, that dreadful fellow who—But no; out of respect for the venerable hermit of Lynrass I will not make so odious a comparison. Neither was there anything peculiar about his gloves; it is quite cold enough to wear them; and his salty beverage does not surprise me either. Catholic anchorites often follow singular examples; the very same thing, master, is alluded to in this line by the famous Urensius, the monk of Mount Caucasus:—

'Rivos despicieus, maris undam potat amaram.'

Why didn't I think of that verse while I was in that confounded ruin at Vygla? A little better memory would have spared me much needless alarm. To be sure, it is not easy, is it, sir, to collect your thoughts in such a den, seated at the table of a hangman, — a hangman, a creature given over to universal scorn and execration, who only differs from an assassin in the frequency and impunity of his murders; whose heart to all the atrocity of the most awful brigands unites the cowardice of which at least their daring crimes do not admit; a being who offers food and drink with the same hand that wields the instruments of torture, and crushes the bones of his miserable victims between the planks of the rack! Think of breathing the same air with a hangman! And the vilest beggar, if polluted by his loathsome touch, would cast aside with horror the last rags which protected his nakedness and his disease from the wintry blast! And the chancellor, after sealing his commission, flings the paper under the table in token of his malediction and his disgust! And in France, when the hangman dies in his turn, the provost's assistants would rather pay a fine of forty pounds than succeed him! And at Pesth, when Churchill was condemned to die, and they offered to pardon him if he would turn executioner, he preferred death to such a trade. Is it not still notorious, noble sir, that Turmeryn, bishop of Mäestricht, ordered a church to be purified because the hangman had entered it; and that Czarina Petrowna washed her face whenever she witnessed an execution? You know also that the kings of France, to honor warriors, permit them to be punished by their comrades, so that these brave men, even if they be criminals, may not be made infamous by contact with the hangman. And finally, which is decisive, in the 'Descent of Saint George into Hell,' by the learned Melasius Iturham, does not Charon give the robber, Robin Hood, precedence over the hangman, Philip Crass? Truly, master, if ever I attain to power, which God alone can foresee, I shall put down hangmen, and restore the ancient custom and the ancient tariff. For the murder of a prince a man shall pay, as in 1150, fourteen hundred and forty double-crown pieces; for the murder of a count, fourteen hundred and forty plain crowns; for that of a baron, fourteen hundred and forty half-crowns; the killing of a mere noble shall be rated at fourteen hundred and forty escalins; and that of a citizen—"

"Don't I hear the tread of a horse coming toward us?" interrupted Ordener.

They looked back, and, as day had dawned during Spiagudry's long soliloquy, they could distinguish, a hundred paces behind them, a man dressed in black waving one hand to them, and with the other urging on one of those small dingy white ponies so often seen, either wild or domesticated, in the lower mountain ranges of Norway.

"For mercy's sake, master," said the timid keeper, "let us hasten; that black fellow looks to me just like an archer!"

"What, old man; we are two, and we should fly before a single man!"

"Alas! twenty sparrows fly before an owl. What glory is there in waiting for an officer of the law?"

"And who tells you that this is one?" rejoined Ordener, whose eyes were not blinded by fear. "Keep up your courage, my valiant guide; I recognize this traveller. Let us wait for him."

The keeper was forced to submit. A moment later the horseman came up with them, and Spiagudry ceased to tremble when he saw the grave, calm face of the chaplain, Athanasius Munder.

The latter greeted them with a smile, and reined in his steed, saying in an almost breathless voice, "My dear children, it is for your sake that I retrace my steps; and the Lord will surely not permit my absence, prolonged with a charitable intent, to injure those who sorely need my presence."

"Sir minister," answered Ordener, "we shall be happy to aid you in any way we can."

"On the contrary, it is I, noble young man, who desire to serve you. Will you deign to tell me the object of your journey?"

"Reverend sir, I cannot."

"All I ask, my son, is that your refusal may proceed from inability, and not from distrust. If not, I am indeed unhappy! Unhappy is he whom the good man distrusts, even if he have seen him but once!"

The priest's modesty and unction touched Ordener deeply.

"All that I can tell you, Father, is that we are bound to the mountains of the North."

"So I thought, my son, and that is why I followed you. There are bands of roving hunters and miners in those mountains who might injure travellers."

"What then?"

"Well, I know that it is useless to dissuade a noble young man in search of adventure; but the esteem I feel for you inspires me with another plan for helping you. The unfortunate counterfeiter to whom I bore the last consolations of religion yesterday was a miner. Just before he died he gave me a paper inscribed with his name, saying that this passport would protect me from all danger if I ever had to travel among those mountains. Alas! what can it avail a poor priest who must live and die among prisoners, and who, moreover, *inter castra latronum*, should seek no other defence than patience and prayer, the only weapons of God! I did not decline the pass, because we should never distress by refusal the heart of one who in a few minutes more will have nothing to receive or to give on earth. The good God deigned to inspire me, for now I can offer you this parchment, that it may go with you in all the perils of your journey, and that the gift of the dying man may benefit the traveller."

Ordener accepted the old priest's gift with emotion.

"Sir Chaplain," said he, "God grant that your prayer may be heard! Thank you. But," he added, laying his hand on his sword, "I already carry my passport at my side."

"Young man," said the priest, "that poor parchment may perhaps protect you better than your steel blade. The gaze of a penitent man is more potent than the archangel's sword. Farewell! My prisoners await me. Pray sometimes for them and me."

"Holy priest," rejoined Ordener, with a smile, "I told you that your prisoners should be pardoned, and they shall be."

"Oh, do not speak with such assurance, my son! Do not tempt the Lord! No man can know what passes in the mind of another, and you cannot tell what the viceroy's son may decide to do. Perhaps, alas! he will never condescend to admit a humble chaplain to his presence. Farewell, my son; may your journey be blessed, and may you sometimes remember the poor priest and pray for his unhappy prisoners."

XV

Welcome, Hugo; tell me, did you ever see so terrible a
storm!—Maturin: *Bertram*.

IN a room communicating with the apartments of the Governor of
Throndhjem, three of his Excellency's secretaries sat at a table loaded with
parchments, papers, inkstands, and seals, a fourth chair, left vacant, showing
that one of the scribes was late. They had been silently writing and thinking
for some time, when one of them exclaimed: "Did you know, Wapherney,
that the poor librarian, Foxtipp, is to be dismissed by the bishop, owing to
the letter which you wrote recommending Dr. Anglyvius's petition to his
favorable notice?"

"What nonsense are you talking, Richard?" hastily inquired the
secretary to whom Richard had not spoken. "Wapherney could not have
written in favor of Anglyvius, for the fellow's petition disgusted the general
when I read it to him."

"So you told me," answered Wapherney; "but I found the word *tribuatur*
[10] written on the petition in his Excellency's own hand."

"Indeed!" exclaimed the other.

"Yes, my dear fellow; and several other of his Excellency's decisions of
which you told me, were also altered in marginal notes. For instance, on the
petition of the miners, the general wrote, *negetur*."

"What! I can't understand that; the general dreaded the turbulent spirit
of those miners."

"Perhaps he wanted to frighten them into submission by his severity.
What makes me think so is that Chaplain Munder's request for the pardon
of twelve condemned prisoners is also refused."

The secretary whom Wapherney addressed, rose abruptly, saying, "Oh,
come now, I can't believe that; the governor is too kind, and expressed too
much compassion for those prisoners to—"

"Very well, Arthur," answered Wapherney; "read it for yourself."

Arthur took the petition and saw the fatal words.

"Really," said he, "I can scarcely credit my own eyes. I must present this to the governor again. What day did his Excellency mark these papers?"

"I believe it was some three days ago," replied Wapherney.

"That was," said Richard in a low voice, "the morning before Baron Ordener's brief appearance and mysteriously sudden disappearance."

"Stay!" quickly exclaimed Wapherney, before Arthur had time to answer; "if here is not another *tribuatur* on Benignus Spiagudry's ridiculous petition!"

Richard burst out laughing.

"Didn't that old keeper of corpses disappear in a strange way, too?"

"Yes," replied Arthur; "a body was found in his charnel-house so mutilated that the officers of the law are in pursuit of him on a charge of sacrilege. But a little Lapp, who acted as his servant, and who was left alone at the Spladgest, thinks, as do most people, that the Devil carried him off for a sorcerer."

"Here," said Wapherney, laughing, "is a fellow who leaves a good reputation behind him!"

He had hardly had his laugh out when the fourth secretary came in.

"Upon my honor, Gustavus, you are very late this morning. Did you happen to get married yesterday?"

"Oh, no!" answered Wapherney; "he only took the longest way round, so that he might pass under the fair Rosalie's windows in his new cloak."

"Wapherney," said the new-comer, "I only wish that you were right. But the cause of my delay is not half so agreeable; and I doubt if my new cloak produced the slightest effect upon the persons whom I visited."

"Where have you been, then?" asked Arthur.

"To the Spladgest."

"Heaven is my witness," cried Wapherney, dropping his pen, "that we were just now speaking of that place! But though it may be talked of to pass away the time, I cannot conceive how anybody can enter it."

"And still less," said Richard, "how anybody can linger there. But what did you see, my dear Gustavus?"

"Yes," said Gustavus, "you are curious to hear about it, if not to see it; and it would serve you right if I refused to describe those horrors which you would shudder to behold."

The three secretaries crowded about Gustavus, who waited to be urged, although his desire to tell what he had seen was secretly no less lively than their curiosity to hear.

"Well, Wapherney, you can repeat my story to your little sister, who is so fond of frightful tales. I was pushed into the Spladgest by the crowd which thronged about it. The bodies of three soldiers and two bowmen from the Munkholm regiment had just been brought in, having been found yesterday some four miles away, in the ravine at the foot of Cascadthymore cliff. Some of the spectators declared that the poor fellows were the very ones sent out three days ago in the direction of Skongen to catch the runaway keeper of the Spladgest. If this be true, it is impossible to imagine how so many well-armed men could be murdered. The mutilation of the bodies seems to prove that they were flung from the top of the rocks. It made my hair stand on end to look at them."

"What, Gustavus! did you see them?" eagerly inquired Wapherney.

"They are still before my eyes."

"And has any one an idea as to the authors of the crime?"

"Some think that it may have been a band of miners, and assert that they heard the sound of the horn with which the soldiers call to one another, only yesterday among the mountains."

"Really!" said Arthur.

"Yes; but an old peasant demolished this supposition by remarking that there were neither mines nor miners in the neighborhood of Cascadthymore."

"Then who could it have been?"

"No one knows. If the bodies were not intact, it might be supposed the work of wild beasts, for their limbs are covered with long, deep scratches. The same is the case with the corpse of a white-bearded old man brought into the Spladgest day before yesterday, after that fearful storm which prevented you, my dear Leander Wapherney, from visiting your Hero across the fjord, on the Larsynn shore."

"All right, Gustavus," said Wapherney, laughing. "But who was this old man?"

"From his height, his long white beard, and a rosary still clasped tightly in his hands, although he had been stripped of everything else, he was recognized as a hermit of the neighborhood; I believe they called him the Monk of Lynrass. It is evident that this poor man was murdered also; but for what purpose? People are not slaughtered now for their religious opinions, and the old hermit possessed nothing in the world but his serge gown and the good-will of all who knew him."

"And you say," observed Richard, "that his body was mangled, like those of the soldiers, as if by the claws of some savage animal?"

"Yes, my dear boy; and a fisherman declares that he noticed the same marks upon the body of an officer found murdered a few days since upon Urchtal Sands."

"That is strange," said Arthur.

"It is frightful," said Richard.

"Come," said Wapherney, "silence, and to work, for I think the general will be here soon. My dear Gustavus, I am curious to see those corpses. If you like, we will stop a moment at the Spladgest when we leave here this evening."

XVI

She with young unwakened senses,
Within her cabin on the Alpine field
Her simple homely life commences,
Her little world therein concealed.
And I, God's hate flung o'er me,
Had not enough, to thrust
The stubborn rocks before me
And strike them into dust!
She and her peace I yet must undermine:
Thou, Hell, hast claimed this sacrifice as thine!
Goethe: *Faust, Bayard Taylor's Translation.*

IN 1675, twenty-four years previous to the date of this story, sooth to say, the whole village of Thoctree rejoiced and made merry over the marriage of sweet Lucy Pelryhn and that tall, handsome, upright youth, Carroll Stadt. They had long been lovers, and every one felt a warm interest in the happy pair upon the day which was to change so many restless hopes and eager longings into assured and quiet bliss. Born in the same village, reared in the same fields, Carroll had often in their childhood slept in Lucy's lap when tired of play; Lucy had often, as a young girl, leaned on Carroll's arm as she returned from work. Lucy was the loveliest and most modest maiden in the land; Carroll the bravest and noblest lad in the village. They loved each other, and they could no more remember the day when their love began than they could recall the day when they were born.

But their marriage did not come, like their love, easily and as a matter of course. There were domestic interests to be consulted,—family feuds, relations, obstacles. They were parted for a whole year; and Carroll suffered sadly far from Lucy, and Lucy wept bitter tears far from Carroll, before the dawn of that happy day which united them, thereafter never to suffer or to weep apart.

It was by saving her from great danger that Carroll finally won his Lucy. He heard cries from the woods one day; they were uttered by his Lucy, surprised by a brigand dreaded by all the mountain folk, and on the point of carrying her off to his den. Carroll boldly attacked this monster in human shape, who gave vent to strange growls like those of a wild beast. Yes, he attacked the wretch, whom none before had ventured to resist. Love lent him a lion's strength. He rescued his beloved Lucy, restored her to her father, and her father gave her to her deliverer.

Now, the whole village made merry upon the day which united these two lovers. Lucy alone seemed depressed; and yet never had she gazed more tenderly at her dear Carroll. But her gaze was as sad as it was loving, and amid the universal rejoicing this was a subject for surprise. Every moment, as her husband's happiness seemed to increase, her eyes expressed more and more love and despair.

"Oh, my Lucy," said Carroll, when the sacred rites were over, "the coming of that robber, a curse to the entire country, was the greatest blessing for me!" She shook her head, and made no answer.

Night came; they were left alone in their new abode, and the sports and dancing on the village green went on more merrily than before, to celebrate the happiness of the bridal pair.

Next morning Carroll Stadt had vanished. A few words in his handwriting were brought to Lucy's father by a hunter from the mountains of Kiölen, who met him before daylight wandering along the shore of the fjord.

Old Will Pelryhn showed the paper to his pastor and the mayor, and nothing was left of last night's festival but Lucy's gloom and dull despair.

This mysterious catastrophe dismayed the entire village, and vain efforts were made to explain it. Prayers for Carroll's soul were said in the same church where but a few days before he himself sang hymns of thanksgiving for his happiness.

No one knew what kept Widow Stadt alive. At the end of nine months of solitary grief she brought into the world a son, and on the same day the village of Golyn was destroyed by the fall of the hanging cliff above it.

The birth of this son did not dissipate his mother's deep depression. Gill Stadt showed no signs of resemblance to Carroll. His fierce, angry infancy seemed to prophecy a still more ferocious manhood. Sometimes a little wild man—whom those mountaineers who saw him from a distance asserted to be the famous Hans of Iceland—entered the lonely hut of Carroll's widow, and the passers-by would then hear a woman's shrieks and what seemed the roar of a tiger. The man would carry off young Gill, and months would elapse; then he would restore him to his mother, more sombre and more terrible than before.

Widow Stadt felt a mixture of horror and affection for the child. Sometimes she would clasp him in her maternal arms, as the only tie which still bound her to earth; again she would repulse him with terror, calling upon Carroll, her dear Carroll. No one in the world knew what agitated her soul.

Gill reached his twenty-third year; he saw Guth Stersen, and loved her madly.

Guth Stersen was rich, and he was poor; therefore he set off for Roeraas and turned miner, in order to make money. His mother never heard from him again.

One night she sat at the wheel, by which she earned her daily bread; the lamp burned low as she worked and waited in her cabin, beneath those walls which had grown old like herself, in solitude and grief, the silent witnesses of her mysterious wedding-night. She thought anxiously of her son, whose presence, ardently desired as it was, would recall much sorrow, perhaps bring more in its train. The poor mother loved her son, ungrateful as he was. And how could she help loving him, she had suffered so much for him?

She rose and took from an antique wardrobe a crucifix thickly coated with dust. For an instant she looked at it imploringly; then suddenly casting it from her in horror, she cried: "I pray! How can I pray? Your prayers can only be addressed to hell, poor woman! You belong to hell, and to hell alone."

She had relapsed into her mournful revery, when there was a knock at the door.

This was a rare event with Widow Stadt. For many long years, in consequence of the strange incidents connected with her history, the whole village of Thoctree believed that she had dealings with evil spirits; no one therefore ever ventured near her hut,—strange superstitions of that age and ignorant region! She owed to her misfortunes the same reputation for witchcraft that the keeper of the Spladgest owed to his learning.

"What if it were my son, if it were Gill!" she exclaimed; and she rushed to the door.

Alas! it was not her son. It was a little monk clad in serge, his cowl covering all of his face but a black beard.

"Holy man," said the widow, "what would you have? You do not know the house to which you come."

"Yes, truly!" replied the hermit in a hoarse and all too familiar voice.

And tearing off his gloves, his black beard, and his cowl, he revealed a fierce countenance, a red beard, and a pair of hands armed with tremendous claws.

"Oh!" cried the widow, burying her head in her hands.

"Well," said the little man, "have you not in four-and-twenty years grown used to seeing the husband upon whom you must gaze through all eternity?"

"Through all eternity!" she repeated in a terrified whisper.

"Hark ye, Lucy Pelryhn, I bring you news of your son."

"My son! Where is he? Why does he not come?"

"He cannot."

"But you have news of him. I thank you. Alas! and can you bring me pleasure?"

"They are pleasant tidings indeed that I bring you," said the man in hollow tones; "for you are a weak woman, and I wonder that you could bring forth such a son. Rejoice and be glad. You feared that your son would follow in my footsteps; fear no longer."

"What!" cried the enraptured mother, "has my son, my beloved Gill, changed?"

The hermit watched her raptures with an ominous sneer.

"Oh, greatly changed!" said he.

"And why did he not fly to my arms? Where did you see him? What was he doing?"

"He was asleep."

In the excess of her joy, the widow did not notice the little man's ominous look, nor his horrible and scoffing manner.

"Why did you not wake him? Why did not you say to him, 'Gill, come to your mother?'"

"His sleep was too sound."

"Oh, when will he come? Tell me, I implore, if I shall see him soon."

The mock monk drew from beneath his gown a sort of cup of singular shape.

"There, widow," said he, "drink to your son's speedy return!"

The widow uttered a shriek of horror. It was a human skull. She waved it away in terror, and could not utter a word.

"No, no!" abruptly exclaimed the man, in an awful voice, "do not turn away your eyes, woman; look. You asked to see your son. Look, I say! for this is all that is left of him."

And by the red light of the lamp, he offered the dry and fleshless skull of her son to the mother's pale lips.

Too many waves of misfortune had passed over her soul for one misery the more to crush her. She gazed at the cruel monk with a fixed and meaningless stare.

"Dead!" she whispered; "dead! Then let me die."

"Die, if you choose! But remember, Lucy Pelryhn, Thoctree woods; remember the day when the demon, taking possession of your body, gave your soul to hell! I am that demon, Lucy, and you are my wife forever! Now, die if you will."

It is the belief in those superstitious regions that infernal spirits sometimes appear among men to lead lives of crime and calamity. In common with other noted criminals, Hans of Iceland enjoyed this fearful renown. It was also believed that a woman, who by seduction or by violence, became the prey of one of these monsters in human form, by that misfortune was doomed to be his companion in hell.

The events of which the hermit reminded the widow seemed to revive in her these thoughts.

"Alas!" she sobbed, "then I cannot escape from this wretched existence! And what have I done? for you know, my beloved Carroll, I am innocent. A young girl's arm is without strength to resist the arm of a demon."

She rambled on; her eyes were wild with delirium, and her incoherent words seemed born of the convulsive quiver of her lips.

"Yes, Carroll, since that day, though polluted, I am innocent; and the demon asks me if I remember that horrible day! Carroll, I never deceived you; you came too late. I was his before I was yours, alas! Alas! and I must be forever punished. No, I can never rejoin you,—you for whom I weep. What would it avail me to die? I should follow this monster into a world as fearful as himself,—the world of the damned! And what have I done? Must my misfortunes in this life become my crimes in the next?"

The little monk bent a look of triumph and command upon her face.

"Ah!" she suddenly exclaimed, turning toward him; "ah, tell me, is not this some fearful dream induced by your presence? For you know but too well, alas! that since the day of my ruin, every night that I am visited by your fatal spirit is marked by foul apparitions, awful dreams, and frightful visions."

"Woman, woman, cease your raving; it is as true that you are wide awake as it is true that Gill is dead."

The memory of her past misfortunes had, as it were, blotted out all thought of her fresh grief; these words revived it.

"Oh, my son! my son!" she moaned; and the tones of her voice would have moved any but the wicked being who heard it. "No, he will return; he is not dead; I cannot believe that he is dead."

"Well, go ask him of Roeraas rocks, which crushed out his life; of Throndhjem Fjord, which swallowed up his body."

The widow fell upon her knees, crying convulsively, "God! great God!"

"Be silent, servant of hell!"

The wretched woman was silent. He added: "Do not doubt your son's death; he was punished for the sins of his father. He let his granite heart melt in the sunlight of a woman's eyes. I possessed you, but I never loved you. Your Carroll's misfortune was also his. My son and yours was deceived by his betrothed, by her for whom he died."

"Died!" she repeated, "died! Then it is really true? Oh, Gill, you were born of my misery; you were conceived in terror and born in sorrow; your lips lacerated my breast; as a child, you never returned my caresses or embraces; you always shunned and repulsed your mother, your lonely and forsaken mother! You never tried to make me forget my past distress, save by causing me fresh injury. You deserted me for the demon author of your existence and of my widowhood. Never, in long years, Gill, never did you procure me one thrill of pleasure; and yet to-day your death, my son, seems to me the most insupportable of all my afflictions. Your memory to-day seems to me to be twined with comfort and rapture. Alas! alas!"

She could not go on; she covered her head with her coarse black woollen veil, and sobbed bitterly.

"Weak woman!" muttered the hermit; then he continued in a firm voice: "Control your grief; I laugh at mine. Listen, Lucy Pelryhn. While you still weep for your son, I have already begun to avenge him. It was for a soldier in the Munkholm regiment that his sweetheart betrayed him. The whole regiment shall perish by my hands. Look, Lucy Pelryhn!"

He had rolled up the sleeves of his gown, and showed the widow his misshapen arms stained with blood.

"Yes," he said with a fierce roar, "Gill's spirit shall delight to haunt Urchtal Sands and Cascadthymore ravine. Come, woman, do you not see this blood? Be comforted!"

Then all at once, as if struck by a sudden thought, he interrupted himself: "Widow, did you not receive an iron casket from me? What! I sent you gold and I bring you blood, and you still weep. Are you not human?"

The widow, absorbed in her despair, was silent.

"What!" said he, with a fierce laugh, "motionless and mute. You are no woman, then, Lucy Pelryhn!" and he shook her by the arm to rouse her. "Did not a messenger bring you an iron casket?"

The widow, lending him a brief attention, shook her head, and relapsed into her gloomy revery.

"Ah, the wretch!" cried the little man, "the miserable traitor! Spiagudry, that gold shall cost you dear!"

And stripping off his gown, he rushed from the hut with the growl of a hyena that scents a corpse.

XVII

My lord, I braid my hair; I braid it with salt tears because
you leave me alone, and because you go hence into the
hills. — *The Count's Lady* (*Old Romance*).

ETHEL, meantime, had already reckoned four long and weary days
since she was left to wander alone in the dark garden of Schleswig tower;
alone in the oratory, the witness of so many tears, the confidant of so many
longings; alone in the long gallery, where once upon a time she had failed
to hear the midnight bell. Her aged father sometimes accompanied her, but
she was none the less alone, for the true companion of her life was absent.

Unfortunate young girl! What had that pure young soul done that it
should be thus early given over to so much sorrow? Taken from the world,
from honors, riches, youthful delights, and from the triumphs of beauty, she
was still in the cradle when she was already in a prison cell; a captive with
her captive father, she had grown up watching his decay; and to complete
her misery, that she might not be ignorant of any form of bondage, love had
sought her out in prison.

Even then, could she but have kept her Ordener at her side, would
liberty have tempted her? Would she ever have known that a world existed
from which she was cut off? Moreover, would not her world, her heaven,
have been with her in that narrow keep, within those gloomy towers
bristling with soldiers, toward which the passer-by would still have cast a
pitying glance?

But, alas! for the second time her Ordener was absent; and instead of
spending all too brief but ever recurring hours with him in holy caresses
and chaste embraces, she passed days and nights in bewailing his absence,
and praying that he might be shielded from danger. For a maiden has only
her prayers and her tears.

Sometimes she longed for the wings of the free swallow which came
to her to be fed through her prison bars. Sometimes her thought escaped
upon the cloud which a swift breeze drove northward through the sky;
then suddenly she would turn away her head and cover her eyes, as if she

dreaded to see a gigantic brigand appear and begin the unequal contest upon one of the distant mountains whose blue peaks hung on the horizon like a stationary cloud.

Oh, it is cruel to live when we are parted from the object of our love! Few hearts have known this pang in all its extent, because few hearts have known love in all its depth. Then, in some sort a stranger to our ordinary existence, we create for ourselves a melancholy waste, a vast solitude, and for the absent one some terrible world of peril, of monsters, and of deceit; the various faculties which make up our being are changed into and lost in an infinite longing for the missing one; everything about us seems utterly indifferent to us. And yet we still breathe, and move, and act, but without our own volition. Like a wandering planet which has lost its sun, the body moves at random; the soul is elsewhere.

XVIII

On a vast buckler those relentless men
Terrified hell with fearful oaths;
And beside a black bull which they had slain,
All, bathing their hands in blood, swore to be revenged.
The Seven Chiefs before Thebes.

THE coast of Norway abounds in narrow bays, in creeks, coves, reefs, lagoons, and little headlands so numerous as to weary the traveller's memory and the topographer's patience. Formerly, if we are to credit popular tradition, every isthmus was haunted by some demon, each bay inhabited by some fairy, each promontory protected by some saint; superstition mingles all beliefs to create for itself imaginary terrors. Upon Kelvel strand, some miles to the north of Walderhog cave, there was but a single spot, they said, which was free from all jurisdiction either of infernal, intermediary, or celestial spirits. It was the glade lying along the shore, overhung by a cliff, on the top of which could still be seen vestiges of the manor of Ralph, or Rudolf, the Giant. This little wild meadow, bordered on the west by the sea, and closely shut in by rocks clad with heather, owed its exemption solely to the name of that ancient Norwegian lord, its first possessor. For what fairy, what devil, or what angel would venture to become master or guest of a domain once occupied and guarded by Ralph the Giant?

It is true that the mere name of the much dreaded Ralph sufficed to give an alarming character to a region wild in itself. But after all, a memory is not so much to be feared as a spirit; and no fisher, belated in rough weather, and mooring his bark in Ralph's creek, had ever seen the will-o'-the-wisp sport and dance upon the summit of a rock, or a fairy ride through the heather in her phosphorescent car drawn by glow-worms, or a saint ascend toward the moon, after his prayers were said.

And yet, if the angry waves and wind had allowed a wandering mariner to land in that hospitable harbor upon the night after the great storm, he might have been struck with superstitious fear at the sight of three men, who upon that same night sat around a huge fire, blazing in the middle of the meadow. Two of them wore the broad felt hat and loose trousers of royal miners. Their arms were bare to the shoulder, their feet were cased in fawn-colored leather boots; a red sash held their crooked swords and heavy pistols; each had a hunter's horn slung about his neck. One was old, the other was young; the old man's thick beard and the young man's long hair lent a wild and barbarous look to their faces, which were naturally hard and stern.

By his bearskin cap, his tanned leather jacket, the musket slung across his back, his short, tight-fitting drawers, his bare knees, his bark shoes, and the glittering axe in his hand, it was easy to guess that the companion of the two miners was a mountaineer from the north of Norway.

Certainly, any one who saw from afar these three weird figures, upon which the flames, fanned by the salt breeze, cast a red, flickering light, might well have been frightened, even had he no faith in spectres and demons; it would have been enough that he believed in thieves and was somewhat richer than the ordinary poet.

The three men constantly turned their heads toward the winding path through the wood which fringes Ralph's meadow, and judging by such of their words as were not carried off by the wind, they were expecting a fourth person.

"I say, Kennybol, do you know that we should not be allowed to wait so peacefully for this envoy from Count Griffenfeld, if we were in the neighboring meadow, Goblin Tulbytilbet's meadow, or yonder in St. Cuthbert's bay?"

"Don't talk so loud, Jonas," replied the mountaineer; "blessed be Ralph the Giant, who protects us! Heaven save me from setting foot in Tulbytilbet's meadow! The other day I thought I was picking hawthorn there, and I gathered mandrake instead, which began to bleed and shriek, and nearly drove me mad."

The young miner laughed.

"Nearly, Kennybol? For my part, I think that the mandrake's shriek produced its full effect upon your feeble brains."

"Feeble brains yourself!" said the vexed mountaineer; "just see, Jonas, he jests at mandrake. He laughs like a lunatic playing with a death's-head."

"Hum!" answered Jonas. "Let him go to Walderhog cave, where the heads of those whom Hans, the foul fiend of Iceland, has murdered, come back every night to dance about his bed of withered leaves, and gnash their teeth to lull him to sleep."

"That's so," said the mountaineer.

"But," rejoined the young man, "did not Mr. Hacket, for whom we are waiting, promise us that Hans of Iceland would take the lead in our rebellion?"

"He did," replied Kennybol; "and with the help of that demon we are sure to conquer the green jackets of Throndhjem and Copenhagen."

"So much the better!" cried the old miner. "But I'm not the man to stand guard beside him at night."

At this moment the rustle of dead leaves beneath the tread of a man drew the attention of the speakers; they turned, and the firelight gleamed on the new-comer's face.

"It is he! it is Mr. Hacket! Welcome, Mr. Hacket; you have kept us waiting. We have been here this three quarters of an hour."

"Mr. Hacket" was a short, fat man, dressed in black, and his jovial countenance wore a forbidding expression.

"Well, friends," said he, "I was delayed by my ignorance of the road and the necessary precautions. I left Count Schumacker this morning; here are three purses of gold which he bade me give you."

The two old men flung themselves upon the gold with the eagerness common among the peasants of barren Norway. The young miner declined the purse which Hacket offered him.

"Keep your gold, Sir Envoy; I should lie if I said that I had joined the revolt for your Count Schumacker's sake. I rebel to free the miners from the guardianship of the crown; I rebel that my mother's bed may have a blanket less ragged than the coast of our good country, Norway."

Far from seeming disconcerted, Mr. Hacket answered smilingly, "Then I will send this money to your poor mother, my dear Norbith, so that she may have two new blankets to shield her from the cold wind this winter."

The young man assented with a nod, and the envoy, like a skilful orator, made haste to add:—

"But be careful not to repeat what you just now inconsiderately said, that you are not taking up arms in behalf of Schumacker, Count Griffenfeld."

"But—but," muttered the two old men, "we know very well that the miners are oppressed, but we know nothing about this count, this prisoner of state."

"What!" sharply rejoined the envoy; "are you so ungrateful? You groan in your subterranean caves, deprived of light and air, robbed of all your property, slaves to the most onerous tutelage! Who came to your rescue?

Who revived your failing courage? Who gave you gold and arms? Was it not my illustrious master, noble Count Griffenfeld, more of a slave and more unfortunate even than you? And now, loaded with his favors, would you refuse to use them to acquire his liberty with your own?"

"You are right," interrupted the young miner; "that would be an ill deed."

"Yes, Mr. Hacket," said the two old men, "we will fight for Count Schumacker."

"Courage, my friends! Rise in his name; bear your benefactor's name from one end of Norway to the other. Only listen; everything seconds your righteous enterprise; you are about to be freed from a formidable enemy, General Levin de Knud, governor of the province. The secret power of my noble master, Count Griffenfeld, will soon procure his recall to Bergen. Come, tell me, Kennybol, Jonas, and you, my dear Norbith, are all your comrades ready?"

"My brethren of Guldbrandsdal," said Norbith, "only await my signal. To-morrow, if you wish—"

"To-morrow; so be it. The young miners under your leadership must be the first to raise the standard. And you, my brave Jonas?"

"Six hundred heroes from the Färöe Islands, who for three days have lived on chamois flesh and bear's fat in Bennallag forest, only ask a blast from the horn of their old captain, Jonas of Loevig town."

"Good! And you, Kennybol?"

"All those who carry an axe in the gorges of Kiölen, and climb the rocks with bare knees, are ready to join their brothers, the miners, when they need them."

"Enough. Tell your comrades that they need not doubt their victory," added the envoy, raising his voice; "for Hans of Iceland will be their captain."

"Is that certain?" asked all three at once, in a voice of mingled hope and fear.

The envoy answered: "I will meet you four days hence, at the same hour, with your united forces, in Apsyl-Corh mine, near Lake Miösen, on Blue Star plain. Hans of Iceland will be with me."

"We will be there," said the three leaders. "And may God not desert those whom the Devil aids!"

"Fear nothing from God," said Hacket, with a sneer. "Stay; you will find flags for your troops among the ruins of Crag. Do not forget the war-cry,

'Long live Schumacker! We will rescue Schumacker!' Now we must part; day will shortly break. But first, swear the most profound secrecy as to what has passed between us."

Without a word each of the three chiefs opened a vein in his left arm with the point of his sword; then, seizing the envoy's hand, each let a few drops of blood trickle into it.

"You have our blood," they said.

Then the young man exclaimed: "May all my blood flow forth like that which I now shed; may a malicious spirit destroy my plans, as the hurricane does a straw; may my arm be of lead to avenge an insult; may bats dwell in my tomb; may I, still living, be haunted by the dead, and dead, be profaned by the living; may my eyes melt with tears like those of a woman, if ever I speak of what has occurred at this time in Ralph the Giant's meadow. And may the blessed saints deign to hear this, my prayer!"

"Amen!" repeated the two old men.

Then they parted, and nothing was left in the meadow but the smouldering fire, whose expiring embers burned up at intervals, and gleamed upon the summit of Ralph the Giant's ruined and deserted towers.

XIX

Theodore. Tristam, let us be gone.
Tristam. This is a strange disgrace.
Theodore. Did any one see us?
Tristam. I know not, but I fear they did.
Lope da Vega: *The Gardener's Dog.*

BENIGNUS SPIAGUDRY found it hard to guess the motives which led a youth of fine appearance, and apparently likely to live for many long years, to become the voluntary antagonist of the much-dreaded Hans of Iceland. He had frequently and with much ingenuity broached the question since they started on their travels; but the young adventurer preserved a stubborn silence as to the cause of his journey. Nor was the poor fellow any more successful in satisfying his curiosity concerning various other details as to his strange comrade. Once he ventured to ask a question about his young master's family and his name. "Call me Ordener," was the reply; and this very unsatisfactory answer was given in a tone which forbade further question. He was forced to submit; every one has his secrets, and good Spiagudry himself carefully concealed in his wallet, under his cloak, a certain mysterious casket, any inquiry as to which he would certainly have considered very disagreeable and greatly out of place.

Four days had passed since they left Throndhjem, but they had made little progress, owing to the bad state of the roads after the storm, and the multiplicity of crosscuts and roundabout routes which the runaway keeper thought it prudent to take in order to avoid too thickly settled regions. Leaving Skongen on their right, toward evening of the fourth day they reached the shores of Lake Sparbo.

The vast stretch of water reflecting the last gleams of daylight and the first stars of coming night set in a frame of tall cliffs, black firs, and lofty oaks, presented a gloomy but magnificent picture. The sight of a lake at evening sometimes produces, at a certain distance, a peculiar optical illusion; it seems as if a vast abyss, cleaving the earth from side to side, revealed the heavens beneath our feet.

Ordener paused to contemplate the old Druidical forests, which cover the steep shores of the lake as with a garment, and the chalky huts of Sparbo, scattered over the slope like a stray flock of white goats. He listened to the distant clink of the forges,[11] mingled with the dull roar of the weird forests, the intermittent cry of wild birds, and the solemn music of the waves. To the north a huge granite bowlder, still gilded by the rays of the sun, rose majestically above the little village of Oëlmœ, its summit bending beneath a mass of ruined towers, as if the giant were weary of his load.

When the soul is sad, it delights in melancholy scenes; it adds to them its own gloom. Let an unhappy man be thrown among wild, high mountains beside some black lake in the heart of a dark forest, at the close of day, and he will see this solemn scene through a funereal veil; he will not feel that the sun is setting, but that it is dying.

Ordener lingered, motionless and mute, until his companion exclaimed: "Capital, sir! You do well to ponder thus beside the most miasma-laden lake in Norway."

This remark and the gesture which accompanied it, would have brought a smile to the lips of any but a lover parted from his mistress perhaps never again to meet her. The learned keeper added:—

"And yet I must rouse you from your meditations to remind you that day is drawing to a close, and we must make haste if we would reach Oëlmœ village before twilight overtakes us."

The observation was correct. Ordener resumed his journey, and Spiagudry followed him, continuing his unheeded reflections upon the botanic and physiologic phenomena which Lake Sparbo affords the naturalist.

"Mr. Ordener," said he, "if you will listen to your devoted guide, you will give up your fatal enterprise; yes, sir, and you will take up your abode upon the shores of this most curious lake, where we can devote ourselves to all sorts of learned research; for instance, to the study of the *stella canora palustris,*—a singular plant, which many scholars consider to be fabulous, but which Bishop Arngrimmsson asserts that he both saw and heard on the shores of Lake Sparbo. Added to this, we shall have the satisfaction of feeling that we dwell upon soil which contains more gypsum than any other in Europe, and where the hired assassins of Thronodhjem are least likely to find their way. Doesn't it attract you, young master? Come, renounce your senseless journey; for, not to offend you, your scheme is dangerous, without being profitable,—*periculum sine pecunia*; that is to say, senseless, and conceived at a moment when you might better have been thinking of other things."

Ordener, who paid no attention to the poor man's words, merely kept up the conversation by those occasional meaningless monosyllables which great talkers are ready to accept in lieu of answers. Thus they reached Oëlmœ village, where they found an unusual bustle and stir.

The inhabitants—hunters, fishers, and blacksmiths—had left their houses, and hastily collected about a central mound occupied by a group of men, one of whom blew a horn and waved a small black-and-white banner over his head.

"Probably some quack doctor," said Spiagudry,—"*ambubaiarum collegia, pharmacopolœ*; some scamp who turns gold into lead and wounds into sores. Let us see. What invention of the Evil One will he sell these poor rustics? It would be bad enough if these impostors confined themselves to kings, if they all imitated Borch the Dane and Borri of Milan, those alchemists who so completely duped our Frederic III.;[12] but they are just as greedy for the peasant's mite as for the prince's million."

Spiagudry was mistaken. As they approached the mound they recognized by his black gown and round, pointed cap, the mayor, surrounded by a number of bowmen. The man blowing the horn was the town crier.

The fugitive keeper, somewhat disturbed, muttered: "Truly, Mr. Ordener, I did not expect to stumble upon the mayor when I came into this hamlet. Great Saint Hospitius, protect us! What does he say?"

His uncertainty was of brief duration, for the crier's shrill voice was quickly raised, and religiously heeded by the little group of villagers.

"In the name of his Majesty and by order of his Excellency, General Levin de Knud, governor, the lord mayor of Throndhjem notifies the inhabitants of all cities, towns, and villages in the province, that a reward of one thousand crowns is offered for the head of Hans, a native of Klipstadur, in Iceland, a murderer and incendiary."

A vague murmur ran through the crowd. The crier continued:—

"A reward of four crowns is offered for the head of Benignus Spiagudry, ex-keeper of the Spladgest at Throndhjem, accused of necromancy and sacrilege. This proclamation shall be published throughout the province by the mayors of all cities, towns, and villages, who will see that it is carried out."

The mayor took the proclamation from the crier's hands, and added in a lugubrious and solemn voice:—

"The life of these men is offered to whosoever will take it."

The reader will readily believe that this reading was not heard unmoved by our poor, unfortunate Spiagudry. No doubt, the unusual signs of terror which he showed would have roused the attention of the bystanders, had it not just then been wholly absorbed by the first clause of the proclamation.

"A reward for the head of Hans!" cried an old fisherman, who had hastened to the spot, trailing his wet nets behind him. "They might as well, by Saint Usuph, set a price upon the head of Beelzebub!"

"To keep up a proper balance between Hans and Beelzebub," said a hunter, recognizable by his chamois-skin jerkin, "they should only offer fifteen hundred crowns for the head and horns of the latter fiend."

"Glory be to the holy mother of God!" cried an old woman, her bald head shaking as she twirled her distaff. "I only wish I might see the head of that Hans, so that I might make sure if his eyes are really live coals, as they say."

"Yes, to be sure," replied another old woman; "it was just by looking at it that he set Throndhjem cathedral on fire. Now I should like to see the monster whole, with his serpent's tail, cloven foot, and broad wings like a bat."

"Who told you such nonsense, good mother?" broke in the hunter, with a self-satisfied air. "I've seen this Hans of Iceland with my own eyes in the gorges of Medsyhath; he is a man like ourselves, only he is as tall as a forty-year-old poplar."

"Indeed!" said a voice from the crowd, with singular emphasis.

This voice, which made Spiagudry shudder, proceeded from a short man whose face was hidden by the broad felt hat of a miner, his body wrapped in rush matting and sealskin.

"Faith!" cried, with a coarse laugh, a smith who wore his heavy hammer slung across his shoulder, "they may offer one thousand or ten thousand crowns for his head, and he may be four or forty feet tall, but I'll not offer to go in search of him."

"Nor I," said the fisherman.

"Nor I; nor I," repeated every voice.

"And yet any one who may feel tempted," rejoined the little man, "will find Hans of Iceland to-morrow at the ruins of Arbar, near Lake Miösen; the day after that at Walderhog cave."

"Are you sure, my good man?"

This question was asked at one and the same time by Ordener, who listened to this scene with an interest easily understood by any one but Spiagudry, and by another short and tolerably stout man, dressed in black, with a merry countenance, who had issued from the only inn which the village contained, at the first sound of the crier's horn.

The little man with the broad-brimmed hat seemed to be studying them both for a moment, and then answered in hollow tones: "Yes."

"And how can you be so certain?" asked Ordener.

"I know where Hans of Iceland is, just as well as I know where Benignus Spiagudry is; neither of them is far off at this instant."

All the poor keeper's terrors were revived, and he scarcely dared look at the mysterious little man. Fancying that his French periwig had failed to disguise him, he began to pluck at Ordener's cloak and to whisper: "Master, sir, in Heaven's name, have mercy! have pity let us be off! let us leave this accursed suburb of hell!"

Ordener, although equally surprised, carefully examined the little man, who, turning his back to the light, seemed anxious to conceal his face.

"I've seen that Benignus Spiagudry," cried the fisherman, "at Throndhjem Spladgest. He's a tall fellow. They offer four crowns for him."

The hunter burst out laughing.

"Four crowns! I shan't go a-hunting for him. I can get more for the skin of a blue fox."

This comparison, which at any other time would have greatly offended the learned keeper, now comforted him. Still, he was about to address another prayer to Ordener to persuade him to continue his journey, when the latter, having learned all that he wished to know forestalled him by making his way out of the crowd, which was beginning to disperse.

Although when they entered Oëlmœ village they had intended passing the night there, they quitted it, as if by common consent, without even alluding to the motive for their abrupt departure. Ordener was moved by the hope of a more speedy meeting with the brigand, Spiagudry by a desire to get away from the archers as speedily as might be.

Ordener was in too serious a mood to laugh at his comrade's misadventures. He broke the silence in kindly tones.

"Old man, what is the name of the ruin where Hans is to be found tomorrow, according to that little man who seemed to know everything?"

"I don't know; I didn't quite catch the name, noble master," replied Spiagudry, who uttered no falsehood in so saying.

"Then," continued the young man, "I must make up my mind not to meet him until the day after to-morrow at Walderhog cave."

"Walderhog cave, sir! Indeed, that is Hans of Iceland's favorite haunt."

"Let us take that road," said Ordener.

"We must turn to the left, behind Oëlmœ cliff. It will take us at least two days to get to Walderhog cave."

"Do you know, old man," cautiously observed Ordener, "who that odd fellow was, who seemed to be so well acquainted with you?"

This question again awakened Spiagudry's fears, which had been lulled to sleep as the village of Oëlmœ faded in the distance.

"No, truly, sir," he answered, in trembling accents. "But he had a very strange voice."

Ordener tried to encourage him.

"Fear nothing, old man; serve me well, and I will protect you. If I return victorious over Hans, I promise you not only a pardon, but I will also give you the thousand crowns reward offered by the officers of the law."

Honest Benignus dearly loved his life, but he also loved gold. Ordener's promises sounded like magic in his ears; they not only banished all his terrors, but they excited in him a kind of garrulous mirth, which found vent in lengthy discourses, queer gestures, and learned quotations.

"Mr. Ordener," said he, "if I should ever have occasion to discuss the subject with Over-Bilseuth, otherwise called 'the Babbler,' nothing shall prevent me from maintaining that you are a wise and honorable young man. What more worthy and more glorious, in fact, *quid cithara, tuba, vel campana dignius*, than nobly to risk your life to free your country from a monster, a brigand, a demon, in whom all demons, brigands, and monsters seem to be combined? Nobody need tell me that you are moved by mercenary motives. Noble Lord Ordener yields the price of his conflict to the companion of his journey, to the old man who only guided him within a mile of Walderhog cave; for I am sure, young master, that you will allow me to await the result of your illustrious enterprise at the village of Surb, situated in the forest within a mile of Walderhog, will you not? And when your glorious victory is made known, sir, all Norway will thrill with joy like that of Vermund the Refugee, when from the summit of this same Oëlmœ cliff, which we just now passed, he saw the great fire kindled by his brother Halfdan on Munkholm tower in token of his deliverance."

At these words Ordener interrupted him eagerly.

"What! is Munkholm tower visible from the top of this rock?"

"Yes, sir; twelve miles to the south, between the mountains which our fathers called Frigga's Footstools. At this hour you should be able to see the light in the tower distinctly."

"Indeed!" exclaimed Ordener, fired by the idea of another glimpse of the seat of all his happiness. "Old man, of course there is a path leading to the top of the rock, is there not?"

"Yes, to be sure; a path which begins in the wood that lies just before us, and rises by a gentle slope to the bare crown of the cliff, whence it is continued by steps cut in the rock by Vermund's companions, as far as the castle, where it ends. Those are the ruins which you see in the moonlight."

"Well, old man, you shall show me the path; we will spend the night in those ruins,—in those ruins from which Munkholm tower is visible."

"Can you really mean it, sir?" asked Benignus. "The fatigues of the day—"

"Old man, I will support your steps; my footing was never more secure."

"Sir, the brambles that block the path, which has long been deserted, the fallen stones, the darkness—"

"I will take the lead."

"There may be some savage beast, some unclean animal, some hideous monster—"

"I did not undertake this journey to avoid monsters."

The idea of halting so near Oëlmœ was very unpleasant to Spiagudry; the thought of seeing Munkholm light, and possibly the light in Ethel's window, enraptured and transported Ordener.

"Young master," urged Spiagudry, "give up this scheme; take my advice. I have a presentiment that it will bring us bad luck."

This plea was as nothing in the face of Ordener's longing.

"Come," said he, impatiently, "you must remember that you agreed to serve me faithfully. I insist upon your showing me the path; where is it?"

"We shall come across it directly," said the keeper, forced to obey.

In fact, they soon saw the path. They entered it; but Spiagudry observed, with surprise mixed with fright, that the tall grass was broken and trampled, and that Vermund the Refugee's old footpath seemed to have been recently trodden.

XX

Leonardo. The king requires your presence.
Henrique. How so?
Lope da Vega: *La Fuerza Lastinosa.*

GENERAL LEVIN DE KNUD sat at his desk, which was covered with papers and open letters, apparently lost in thought. A secretary stood before him awaiting his orders. The general now struck the rich carpet beneath his feet with his spurs, and now absently toyed with the decoration of the Elephant, hanging about his neck from the collar of the order. Occasionally he opened his lips as if to speak, then stopped, rubbed his head, and cast another glance at the unsealed despatches littering the table.

"How the devil!" he cried at last.

This conclusive exclamation was followed by a brief silence.

"Who would ever have imagined," he resumed, "that those devilish miners would have gone so far? Of course they were secretly egged on to this revolt; but do you know, Wapherney, the thing looks serious? Do you know that five or six hundred scoundrels from the Färöe Islands, headed by a certain old thief named Jonas, have already quitted the mines; that a young fanatic called Norbith has also taken command of the Guldbrandsdal malcontents; that all the hot-heads in Sund-Moer, Hubfallo, and Kongsberg, who were only waiting the signal, may have risen already? Do you know that the mountaineers have joined the movement, and that they are headed by one of the boldest foxes of Kiölen, old Kennybol? And finally, do you know that according to popular report in northern Throndhjem, if we are to believe the lord mayor, who has written me, that notorious criminal, upon whose head we have set a price, the much-dreaded Hans, has taken chief command of the insurrection? What do you say to all this, my dear Wapherney? Ahem!"

"Your Excellency," said Wapherney, "knows what measures—"

"There is still another circumstance connected with this lamentable affair which I cannot explain; that is, how our prisoner Schumacker can be the author of the revolt, as they claim. This seems to surprise no one, but it surprises me more than anything else. It is hard to believe that a man whose company my faithful Ordener loves can be a traitor; and yet it is asserted that the miners have risen in his name,—his name is their watchword. They even give him the titles of which the king deprived him. All this seems certain; but how does it happen that Countess d'Ahlefeld knew all these details a week ago, at a time when the first real symptoms of trouble had scarcely begun to appear in the mines? It is strange! No matter, I must provide for every emergency. Give me my seal, Wapherney."

The general wrote three letters, sealed them, and handed them to his secretary.

"See that this message is sent to Baron Vœthaün, colonel of musketeers, now garrisoned at Munkholm, so that his regiment may march at once to the seat of the revolt; this to the officer in command at Munkholm, an order to guard the ex-chancellor more closely than ever. I must see and question this Schumacker myself. Then despatch this letter to Skongen, to Major Wolhm, who is in command there, directing him to send forward a portion of the garrison to the centre of rebellion. Go, Wapherney, and see that these orders are executed at once."

The secretary went out, leaving the governor plunged in meditation.

"All this is very alarming," thought he. "These miners rebelling in one place, this chancellor intriguing in another, that crazy Ordener—nobody knows where! He may be travelling in the very midst of all these rioters, leaving Schumacker here under my protection to conspire against the State, and his daughter, for whose safety I have been kind enough to remove the company of soldiers to which that Frederic d'Ahlefeld belongs, whom Ordener accuses of—Why, it seems to me that this very company might easily stop the advance columns of the insurgents; it is very well situated for that. Wahlstrom, where it is stationed, is near Lake Miösen and Arbar ruin. That is one of the places of which the rebels will be sure to take possession."

At this point in his revery, the general was interrupted by the sound of the opening door.

"Well, what do you want, Gustavus?"

"General, a messenger asks to speak for a moment with your Excellency."

"Well, what is it now? What fresh disaster! Let the messenger come in."

The messenger entered, and handed a packet to the governor, saying, "From his highness the viceroy, your Excellency."

The general hurriedly tore open the despatch.

"By Saint George!" he cried, with a start of surprise, "I believe that they have all gone mad! If here is not the viceroy requesting me to proceed to

Bergen. He says it is on urgent business, by order of the king. A fine time this to transact urgent business! 'The lord chancellor, now travelling in the province of Throndhjem, will take your place during your absence.' Here's a substitute in whom I have no confidence! 'The bishop will assist him—' Really, these are excellent governors that Frederic chooses for a country in a state of revolt,—two gentlemen of the cloth, a chancellor, and a bishop! Well, no matter, the invitation is express; it is the order of the king. Needs must obey; but before I go I must see Schumacker and question him. I am sure that there is a plot to involve me in a network of intrigue; but I have one unerring compass,—my conscience."

XXI

The voice of thy slain brother's blood cries out,
Even from the ground, unto the Lord!
Cain: A Mystery.

"YES, Count; it was this very day, in Arbar ruin, that we were told he might be found. Countless circumstances lead me to believe in the truth of this valuable information which I accidentally picked up yesterday, as I told you, at Oëlmœ village."

"Are we far from this Arbar ruin?"

"It is close by Lake Miösen. The guide assures me that we shall be there before noon."

These words were spoken by two horsemen muffled in brown cloaks, who early one morning were pursuing one of the many narrow, winding paths which run in every direction through the forest lying between Lakes Miösen and Sparbo. A mountain guide, provided with a huntinghorn and an axe, led the way upon his little gray pony, and behind the travellers rode four men armed to the teeth, toward whom these two persons occasionally turned, as if afraid of being overheard.

"If that Iceland thief is really lurking in Arbar ruin," said one rider, whose steed kept a respectful distance behind the other, "it is a great point gained; for the difficulty hitherto has been to find this mysterious being."

"Do you think so, Musdœmon? And suppose he declines our offers?"

"Impossible, your Grace! What brigand could resist gold and a free pardon?"

"But you know that this is no common scoundrel. Do not judge him by yourself. If he should refuse, how can you keep your promise of night before last to the three leaders of the insurrection?"

"Well, noble Count, in that case, which I regard as impossible if we are lucky enough to find our man, has your Grace forgotten that a false Hans of Iceland awaits me two days hence at the hour and place appointed for meeting the three chiefs, at Blue Star, a place, moreover, conveniently near Arbar ruin?"

"You are right, my dear Musdœmon, as usual," said the count; and each resumed his own particular line of thought.

Musdœmon, whose interest it was to keep his master in good humor, for the purpose of diverting him, asked the guide a question.

"My good man, what is that ruined stone cross yonder, behind those young oaks?"

The guide, a man with fixed stare and stupid mien, turned his head and shook it several times, as he said: "Oh, master, that is the oldest gallows in Norway; holy king Olaf had it built for a judge who made a compact with a robber."

Musdœmon saw by his patron's face that the guide's artless words had produced an effect quite contrary to that which he hoped.

"It is a curious story," the guide added; "good Mother Osia told it to me. The robber was ordered to hang the judge."

The poor guide, in his simplicity, did not suppose that the incident with which he meant to entertain his employers was almost an insult to them. Musdœmon stopped him.

"That will do," said he; "we have heard the story before."

"Insolent fellow!" muttered the count, "he has heard the story before. Ah, Musdœmon, you shall pay for your impudence yet."

"Did your Grace speak to me?" obsequiously asked Musdœmon.

"I was thinking how I could obtain the Order of the Dannebrog for you. The marriage of my daughter Ulrica and Baron Ordener would be an excellent opportunity."

Musdœmon was profuse in protestations and thanks.

"By the way," added his Grace, "let us talk business. Do you suppose that the temporary recall which we sent him has reached the Mecklenburger?"

The reader may remember that the count was in the habit of thus designating General Levin de Knud, who was indeed a native of Mecklenburg.

"Let us talk business!" thought the injured Musdœmon; "it seems that my affairs are not 'business.' Count," he replied aloud, "I think that the viceroy's messenger must be in Throndhjem by this time, and therefore General Levin must be getting ready to start."

The count assumed a kindly tone.

"That recall, my dear fellow, was one of your masterstrokes,—one of your best planned and most skilfully executed intrigues."

"The credit belongs as much to your Grace as to me," replied Musdœmon, careful, as we have already remarked, to mix the count in all his machinations.

The master understood this secret desire of his confidant, but chose to seem unconscious of it.

He smiled.

"My dear private secretary, you are always modest; but nothing can make me depreciate your most eminent services. Elphega's presence and the Mecklenburger's absence assure my triumph in Throndhjem. I am now at the head of the province; and if Hans of Iceland accepts the command of the rebels, which I intend to offer him in person, to me will fall, in the eyes of the king, the glory of putting down this distressing insurrection and capturing this terrible brigand."

They were chatting thus in low voices when the guide rode back to them.

"Masters," said he, "here on our left is the hillock upon which Biorn the Just had the double-tongued Vellon beheaded in the presence of his entire army, the traitor having driven off the king's allies and summoned the enemy to the camp, that he might have the appearance of saving Biorn's life."

All these reminiscences of old Norway did not seem to be to Musdœmon's taste, for he hurriedly interrupted the guide.

"Come, come, good man, be silent and go your way, without turning back so often. What do we care about the foolish stories of which these ruins and dead trees remind you? You annoy my master with your old wives' tales."

XXII

Now the hungry lion roars,
And the wolf behowls the moon;
While the heavy ploughman snores,
All with weary task foredone.
Now the wasted brands do glow,
Whilst the screech-owl, screeching loud.
Puts the wretch that lies in woe
In remembrance of a shroud.
Now it is the time of night,
That the graves, all gaping wide,
Every one lets forth his sprite,
In the church-way paths to glide.
Shakespeare: *Midsummer Night's Dream.*

LET us now retrace our steps. We left Ordener and Spiagudry struggling laboriously up the brow of Oëlmœ cliff by the light of the rising moon. This rock, bare of vegetation at the point where it begins to curve, is, from this peculiarity, called by the Norwegian peasants the Vulture's Neck, — a name which gives an excellent idea of the aspect of this huge granite bowlder as seen from a distance.

As our travellers approached this part of the rock, the forest changed to heather. Grass gave place to moss; wild brier-roses, broom, and holly were substituted for oaks and beeches, — a scantier growth, which in mountainous regions always shows that the summit is near, as it indicates the gradual diminution of the stratum of earth covering what may be termed the skeleton of the mountain.

"Mr. Ordener," said Spiagudry, whose lively mind seemed ever a prey to a varying world of ideas, "this is a very tiresome climb, and it takes all my devotion to follow you. But it seems to me that I see a superb *convolvulus* yonder to the right; how I should like to examine it. Why is it not broad daylight? Don't you think it was a great piece of impertinence to value a learned man like me at no more than four paltry crowns? 'Tis true, the famous Phædrus was a slave, and Æsop, if we are to believe the learned

Planudes, was sold at a fair like a beast of burden or household chattel. And who would not be proud to bear any sort of resemblance to the great Æsop?"

"Or to the celebrated Hans?" added Ordener, with a smile.

"By Saint Hospitius," replied the keeper, "do not utter that name so lightly; I swear I could readily forego the latter comparison. But wouldn't it be strange if Benignus Spiagudry, his companion in misfortune, should win the reward for his head? Mr. Ordener, you are more generous than Jason, for he did not give the golden fleece to the Argonaut pilot; and I am sure that your mission, although I do not clearly understand its object, is no less perilous than that of Jason."

"Well," said Ordener, "since you know Hans of Iceland, tell me something about him. You say that he is by no means a giant, as is generally supposed."

Spiagudry interrupted him: "Stop, master! Don't you hear footsteps behind us?"

"Yes," quietly answered the young man; "don't be alarmed; it is some animal frightened at our coming, and brushing against the bushes in its flight."

"You are right, my young Cæsar; it is so long since these woods have seen the face of man! If we may judge by its heavy tread, it must be a good-sized animal. It may be an elk or a reindeer; this part of Norway abounds in these beasts. Wildcats are also found here; I saw one myself, which was brought to Copenhagen; he was monstrous big. I must give you a description of this ferocious animal."

"My dear guide," said Ordener, "I would rather that you would give me a description of another and no less ferocious monster, the horrible Hans."

"Speak lower, sir! How calmly you utter that name! You do not know — Good Heavens, sir! just hear that!"

As Spiagudry said this, he drew closer to Ordener, who did indeed distinctly hear a cry similar to the growl which, as the reader may remember, had so alarmed the timid keeper on the stormy night of their departure from Throndhjem.

"Did you hear that?" he whispered, breathless with fright.

"To be sure I did," said Ordener; "but I don't see why you tremble so violently. It is the howl of some wild beast, possibly the cry of one of those very wildcats of which you were just talking. Did you expect to pass through such a place at this time of night without disturbing any of its inhabitants? I'll warrant you, old man, they are far more frightened than you are."

Spiagudry, seeing his young companion's composure, was somewhat reassured.

"Well, it may be, sir, that you are right. But that yell sounded terribly like a voice that I—It was a very poor idea, let me tell you, sir, to insist upon climbing up to this Vermund's castle. I fear we shall meet with some accident on the Vulture's Neck."

"Fear nothing while you are with me," answered Ordener.

"Oh, nothing disturbs you; but, sir, nobody but the blessed Saint Paul can handle vipers without getting bitten. You did not even notice, when we struck into this confounded footpath, that it seemed to have been recently trodden, and that the grass had not had time to lift its head since it was trampled."

"I confess that I did not pay much heed to it, and that my peace of mind is not dependent upon the state of a few blades of grass. See, we are now out of the thicket; we shall hear no more from the wild beasts; I need not therefore tell you, my brave guide, to summon all your courage, but rather bid you muster all your strength, for this path, cut in the rock, will doubtless be even steeper than the one we have left."

"It is not that it is steeper, sir, but the learned traveller, Suckson, says that it is often impeded by rocks or heavy stones too big to be handled, over which it is not easy to clamber. Among others, there is, just beyond the Maläer postern, which must be close at hand, a huge triangular granite bowlder, which I have always had the greatest desire to see. Schoenning asserts that he discovered the three primitive Runic characters on it."

The travellers had for some time been climbing the face of the rock; they now reached a small, ruined tower, through which their path led, and to which Spiagudry drew Ordener's attention.

"This is the Maläer postern, sir. This path hewn in the living rock contains several curious structures, which show the ancient style of fortification used in our Norwegian manor-houses. This postern, which was always guarded by four men-at-arms, was the first outwork of Vermund's fort. Speaking of posterns, the monk Urensius makes an odd remark; he asks whether the word *janua*, derived from Janus, whose temple doors were so widely celebrated, has any connection with 'Janissary,' a name applied to the troops who guard the sultan's gate. It would be strange enough if the name of the mildest prince known to history should have passed to the most ferocious soldiers upon earth."

In the midst of all the keeper's scientific twaddle, they journeyed laboriously along, over loose stones and sharp pebbles, mingled with the short, slippery grass which sometimes grows upon rocks. Ordener beguiled his weariness by thinking how delightful it would be to gaze once more upon distant Munkholm; all at once Spiagudry exclaimed: "Oh, I see it! This sight alone repays me for all my trouble. I see it, sir, I see it!"

"See what?" said Ordener, who was just then thinking of Ethel.

"Why, sir, the three-sided pyramid described by Schoenning. I shall be the third scientific man, with Professor Schoenning and Bishop Isleif, to have the pleasure of studying it. Only it is a great pity that there is no moon."

As they approached the famous bowlder, Spiagudry uttered an exclamation of horror and distress. Ordener, in surprise, asked with some interest the cause of this new emotion; but the archæologist was for a time unable to reply.

"You thought," said Ordener, "that this rock blocked the path; on the contrary, you should be grateful to find that it leaves it entirely open."

"And that is the very thing which provokes me," said Benignus, in piteous accents.

"What do you mean?"   •

"Why, sir," replied the keeper, "do you not see that the position of the pyramid has been changed; that the base, which rested on the path, is now uppermost; and that the bowlder stands upside down, upon the very side on which Schoenning discovered the primordial Runic letters? I am indeed unfortunate!"

"It is a pity," said the young man.

"And besides," hastily added Spiagudry, "the overturning of this mass of stone proves the presence of some superhuman being. Unless it be the work of the Devil, there is but one man in Norway whose arm could—"

"My poor guide, there you are, giving way again to your foolish fears. Who knows but this stone has lain thus for more than a hundred years?"

"It is a hundred and fifty years, it is true," said Spiagudry, more quietly, "since the last scientific man observed it. But it seems to me to have been moved recently; the place which it formerly occupied is still damp. Look, sir."

Ordener, impatient to reach the ruins, dragged his guide away from the marvellous pyramid, and succeeded, by gentle words, in removing the fresh fears with which this strange displacement inspired the aged scholar.

"See here, old man, you can take up your abode on the borders of this lake, and devote yourself to your important studies, when you get the thousand crowns reward for Hans's head."

"You are right, noble sir; but do not speak so lightly of so dubious a victory. I must give you one piece of advice which may help you to overcome the monster."

Ordener drew eagerly toward Spiagudry. "Advice! what is it?"

"The robber," said the latter, in a low voice, casting uneasy glances around him, — "the robber wears at his belt a skull, from which he usually drinks. It is the skull of his son, of the mutilation of whose corpse I am accused."

"Speak a little louder, and don't be frightened; I can hardly hear you. Well, this skull?"

"This skull," said Spiagudry, bending to whisper in the young man's ear, "you must try to obtain. The monster attaches a certain superstitious importance to its possession. His son's skull once yours, you can do what you will with him."

"That is all very well, my good fellow; but how am I to get this skull?"

"By some stratagem, sir. While the monster sleeps, perhaps."

Ordener interrupted him: "Enough. Your good advice is useless. I cannot be supposed to know when my enemy is asleep. My sword is the only weapon which I recognize."

"Sir, sir! it has never been proved that the archangel Michael did not resort to stratagem to vanquish Satan."

Here Spiagudry stopped short, and stretching out his hands, exclaimed in scarcely audible tones, "Oh, heavens! Oh, heavens! What do I see? Look, master; is not that a short man walking before us in the path?"

"Faith," said Ordener, raising his eyes, "I see nothing."

"Nothing, sir? To be sure, the path bends, and he has disappeared behind that rock. Go no farther, sir, I entreat you."

"Surely, if the person whom you imagine that you saw disappeared so quickly, it shows that he has no idea of waiting for us; and if he chooses to run away, that is no reason why we should do the same."

"Watch over us, holy Hospitius!" ejaculated Spiagudry, who in all moments of danger remembered his favorite saint.

"You must," added Ordener, "have taken the flickering shadow of some startled owl for a man."

"And yet I really thought I saw a little man; to be sure, the moonlight often produces strange delusions. It was in the moonlight that Baldan, lord of Merneugh, took a white bed-curtain for his mother's ghost; which led him to go next day and confess himself guilty of parricide before the judges of Christiania, who were about to condemn the dead woman's innocent page. So we may say that the moonlight saved that page's life."

No one was ever more ready than Spiagudry to forget the present in the past. One anecdote from the vast storehouse of his memory was enough to banish all thought of the present. Thus the story of Baldan diverted his fears, and he added in a tranquil voice, "It is quite possible that the moonlight deceived me too."

Meantime, they gained the top of the Vulture's Neck, and began to get another glimpse of the ruins, which the steep slope of the rock had hidden from them as they ascended.

The reader need not be surprised if we frequently encounter ruins on the topmost peak of Norwegian mountains. No one who has travelled among the mountains of Europe can have failed to notice the remains of fortresses and castles clinging to the top of the loftiest peaks, like the deserted nest of a vulture or the eyrie of some dead eagle. In Norway especially, at the period of which we write, the variety of these aerial structures was as amazing as their number. Sometimes they consisted of long dismantled walls, enclosing a rock, sometimes of slender pointed turrets, surmounting a sharp peak, like a crown; or upon the snowy summit of a lofty mountain might be seen great towers grouped about a massive donjon, looking in the distance like an antique diadem. Here were the graceful pointed arches of a Gothic cloister, side by side with the heavy Egyptian columns of a Saxon church; there, close by some pagan chieftain's citadel with its square towers, stood the crenellated fortress of a Christian lord; or, again, a stronghold crumbling with age, neighbored by a monastery ravaged by war. Of all these edifices—a strange medley of architectural styles, now almost forgotten, daringly constructed in apparently inaccessible spots—but a few ruins remained to bear witness alike to the power and the impotence of man. Within their walls deeds were perhaps done far worthier of repetition than all the stories which are written now; but time passed; the eyes which witnessed them are closed; the tradition of them died with the lapse of years, like a fire which is not fed; and when that is lost, who can read the secret of the ages?

The manor-house of Vermund the Refugee, which our two travellers had now reached, was one of those places about which popular superstition has woven endless amazing histories and marvellous legends. By its walls—composed of pebbles bedded in cement, now harder than stone— it was easy to determine that it was built about the fifth or sixth century. But one of its five towers remained standing; the other four, more or less dilapidated, and strewing the top of the rock with broken fragments, were connected by a line of ruins, which also showed the ancient limits of the inner courts of the castle. It was very difficult to penetrate this enclosure, littered as it was with stones and shattered blocks of granite, and overgrown with weeds and brambles which, clambering from ruin to ruin, crowned the broken walls with verdure, or overhung the precipice with long, flexible branches. On these drooping tendrils, it was said, dim ghosts often swung in the moonlight,—the guilty spirits of those who had wilfully drowned themselves in Lake Sparbo; and to these twigs, too, the water-sprite fastened the cloud which was to bear him home again at sunrise. Fearful mysteries were these, more than once witnessed by hardy fishermen, when, to take advantage of the time when dogfish sleep,[13] they ventured to row as far as Oëlmœ cliff, which loomed up in the darkness over their heads like the broken arch of some huge bridge.

Our two adventurers climbed the manor wall, though not without some difficulty, and crept through a crevice, for the door was filled with fragments. The only tower which, as we have said, remained standing, was at the extreme edge of the rock. It was, Spiagudry told Ordener, from the top of this tower that Munkholm lighthouse could be seen. They went towards it, although the darkness was at that moment complete, the moon being hidden by a great black cloud. They were about to cross a breach in another wall, in order to enter what was once the second courtyard of the castle, when Benignus stopped short, and suddenly seized Ordener's arm with such a trembling hand that the young man himself almost fell.

"What now?" asked Ordener in surprise.

Benignus, without answering, pressed his arm more firmly, as if begging him to be silent.

"Well—" said the young man.

Another pressure, accompanied by an ill-suppressed sigh, decided him to wait patiently until this fresh fright should cease.

At last Spiagudry asked, in a stifled voice: "Well, master, what do you say now?"

"To what?" said Ordener.

"Yes, sir," added the other, in the same tone; "I suppose you are sorry now that you came here?"

"No, indeed, my worthy guide; on the contrary, I hope to climb higher still. Why should you think that I am sorry?"

"What, sir, did you not see?"

"See! What?"

"You saw nothing?" repeated the honest keeper, with ever-increasing terror.

"Truly I did not," impatiently answered Ordener; "I saw nothing, and I heard nothing but the sound of your teeth chattering with fright."

"What! not behind that wall, in the shadow, those two flaming eyes, like comets, fixed directly upon us,—did you not see them?"

"Upon my honor, I did not."

"You did not see them move up and down, and then disappear among the ruins?"

"I don't know what you are talking about. Besides, what if I did see them?"

"What! Mr. Ordener, don't you know that there is but one man in Norway whose eyes gleam in that way in the dark?"

"Well, and what then? Who is this man with the eyes of a cat? Is it Hans, your much-dreaded Icelander? So much the better if he be here! It will spare us a journey to Walderhog."

This "so much the better" was not to the taste of Spiagudry, who could not help betraying his secret thought by the involuntary ejaculation: "Oh, sir, you promised to leave me at the village of Surb, a mile away from the battle."

The generous and kindly Ordener understood, and smiled.

"You are right, old man; it would be unfair to make you share my danger; therefore fear nothing. You see this Hans of Iceland everywhere. May there not be some wildcat lurking among these ruins, whose eyes shine quite as fiercely as his do?"

Once more Spiagudry's fears were set at rest, either because Ordener's suggestion struck him as very plausible, or because his young companion's composure proved contagious.

"Ah, sir," said he, "if it had not been for you I should have died a dozen deaths from fright as I climbed these rocks. To be sure, I should never have attempted such a task if it had not been for you."

The moon, which now broke through the clouds, showed them the gateway to the highest tower, the foot of which they had already reached. They entered, after raising a thick curtain of vines, which showered them with drowsy lizards and old decayed bird's-nests. The keeper picked up a couple of pebbles, and striking them together, produced a few sparks, by means of which he soon set fire to a heap of dead leaves and dry branches collected by Ordener. In a few moments a bright column of flame rose into the air, and banishing the darkness about them, permitted them to examine the interior of the tower.

Nothing was left but a circular wall, which was very thick, and was overgrown with moss and vines. The ceiling and floors of its four stories had crumbled away one after the other, and now formed a vast heap of rubbish upon the ground. A narrow spiral staircase, entirely without a railing, and broken in various places, was built in the wall, to the top of which it led. As the fire began to crackle cheerily, a swarm of owls and ospreys flew up heavily, with strange, weird cries, and huge bats now and then hovered above the flames, poised upon their ashen wings.

"Our hosts do not receive us very merrily," said Ordener; "but do not take fright again."

"I, sir," replied Spiagudry, seating himself close to the fire; "I fear an owl or a bat! I have dwelt with corpses, and I do not fear vampires. Ah, I only dread the living! I am not brave, I admit; but at least I am not superstitious. Come, sir, take my advice; let us laugh at these ladies in black petticoats and with such hoarse voices, and let us be thinking of supper."

Ordener thought of nothing but Munkholm.

"I have here a few provisions," said Spiagudry, drawing his knapsack from under his cloak; "but if your appetite be as good as mine, this black bread and mouldy cheese will not go far. I see that we shall have to observe the limits of the law laid down by the French king, Philip the Fair, —*Nemo audeat comedere præter duo fercula cum potagio.* There must be nests of gulls or pheasants on the top of this tower; but how are we to get there by that dilapidated staircase, which does not look as if it would bear the weight of anything but a sylph?"

"Still," answered Ordener, "it must needs bear mine, for I shall certainly climb to the top of this tower."

"What, master! to get a few gull's-nests? Do not, for mercy's sake, be so rash! It is not worth while to kill yourself for the sake of a better supper. Besides, suppose you should make a mistake and take the nests of these owls?"

"Much I care for your nests! Didn't you tell me that I could see Munkholm light from the top of this tower?"

"So you can, young master; it lies to the south. I see that your desire to establish this point, so important to the science of geography, was your motive for taking this fatiguing journey to Vermund castle. But do consider, good Mr. Ordener, that it may sometimes be the duty of a zealous student to brave toil and hardship, but never to run into danger. I implore you, do not attempt that poor broken-down staircase, upon which even a crow would not venture to perch."

Benignus was by no means anxious to be left alone in the tower. As he rose to take Ordener's hand, his knapsack, which was lying across his knees, fell upon some stones, and gave forth a clear metallic ring.

"What have you in your wallet that rings so loudly?" asked Ordener.

This was such a delicate question that Spiagudry lost all desire to restrain his young companion.

"Well," said he, without answering the question, "if, in spite of all my prayers, you persist in climbing to the top of this tower, at least beware of the broken places in the stairs."

"But," repeated Ordener, "you have not told me what you have in your knapsack to make it sound so metallic."

This indiscreet persistence was extremely unpleasant to the old keeper, who cursed the questioner from the bottom of his soul.

"Oh, noble master," he replied, "how can you show such curiosity about a paltry iron barber's-basin, which clinked against a stone? If I cannot persuade you to change your mind," he made haste to add, "come back as soon as you can, and be careful to hold fast to the vines which cover the wall. You will see Munkholm lighthouse to the south, between Frigga's Footstools."

Spiagudry could not have said anything better calculated to drive every other idea out of the young man's head. Ordener, throwing aside his mantle, sprang toward the staircase, up which the keeper followed him with his eyes until he could only see him move like a faint shadow upward to the top of the wall, dimly lighted by the flickering flames and the cold rays of the moon.

Then reseating himself and picking up his knapsack, he said: "Now, my dear Benignus Spiagudry, while that young lynx cannot see you, and you are alone, make haste and break the cumbrous iron envelope which prevents you from taking possession, *oculis et manu*, of the treasure undoubtedly contained in this casket. When it is delivered from its prison, it will be lighter to carry and easier to conceal."

Arming himself with a huge stone, he was about to break the lid of the box, when the firelight, falling on the iron lock, suddenly arrested the antiquarian.

"By Saint Willibrod the Numismatologist, I am not mistaken," he exclaimed, eagerly rubbing the rusty lid; "those are indeed the arms of Griffenfeld. I came near doing a very foolish thing in breaking this lock. This may be the only perfect copy in existence of those famous armorial bearings destroyed in 1676 by the hangman's hand. The devil! I will not touch this box. Whatever may be the value of its contents, unless, as seems scarcely probable, it should be coin of Palmyra or Carthaginian money, this is certainly still more precious. So here I am the sole owner of the now obsolete arms of Griffenfeld! Let me hide this treasure carefully, and I may some time discover the secret of opening the casket without committing an act of vandalism. The Griffenfeld arms! Oh, yes! here are the hand of Justice and the scales upon a gules ground. What luck!"

At each fresh heraldic discovery that he made as he polished the ancient coffer, he uttered a cry of admiration or an exclamation of content.

"By means of a solvent, I can open the box without breaking the lock. It probably contains the ex-chancellor's treasure. If any one, tempted by the bait of the four crowns offered by the council for my head, should recognize me now and stop me, I can readily buy my freedom. So this blessed casket will save me."

As he spoke, he looked up mechanically. All at once his grotesque features changed with lightning speed from an expression of intense delight to that of stupefied dismay; his limbs trembled convulsively, his eyes became fixed, his brow furrowed, his mouth gaped wide, and his voice stuck in his throat.

Before him, on the other side of the fire, stood a little man with folded arms. By his dress of blood-stained skins, his stone axe, his red beard, and the ravenous stare fastened on his face, the wretched keeper at once recognized the frightful character whose last visit he had received in the Spladgest at Throndhjem.

"It is I!" said the little man, with terrible calmness. "That casket will save you," he added with a bitterly sarcastic smile. "Spiagudry, is this the way to Thoctree?"

The unfortunate man tried to stammer a word of excuse.

"Thoctree! Sir—My lord and master,—I was going—"

"You were going to Walderhog," replied the other, in a voice of thunder.

The terrified Spiagudry mustered all his forces to deny the charge.

"You were guiding an enemy to my retreat. I thank you! 'Twill be one living man the less. Fear nothing, faithful guide; he shall follow you."

The luckless keeper strove to shriek, but could with difficulty utter a feeble moan.

"Why are you so frightened at my presence? You were seeking me. Hark ye! Do not speak, or you are a dead man."

The little man swung his stone axe above the keeper's head. He added, in a voice which sounded like the roar of a mountain torrent as it bursts from some subterranean cave: "You have betrayed me."

"No, your Grace! No, your Excellency!" gasped Benignus, scarcely able to articulate these words of apology and entreaty.

The other gave vent to a low growl.

"Ah! you would deceive me again! Hope not to succeed. Listen! I was on the roof of the Spladgest when you sealed your compact with that mad fool; twice you have heard my voice. It was my voice you heard amid the storm upon your road; it was I whom you met in Vygla tower; it was I who said, 'We shall meet again!'"

The terrified keeper looked about him in despair, as if to summon help. The little man went on: "I could not let those soldiers who pursued you, escape my wrath; they belonged to the Munkholm regiment. I knew that I should not lose you. Spiagudry, it was I whom you saw again in Oëlmœ village beneath the miner's hat; it was my footstep and my voice that you heard, and my eyes that you saw as you climbed to these ruins. It was I!"

Alas! the unfortunate man was but too well convinced of these dreadful truths. He rolled upon the ground at the feet of his fearful judge, crying in faint and agonizing accents, "Mercy!"

The little man, his arms still folded, fixed upon him a murderous look, more scorching even than the flames upon the hearth.

"Ask that casket to save you, as you said it would do," he said sarcastically.

"Mercy, sir, mercy!" repeated the expiring victim.

"I warned you to be faithful and to be dumb. You have not been faithful; but in future I protest that you shall be dumb."

The keeper, grasping the horrible meaning of these words, uttered a deep groan.

"Fear nothing," said the man; "I will not part you from your treasure."

At these words, unfastening his leather belt, he passed it through a ring on the cover of the casket, and by this means hung it about Spiagudry's neck, the poor fellow bending beneath its weight.

"Come!" rejoined the monster, "to what devil will you confide your soul? Make haste and summon him, lest another demon whom you do not care about, take possession of it before him."

The desperate old man, past all power of speech, fell at the little man's knees, making countless gestures of terror and entreaty.

"No, no!" said his tormentor; "my faithful Spiagudry, you need not be distressed at leaving your young companion without a guide. I promise you that he shall go where you go. Follow me; you do but show him the way. Come!"

With these words, seizing the wretched man in his powerful arms, he bore him from the tower as a tiger might carry off a writhing serpent, and a moment later a fearful shriek rang through the ruins, mingled with a horrible burst of laughter.

XXIII

Yes, we may reveal to the faithful lover's tear-wet eye the distant object of his adoration. But alas! the moments of expectation, the farewells, the thoughts, the sweet and bitter memories, the enchanting dreams of two beings that love! Who can restore these? — Maturin: *Bertram*.

MEANTIME the venturesome Ordener, after a score or more of narrow escapes from a fall during his perilous ascent, reached the top of the thick, round tower wall. At his unexpected visit, dusky old owls abruptly aroused from their nests, flew up, staring at him as they sailed away, and loose stones, displaced by his tread, rolled into the abyss, rebounding from projections in the masonry with a remote, hollow roar.

At any other time, Ordener's gaze would have roamed far and wide, and his mind would have dwelt upon the depth of the gulf yawning beneath him, which seemed even greater from the thick darkness of the night. His eye, taking in all the great masses of shadow on the horizon, their sombre outlines but half revealed by a nebulous moon, would have striven to distinguish between mist and rocks, between mountains and clouds; his imagination would have lent life to all the gigantic forms, the fantastic shapes with which moonlight clothes hills and vapors. He would have listened to the indistinct murmur of lake and woods blended with the shrill sough of the wind through the crevices in the stones and through the dried grass at his feet, and his fancy would have lent words to all those low voices through which material Nature speaks while man sleeps, in the silence of the night. But although the scene unconsciously acted upon his whole being, other thoughts filled his mind. Hardly had his foot touched the top of the wall, when his eye turned to the southern sky, and he thrilled with unspeakable rapture as he saw beyond and between two small mountains a point of light gleaming upon the horizon like a red star. It was Munkholm beacon.

None but those who have tasted the truest joys which life can give can understand the young man's happiness. His soul was filled with delight; his heart beat violently. Motionless, his eye fixed, he gazed at the star of hope and consolation. It seemed as if that beam of light traversing the darkness, and coming from the spot which held all that made life worth living, bore with it something of his Ethel. Ah! do not doubt it; one soul may sometimes hold mysterious communion with another, though widely parted by time and space. In vain the world of reality rears its barriers between two beings who love; inhabitants of an ideal world, they are present to each other in absence, they are united in death. What can mere bodily separation or physical distance avail if two hearts be indissolubly bound by a single thought and a common desire? True love may suffer, but it cannot die.

Who has not repeatedly lingered on a rainy night beneath some dimly lighted window? Who has not passed and repassed a certain door, rapturously wandered up and down before a certain house? Who has not abruptly retraced his steps, to follow, at evening, along some deserted, winding street, a floating skirt or a white veil suddenly recognized in the twilight? He who has never experienced these feelings may safely say that he has never loved.

As he gazed at the distant lighthouse, Ordener pondered. A sad and ironical contentment took the place of his first transports; a thousand varying thoughts and ideas crowded upon his agitated spirit. "Yes," said he, "a man must labor long and painfully to win at last a ray of happiness in the vast night of existence. So she is there! She sleeps, she dreams, perhaps she thinks of me! But who will tell her that her Ordener even now hangs above an abyss, sad and lonely, surrounded by darkness,—her Ordener, who retains nothing of her but a single ringlet pressed to his heart and a faint light upon the horizon!" Then, looking at the ruddy glow of the huge fire burning in the tower beneath, and escaping through the crevices in the wall, he murmured: "Perhaps from one of her prison windows she casts an indifferent glance at the far-off flame upon this hearth."

All at once, a loud shriek and a prolonged burst of laughter rose from the brink of the precipice below; he turned abruptly, and saw that the interior of the tower was vacant. Alarmed for the safety of the old man, he hurriedly descended; but he had taken but a few steps when he heard a dull splash, as if a heavy body had been thrown into the deep waters of the lake.

XXIV

Count Don Sancho Diaz, lord of Saldana, shed bitter tears in
his prison cell. Full of despair, he sighed forth in solitude his
complaints against King Alfonso: "Oh, sad moments, when
my white locks remind me how many years I have already
passed in this horrible prison!" —*Old Spanish Romance.*

THE sun was setting, and its horizontal beams threw the dark shadow of
the prison-bars upon Schumacker's woollen gown and Ethel's crape dress,
as they sat by the high-arched casement, the old man in a great Gothic chair,
the young girl upon a stool at his feet. The prisoner seemed to be brooding,
in his favorite melancholy attitude. His bald, wrinkled brow rested on his
hand, and his face was hidden save for the long white beard which hung
down his breast in sad disorder.

"Father," said Ethel, trying by every means to rouse him, "my lord and
father, I dreamed last night of a happy future. Look, dear father; raise your
eyes, and see that bright, cloudless sky."

"I can only see the sky," the old man replied, "through my prison-bars,
as I can only see your future, Ethel, through my misfortunes."

Then his head, for an instant lifted, fell back upon his hands, and both
were silent.

"Father," rejoined the young girl, a moment later, in a timid voice, "are
you thinking of Lord Ordener?"

"Ordener?" said the old man, as if striving to recall the name. "Ah, I
know whom you mean! What of him?"

"Do you think that he will soon return, father? He has been gone so
long!—this is the fourth day."

The old man shook his head sadly.

"I think that when four years have passed, his return will be as close at
hand as it is to-day."

Ethel turned pale.

"Heavens! Then you think that he will not come back?"

Schumacker made no answer. The young girl repeated her question in an anxious and beseeching tone.

"Did he not promise to return?" said the old man, curtly.

"Yes, to be sure!" eagerly answered Ethel.

"Well, how can you reckon upon his coming, then? Is he not a man? I believe that the vulture will return to a dead body, but I have no faith in the return of spring when the year is on the wane."

Ethel, seeing that her father had relapsed into his wonted melancholy, took courage; the voice of her young and virginal soul proudly denied the old man's morbid philosophy.

"Father," she said firmly, "Lord Ordener will return; he is not like other men."

"What do you know about it, girl?"

"What you know yourself, my lord and father."

"I know nothing," said the old man. "I heard words from a man, and they promised the actions of a god." Then he added, with a bitter smile: "I have weighed them well, and I see that they are too beautiful to be true."

"And I, sir, believe them because they are so beautiful."

"Oh, girl, if you were what you should be, Countess of Tönsberg and Princess of Wollin, surrounded, as you would be, by a swarm of handsome traitors and selfish adorers, such credulity would be most dangerous."

"It is not credulity, my lord and father, but confidence."

"It is easy to see, Ethel, that there is French blood in your veins."

This idea led the old man, by an imperceptible transition, to a different train of thought, and he added, with a certain complacency:—

"For those who degraded your father to a point lower yet than that from which he had raised himself, cannot deny that you are the daughter of Charlotte, Princess of Tarentum, or that one of your ancestresses was Adela (or Edila), Countess of Flanders, whose name you bear."

Ethel's mind was running on quite other things.

"Father, you misjudge the noble Ordener."

"Noble, my daughter! What do you mean by that? I have made men noble who proved themselves very vile."

"I do not mean, sir, that his nobility is of the kind conferred by man."

"Do you know that he is descended from some 'jarl' or 'hersa'?"[14]

"I know as little of his descent as you do, father. He may be," she added, with downcast eyes, "the son of a vassal or a serf. Alas! crowns and lyres may be painted upon the velvet covering of a footstool. I only mean that, judged by your own standard, my revered sire, he has a noble heart."

Of all the men whom she had seen, Ordener was the one whom Ethel knew at once best and least. He had dawned upon her destiny, like one of those angels who visited the first men, wrapped alike in mystery and in radiant light. Their mere presence revealed their nature, and they were at once adored. Thus Ordener had shown Ethel what men usually conceal, his heart; he had been silent concerning that of which they usually make boast, his country and his family. His look was enough for Ethel, and she had faith in his words. She loved him, she had given him her life, she was intimate with his soul, and she did not know his name.

"A noble heart!" repeated the old man; "a noble heart! Such nobility is higher than any in the gift of kings; it is the gift of God. He is less lavish with it than are they."

The prisoner raised his eyes to his shattered escutcheon as he added: "And he never withdraws it."

"Then, father," said the girl, "he who retains the one should be easily consoled for the loss of the other."

These words startled her father and restored his courage. He replied in a firm voice:—

"You are right, girl. But you do not know that the disgrace held by the world to be unjust is sometimes confirmed by our secret conscience. Such is our poor nature; once unhappy, countless voices which slumbered in the time of our prosperity wake within us and accuse us of faults and errors before unnoted."

"Say not so, illustrious father," said Ethel, deeply moved; for by the old man's altered voice, she felt that he had allowed the secret source of one of his greatest sorrows to escape him.

She raised her eyes to his face, and kissing his pallid, withered hand, she added gently: "You are severe in your judgment of two noble men, Lord Ordener and yourself, my revered father."

"You decide lightly, Ethel. One would say that you did not know that life is a serious matter."

"Am I wrong then, sir, to do justice to the generous Ordener?"

Schumacker frowned, with a dissatisfied air.

"I cannot approve, my daughter, of such admiration for a stranger whom you may never see again."

"Oh," said the young girl, upon whose soul these cold words fell like a heavy weight, "do not believe it. We shall see him again. Was it not for your sake that he went forth to brave such danger?"

"Like yourself, I confess that I was at first deceived by his promises. But no; he will never go upon his mission, and therefore he will never return to us."

"He did go, sir; he did go."

The tone in which the young girl pronounced these words was almost that of one offended and insulted. She felt herself outraged in her Ordener's person. Alas! she was only too sure in her own soul of the truth which she asserted.

The prisoner replied, seemingly unmoved: "Very well. If he has really gone to fight that brigand, if he has rushed into such danger, it comes to the same thing, — he will never return."

Poor Ethel! how often a word indifferently uttered, painfully galls the hidden wound in an anxious and tortured heart! She bent her pale face to hide from her father's stern gaze the tears which, in spite of all her efforts, fell from her burning eyes.

"Oh, father," she sighed, "while you speak thus, this noble and unfortunate youth may be dying for your sake!"

The aged minister shook his head doubtfully.

"That I can neither believe nor wish. And even so, how am I to blame? I should merely show myself ungrateful to the young man, as so many others have shown themselves to me."

A deep sigh was Ethel's only answer; and Schumacker, turning to his table, tore up with an absent air a few leaves of "Plutarch's Lives," which volume lay before him, already tattered in countless places, and covered with marginal notes. A moment later the door opened, and Schumacker, without looking up, cried out as usual: "Do not enter! do not disturb me! I will see no one!"

"It is his Excellency the governor," was the answer.

An elderly man dressed in the uniform of a general, with the collars of the Elephant, the Dannebrog, and the Golden Fleece about his neck, advanced toward Schumacker, who half rose, muttering, "The governor! the governor!" The general bowed respectfully to Ethel, as she stood at her father's side, timidly and anxiously watching him.

Perhaps before proceeding further, it will be well briefly to recall the motives of General Levin's visit to Munkholm. The reader will remember the unpleasant news which disturbed the old governor, in the twentieth chapter of this truthful narrative. On receiving it, he at once saw the importance of questioning Schumacker; but he was extremely reluctant to do so. The idea of tormenting a poor prisoner, already a prey to so much that was painful, and whom he had known in his days of power, of severely scanning the secrets of an unfortunate man, even if guilty, was most unpleasant to his kind and generous soul. Still, his duty to the king required it. He ought not to leave Throndhjem without such fresh light as might be gained by questioning the apparent author of the rebellion among the miners. Accordingly, the night before his departure, after a long and confidential talk with Countess d'Ahlefeld, the governor made up his mind to visit the prisoner. As he approached the fortress, thoughts of the interests of the State, of the advantage to which his many personal enemies might turn what they would style his negligence, and perhaps too the crafty words of the chancellor's wife, worked within him, and confirmed him in his purpose. He therefore climbed to the Lion of Schleswig tower with every intention to be severe; he resolved to bear himself toward Schumacker the conspirator as if he had never known Griffenfeld the chancellor,—to cast aside all his memories, and even his natural disposition, and to speak as a firm judge to this former fellow-sharer in the royal favor.

So soon, however, as he entered the ex-chancellor's apartment, the old man's venerable though sombre face made a strong impression upon him; Ethel's sweet though dignified expression touched him; and with his first glance at the two prisoners, his stern intentions died within him.

He advanced toward the fallen minister, and involuntarily offered him his hand, saying, without remarking that his politeness met with no response:—

"How are you, Count Griffenf—" His old habit overcame him for the moment; then he corrected himself quickly—"Mr. Schumacker?" With this he paused, satisfied and exhausted by such an effort.

Silence ensued. The general racked his brain to find words harsh enough to correspond with this brutal beginning.

"Well," Schumacker said at last, "are you the governor of the province of Throndhjem?"

The governor, somewhat surprised to find himself questioned by the man he had meant to question, bowed his head.

"Then," added the prisoner, "I have a complaint to lay before you."

"A complaint! What is it? what is it?" And the kind-hearted Levin's countenance assumed a look of interest.

Schumacker went on, in a tone of considerable annoyance: "By order of the viceroy I am to be left free and undisturbed in this donjon."

"I am aware of the order."

"And yet, Governor, I am importuned and annoyed by visits."

"Visits! and from whom?" cried the general; "tell me who dares—"

"You, Governor."

These words, uttered in a haughty tone, offended the general. He answered, in a somewhat irritated voice: "You forget that my power knows no limits when it is a question of serving the king."

"Unless," said Schumacker, "it were those of the respect due to misfortune. But men know nothing of that."

The ex-chancellor said this as if speaking to himself. The governor heard him.

"Yes, indeed! yes, indeed! I was wrong, Count Griff—Mr. Schumacker, I should say; I should leave the privilege of anger to you, since the power is mine."

Schumacker was silent for a moment. "There is," he resumed thoughtfully, "something about your face and voice, Governor, which reminds me of a man I once knew. It was very long ago. No one but myself can remember those days. It was in the time of my prosperity. He was one Levin de Knud, of Mecklenburg. Did you ever know the foolish fellow?"

"I knew him," quietly replied the general.

"Oh, you remember him! I thought it was only in adversity that we remembered."

"Was he not a captain in the Royal Guards?" added the governor.

"Yes, a mere captain, although the king loved him dearly. But he thought of nothing but pleasure, and seemed to have no ambition. He was a strange, mad fellow. Can you conceive that a favorite could be so moderate in his desires?"

"I can understand it."

"I was fond of this Levin de Knud, because he never gave me any alarm. He was the king's friend as he might have been the friend of any other man. It seemed as if he loved him for his own sake, and not for his position."

The general would have interrupted Schumacker; but the latter persisted, either from a spirit of contradiction, or because the train of thought into which he had drifted really pleased him.

"Since you knew this Captain Levin, Governor, you probably know that he had a son who died young. But do you remember what happened at the birth of this son?"

"I can better recall what occurred at the time of his death," said the general, covering his eyes with his hand, and in a faltering voice.

"But," continued the heedless Schumacker, "this fact was known to very few persons, and it will show you just how peculiar this Levin was. The king wished to be the child's godfather; would you believe that Levin refused? He did more; he chose an old beggar who hung about the palace gates, to hold his son at the baptismal font. I never could understand the reason for such an act of lunacy."

"I will tell you," replied the general. "In choosing a guardian for his son's soul, this Captain Levin doubtless thought that a poor man had more influence with God than a king."

Schumacker considered for a moment, then said: "You are right."

The governor again attempted to turn the conversation to the object of his visit. But Schumacker cut him short.

"Excuse me; if it be true that you know this Levin of Mecklenburg, let me talk of him. Of all the men whom I knew in the days of my grandeur, he is the only one whose memory does not inspire me with disgust or horror. Although he carried his peculiarity to the verge of folly, his noble qualities, none the less, made him one man in a thousand."

"I do not agree with you. This Levin was no better than other men. In fact, there are many who are better."

Schumacker folded his arms, and raised his eyes to heaven. "Yes, that is the way with them all. You cannot praise a worthy man in their presence, that they do not instantly seek to disparage him. They poison everything, even the pleasure of just praise, rare as it is."

"If you knew me, you would not accuse me of disparaging Gener—I mean, Captain Levin."

"Nonsense! nonsense," said the prisoner; "for loyalty and generosity, there were never two men like this Levin de Knud, and to say a word to the contrary is both an outrageous slander and a flattery of this miserable human race."

"I assure you," returned the general, trying to assuage Schumacker's wrath, "that I have not the slightest intention of wronging Levin de Knud."

"Do not say that. Although he was so foolish, the rest of mankind is anything but like him. They are a false, ungrateful, envious set of slanderers. Do you know that Levin de Knud gave more than half his income to the Copenhagen hospitals?"

"I did not know that you knew it."

"There it is!" triumphantly exclaimed the old man. "You thought that you could safely brand him, trusting to my ignorance of the poor fellow's good deeds!"

"Not at all, not at all!"

"Do you suppose, too, that I don't know that he persuaded the king to give the regiment which he intended for him, to an officer who had wounded him in a duel, because, he said, the other outranked him?"

"I thought that transaction was a secret."

"Well, tell me, Governor of Throndhjem, does that make it any less beautiful? If Levin concealed his virtues, is that a reason for denying them? Oh, how much alike men are! How dare you compare the noble Levin with them,—he who, when he could not save a soldier convicted of an attempt to murder him, settled a pension upon his murderer's widow?"

"Pooh! who would not do as much?"

Here Schumacker exploded. "Who? You! I! Any other man, Sir Governor! Because you wear the showy uniform of a general, and stars and crosses on your breast, do you think yourself a very meritorious person? You are a general, and poor Levin, I dare say, died a captain. True, he was a foolish fellow, and never thought of promotion."

"If he did not think of it himself, the king in his goodness thought of it for him."

"Goodness? Say, rather, justice, if there be such a thing as the justice of a king! Well, what signal reward did he receive?"

"His Majesty paid Levin de Knud far beyond his deserts."

"Capital!" cried the aged minister, clapping his hands. "A faithful captain is perhaps, after thirty years' service, made a major; and this distinguished mark of favor offends you, noble general? The Persian proverb is true which says that the setting sun is jealous of the rising moon."

Schumacker's fury was so great that the general could scarcely get in the words: "If you persist in interrupting me—You will not let me explain—"

"No, no!" continued the other; "I thought at first sight, General, that I caught a certain likeness between you and my good Levin; but no! there is none."

"Do but listen to me—"

"Listen to you! and hear you say that Levin de Knud is unworthy of some trifling reward?"

"I swear it is not—"

"You will presently—I know you men—try to persuade me that he is a knave, a hypocrite, and a villain, like the rest of you."

"No, indeed!"

"How do I know? Or perhaps that he betrayed a friend, persecuted a benefactor, as you all do; or poisoned his father, or murdered his mother?"

"You are mistaken. I have not the slightest desire—"

"Do you know that it was he who compelled Vice-chancellor Wind, as well as Scheele, Vinding, and Justice Lasson, three of my judges, not to sentence me to death? And you would have me hear him calumniated, and not defend him! Yes, that is what he did for me, and yet I had always done him more harm than good; for I am like you, vile and wicked."

The noble Levin was strangely moved by this singular interview. The object alike of the most direct insults and the sincerest praise, he knew not how to take such rough compliments and such flattering abuse. He was shocked and touched. Now he wanted to get into a passion, and now to thank Schumacker. Present and yet unknown, he loved to hear the fierce Schumacker defend in him, and against him, a friend and an absent man; only he would have preferred that his advocate should put a trifle less bitterness and acrimony into his panegyric. But in his innermost heart the exaggerated praise bestowed on Captain Levin pleased him even more than the insults addressed to the governor of Throndhjem wounded him. Fixing his kindly gaze upon the favorite in disgrace, he allowed him to vent his gratitude and his wrath; until at last, after a prolonged invective against human ingratitude, he sank exhausted upon an arm-chair, into the trembling Ethel's arms, saying in a melancholy voice: "Oh, men! what have I done that I should be forced to know you?"

The general had not yet been able to broach the important topic of his visit to Munkholm. All his reluctance to torment the captive by a series of questions, revived; to his pity and emotion were added two powerful motives: Schumacker's present state of agitation made it improbable that he could answer satisfactorily; and, moreover, on considering the affair more closely, it did not seem to the trusting Levin that such a man could be a conspirator. Still, how could he leave Throndhjem without examining Schumacker? This disagreeable necessity of his position as governor once more overcame all his scruples, and he began as follows, softening his voice as much as possible: "Pray, calm your excitement, Count Schumacker."

This compromise struck the good governor as a happy inspiration, well fitted to reconcile the respect due to the sentence pronounced against him, with a proper regard for the prisoner's misfortune, as it combined his noble title and his humble cognomen. He added: "It is my painful duty—"

"First," interrupted the prisoner, "allow me, Governor, to return to a subject which interests me far more than anything that your Excellency can have to say to me. You assured me just now that that madcap Levin had been rewarded for his services. I am most anxious to know in what way."

"His Majesty, my lord Griffenfeld, raised Levin to the rank of general, and for more than twenty years the foolish fellow has grown old in peace, honored with this military dignity and the favor of his king."

Schumacker's head drooped.

"Yes; that foolish Levin, who cared so little whether he ever lived to be more than a captain, will die a general; and the wise Schumacker, who expected to die Lord Chancellor, grows old a prisoner of State."

As he uttered these words, he hid his face in his hands and heaved a deep sigh. Ethel, who understood nothing of the conversation, save that it distressed her father, instantly strove to divert him.

"Look yonder, father, to the north; I see a gleam of light which I never noticed before."

In fact, the night, which had now closed in, revealed a faint and distant light upon the horizon, apparently coming from some far-off mountain. But Schumacker's mind and eye were not, like those of Ethel, ever bent on the north; therefore he made no reply. The general alone was struck by the young girl's remark.

"It may be," thought he, "a fire kindled by the rebels;" and this idea forcibly reminding him of the purpose of his visit, he thus addressed the prisoner: "Mr. Griffenfeld, I am sorry to distress you, but you must allow me—"

"I understand you, Governor; it is not enough to spend my days in this dungeon, to lead a lonely, disgraced existence, to have nothing left but bitter memories of past grandeur and power, you must also intrude upon my solitude, gaze upon my sorrow, and enjoy my misfortune. Since that noble Levin de Knud, whom some of your outward features recall to me, is a general like yourself, why was not he permitted to fill your post; for he would never, I swear, Sir Governor, have come to torture a miserable prisoner."

During the course of this strange interview the general had more than once been on the point of revealing himself, that he might bring it to a close. This indirect reproach made it impossible; it accorded so well with his secret feelings that it almost made him feel ashamed of himself. Still, he tried to answer Schumacker's injurious charge. Strange to say, from their mere difference of character, the two men had mutually changed their position; the judge was in some sort obliged to justify himself to the prisoner.

"But," said the general, "if his duty compelled him, do not doubt that Levin de Knud—"

"I do doubt it, noble Governor," exclaimed Schumacker; "do not doubt in your turn that he would have rejected, with all the generous indignation of his soul, the office of spy, or of increasing the agony of a wretched prisoner! No, I know him better than you; he would never have accepted the duties of an executioner. Now, General, I am at your service; do what you consider your duty. What does your Excellency require of me?"

And the old minister fixed his haughty gaze upon the governor, all whose resolution was gone. His first reluctance had returned, and was not to be overcome.

"He is right," thought he; "why should I torture an unfortunate man upon mere suspicion? Let some one else undertake the task!"

The effect of these reflections was prompt; he walked up to the astonished Schumacker and pressed his hand. Then he hurriedly left the room, saying: "Count Schumacker, always preserve the same esteem for Levin de Knud."

XXV

Lion (roaring). Oh—
Demetrius. Well roared, lion!
Shakespeare: *Midsummer Night's Dream.*

THE traveller of the present day who visits the snow-clad mountains which surround Lake Miösen like a white girdle, will scarcely find a vestige of what Norwegians of the seventeenth century knew as Arbar ruin. No one was ever able to decide the architectural period or the purpose for which this ruin, if we may give it the name, was built. As you left the forest which covered the southern shore of the lake, after climbing a slope crowned with here and there a fragment of wall or a bit of masonry once a tower, you reached an arched opening leading into the side of the mountain. This entrance, now completely closed by landslips, led into a species of gallery cut in the living rock, and piercing the mountain from side to side.

This tunnel, dimly lighted by conical air-holes made in the arched roof at regular intervals, ended in an oval hall in part excavated from the rock, and terminating in a cyclopean stone wall. Around this hall, in deep niches, were rude images carved from granite. Some of these mysterious figures, which had fallen from their pedestals, lay heaped in confusion on the ground with other shapeless rubbish, covered with grass and weeds, among which crawled lizards, spiders, and all the hideous vermin born of damp earth and ruins.

Daylight penetrated to this place only through a door opposite the mouth of the gallery. This door, viewed in a certain light, was seen to be of pointed construction, of no especial date, and evidently the work of the architect's whim.

This door might as well have been styled a window, although it was on a level with the ground, for it opened upon a fearful precipice; and it was impossible to imagine whither a short flight of stairs which overhung the abyss could possibly lead.

The hall formed the interior of a huge turret which from a distance, seen from the other side of the precipice, looked like any high mountain peak. It stood alone, and, as has already been said, no one knew to what sort of structure it had belonged. Above it, however, upon a plateau inaccessible even to the boldest hunter, was a mass of masonry which might be taken, being so remote, either for a rounded rock or for the remains of a colossal arch. This turret and crumbling arch were known to the peasants as Arbar ruin, the origin of the name being fully as obscure as that of the buildings themselves.

On a stone in the centre of this oval hall sat a little man dressed in the skins of wild beasts, whom we have already had occasion to mention several times in the course of our story.

His back was turned to the light, or rather to the faint twilight which filtered into the gloomy turret when the sun reached high noon. This light, the strongest natural light which ever entered the tower, was not sufficient to reveal the nature of the object over which the little man was stooping. An occasional muffled groan was heard, and it seemed to proceed from this object, judging by the feeble movement which it now and then made. Sometimes the little man straightened himself, and raised to his lips a cup, by its form apparently a human skull, filled with steaming liquid of some indistinguishable hue, and drank deep draughts.

All at once he started up.

"I hear steps in the gallery, I believe; can it be the chancellor of the two kingdoms already?"

These words were followed by a horrible burst of laughter ending in a savage roar, which met with an instant response in a howl from the gallery.

"Oh, ho!" rejoined the lord of Arbar ruin; "it is not a man. But it is an enemy all the same; it is a wolf."

In fact, a huge wolf suddenly emerged from the vaulted gallery, paused a moment, then advanced stealthily toward the man, crouching to the ground and fixing upon him burning eyes which gleamed through the darkness. The man stood with folded arms, and watched him.

"Ah! 'tis the old gray wolf,—the oldest wolf in Miösen woods! Good-morning, wolf; your eyes glitter; you are hungry, and the smell of dead bodies attracts you. You too shall soon attract other hungry wolves. Welcome, wolf of Miösen; I have always longed to make your acquaintance. You are so old that they say you cannot die; they will not say so to-morrow."

The animal answered with a frightful yell, sprang back, and then bounded upon the little man.

He did not budge an inch. As quick as a flash, with his right arm he grasped the body of the wolf, which, standing on two legs before him, had thrown his fore-paws upon his shoulders; with his left hand he guarded his face from the gaping jaws of his enemy, seizing it by the throat with such force that the creature, compelled to raise his head, could scarcely utter a sound.

"Wolf of Miösen," said the triumphant man, "you tear my jerkin, but your skin shall replace it."

As he mingled with these words of victory a few words in a strange jargon, a convulsive movement made by the dying wolf caused him to stumble upon the stones which were thickly strewn over the floor. The two fell together, and the roars of the man were blended with the howls of the beast.

Obliged in his fall to relax his grasp of the wolfs throat, the man felt the sharp teeth buried in his shoulder, when, as they rolled over one another, the two combatants struck against an enormous shaggy white body lying in the darkest corner of the room. It was a bear, who waked from his heavy sleep with a growl.

No sooner were the drowsy eyes of this new-comer opened wide enough to see the fight, than he rushed furiously, not upon the man, but upon the wolf, just then victorious in his turn, seized him violently by the back, and thus freed the human combatant.

This latter, far from showing any gratitude for so great a service, rose, covered with blood, and springing upon the bear, gave him a vigorous kick, such as a master might bestow on a dog guilty of some misdemeanor.

"Friend, who called you? Why do you meddle?"

These words were interspersed with furious ejaculations and gnashing of teeth.

"Begone!" he added with a roar.

The bear, who had received at one and the same time a kick from the man and a bite from the wolf, uttered a plaintive remonstrance; then, hanging his great head, he released the famished beast, who hurled himself upon the man with fresh fury.

While the struggle was renewed, the rebuffed bear went back to his couch, sat gravely down, and gazed indifferently at the two raging adversaries, preserving the utmost silence, and rubbing first one fore-paw and then the other across the tip of his white nose.

But the small man, as the leader of the Miösen wolves returned to the charge, seized his bloody snout; then, by an unparalleled exertion requiring both strength and skill, he managed to clasp his entire jaw in one hand.

The wolf struggled frantically with rage and pain; foam dropped from his compressed lips, and his eyes, distended with rage, seemed starting from their sockets. Of the two foes, the one whose bones were shattered by sharp teeth, whose flesh was rent by cruel claws, was not the man but the wild beast; the one whose howl was most savage, whose expression was most fierce, was not the animal but the man.

Finally, the latter, collecting all his strength, exhausted by the aged wolf's prolonged resistance, squeezed his muzzle in both hands with such force that blood gushed from the creature's nose and mouth; his flaming eyes grew dim, and half closed; he tottered, and fell lifeless at his victor's feet. The feeble twitching of his tail and the convulsive and occasional shudder which shook his entire frame, alone showed that he was not yet quite dead.

All at once a final quiver ran through the expiring frame, and all signs of life ceased.

"There you lie, dead, old wolf," said the little man, kicking him contemptuously. "Did you think that you could live on after you had encountered me? You will hasten no more with muffled step across the snow, following the scent and the track of your prey; you are food for wolves or vultures now yourself; you have devoured many a lost traveller on the shores of Miösen during your long life of murder and carnage; now you yourself are dead, you will eat no more men. 'Tis a pity!"

He took up a sharp stone, crouched beside the wolf's warm, palpitating body, broke the limbs at their joints, severed the head from the shoulders, slit the skin from head to heel, stripped it off, as he might remove his own waistcoat, and in the twinkling of an eye nothing was left of the much-dreaded wolf of Miösen but a bare and bleeding carcass. He flung his trophy over his shoulders, bruised with bites, turning inside out the skin, still reeking and stained with long streaks of blood.

"Needs must," he muttered, "dress in the skins of beasts; that of a man is too thin to keep out the cold."

As he thus talked to himself, more hideous than ever beneath his loathsome burden, the bear, tired no doubt of inaction, furtively approached the other object lying in the shadow, to which we referred in the beginning of this chapter, and a crunching of bones, mingled with faint, agonized moans, soon rose from this gloomy quarter of the hall. The small man turned.

"Friend!" cried he in threatening tones; "ah, you good-for-nothing Friend! Here, come here!"

And picking up a huge stone, he hurled it at the monster's head. The creature, stunned by the blow, reluctantly tore himself from his prey, and crawled, licking his bloody chaps, to fall panting at the little man's feet, lifting his huge head and wriggling, as if to ask pardon for his rash act.

Then ensued between the two monsters—for we may well apply that name to the dweller in Arbar ruin—an exchange of significant growls. Those of the man expressed anger and authority; those of the bear, entreaty and submission.

"There," said the man at last, pointing with his crooked finger to the flayed body of the wolf, "there is your victim; leave mine to me."

The bear, after smelling at the wolf's carcass, shook his head discontentedly, and turned his eye toward the man who seemed to be his master.

"I understand," said the latter; "that is too dead for you, while there is still life in the other. You are refined in your pleasures, Friend,—quite as much so as a man; you like to have your food retain its life until the instant when you tear it limb from limb; you love to feel the flesh expire beneath your teeth; you enjoy nothing unless it suffers. We are alike; for I am not a man, Friend; I am superior to that wretched race; I am a wild beast like you. How I wish that you could speak to me, comrade Friend, to tell me whether my joy equals that which thrills your bearish soul when you devour a man's heart. But no; I should be loath to hear you speak, lest your voice should recall to me the human voice. Yes, growl at my feet with that growl which makes the stray goatherd tremble among the mountains; it pleases me as the voice of a friend, because it proclaims you his enemy. Look up, Friend, look up at me; lick my hands with that tongue which has drunk so often of human blood. Your teeth are white like mine: it is no fault of ours if they be not red as a new-made wound; but blood washes away blood. More than once from the depths of some dark cave I have seen the maidens of Kiölen or Oëlmœ bathe their bare feet in some mountain torrent, singing the while in sweet tones; but I prefer your hairy snout and your hoarse cries to those melodious voices and satin-smooth faces; for they terrify mankind."

As he said this, he sat down and yielded his hand to the caresses of the monster, who, rolling on his back at his master's feet, lavished all sorts of endearments upon him, like a spaniel displaying his pretty tricks before the sofa of his mistress.

Stranger yet was the intelligent attention with which he seemed to follow his master's words. The singular monosyllables with which the latter interspersed them seemed particularly intelligible to his understanding;

and he showed his comprehension by rearing his head suddenly, or by a vague rumbling noise in the back of his throat.

"Men say that I shun them," resumed the little man; "but it is they that shun me; they do through fear what I should do through hate. Still, you know, Friend, that I am always glad to come across a man when I am hungry or thirsty."

All at once he saw a red glow start into life in the depths of the gallery, growing brighter by degrees and faintly tinting the damp old walls.

"Here comes one now. Talk of the Devil and you see his horns. Hullo, Friend!" he added, turning to the bear; "hullo! get up!"

The animal instantly rose.

"Come, I must reward your obedience by gratifying your appetite."

With these words, the man stooped toward the object lying on the ground.

The cracking of bones broken by a hatchet was heard; but no sigh or groan was now blended with it.

"It seems," muttered the small man, "that there are but two of us left alive in Arbar hall. There, good Friend, finish the feast which you began."

He flung toward the aforementioned outer door what he had detached from the object stretched at his feet. The bear threw himself upon his prey so rapidly that the swiftest eye could not have been sure that the fragment was indeed a human arm, clad in a bit of green stuff of the same shade as the uniform worn by the Munkholm musketeers.

"Some one is coming," said the little man, keeping his eye on the light, which was steadily advancing. "Comrade Friend, leave me alone for a moment. Ho there! Away with you!"

The obedient beast rushed to the door, backed down the steps outside, and disappeared, bearing off his disgusting booty with a satisfied howl.

At the same instant a tall man appeared at the mouth of the tunnel, whose sinuous depths still reflected a dim light. He was wrapped in a long brown cloak, and carried a dark-lantern, which he turned full on the small man's face.

The latter, still seated on his stone with folded arms, exclaimed: "Ill befall you, you who come hither guided by an idea, and not by instinct!"

But the stranger, making no reply, seemed studying him carefully.

"Look at me," he continued, raising his head; "an hour hence you may have no voice left with which to boast that you have seen me."

The new-comer, moving his light up and down the little man's person, seemed even more surprised than frightened.

"Well, what astonishes you so much?" rejoined the little man, with a laugh like the breaking of bones. "I have legs and arms like your own; only my limbs will not like yours serve to feed wildcats and crows!"

The stranger at length replied, in a low but confident voice, as if he only feared being heard from without: "Hear me; I come, not as an enemy, but as a friend."

The other interrupted, "Then why did you not strip off your human form?"

"It is my purpose to do you a service, if you be he whom I seek."

"You mean, to ask a service. Man, you waste your breath. I can do no service to any save those who are weary of life."

"By your words," replied the stranger, "I am sure that you are the man I want; but your stature—Hans of Iceland is a giant. You cannot be he."

"You are the first who ever doubted it to my face."

"What! can it be?" And the stranger approached the little man. "But I always heard that Hans of Iceland was of colossal height."

"Add my renown to my height, and you will see that I am taller than Mount Hecla."

"Indeed! Tell me, I pray, are you really Hans, a native of Klipstadur in Iceland?"

"It is not in words that I should answer that question," said the little man, rising; and the look which he cast at the rash stranger made him start back several paces.

"Confine yourself, I beg, to answering it by that glance," he replied in a voice of entreaty, casting a look toward the exit, which showed his regret that he had ever entered; "I came here in your interests alone."

Upon entering the hall, the new-comer, having but a glimpse of the person whom he accosted, had retained his self-possession; but when the master of Arbar rose, with his tigerish visage, his thick-set limbs, his bloody shoulders, but half concealed by a skin still green, his huge hands armed with claws, and his fiery eyes, the bold stranger shuddered, like an ignorant traveller who thinks he is handling an eel and feels the sting of a viper.

"My interests?" repeated the monster. "Have you come to tell me of some spring which I may poison, some village I may burn, or some Munkholm musketeer I may slaughter?"

"Perhaps. Listen: The miners of Norway are in a state of revolt. You know what disaster follows in the train of revolt."

"Yes,—murder, rape, sacrilege, fire, and pillage."

"All these I offer you."

The little man laughed.

"I should not wait for you to offer them."

The brutal sneer accompanying these words made the stranger again shudder. He went on, however:—

"In the name of the miners, I offer you the command of the insurrection."

The small man was silent for an instant. All at once his dark countenance assumed an expression of infernal malice.

"Does the offer really come from them?" said he.

This question seemed to embarrass the new-comer; but as he was sure that he was unknown to his terrible interlocutor, he readily recovered himself.

"Why have the miners rebelled?"

"To throw off the burden of the royal protectorate."

"Only for that?" replied the other in the same mocking tone.

"They also wish to free the prisoner of Munkholm."

"Is this the sole purpose of the movement?" repeated the small man in a voice which confused the stranger.

"I know of no other," he stammered.

"Oh, you know of no other!"

These words were pronounced in the same sarcastic tone. The stranger, to hide the embarrassment which they caused him, hastily drew from beneath his cloak a heavy purse which he flung at the monster's feet.

"Here is your pay as commander-in-chief."

The small man spurned the purse with his foot.

"I will not have it. Do you imagine that if I wanted your gold or your blood I should wait for your permission to gratify my desire?"

The stranger made a gesture of surprise, almost of terror.

"It is a present from the royal miners."

"I will not have it, I tell you. Gold is useless to me. Men will sell their soul, but they do not sell their life. That must be taken by force."

"Then I may tell the miners that the terrible Hans of Iceland accepts their leadership, but not their gold?"

"I do not accept it."

These words, uttered in curt tones, seemed to strike the pretended envoy from the rebellious miners very unpleasantly.

"What?" he asked.

"No!" repeated the other.

"You refuse to take part in an expedition which presents so many advantages?"

"I am quite able to pillage farms, lay waste villages, and massacre peasants or soldiers, single-handed."

"But consider that by accepting the offer of the miners you are assured of a free pardon."

"Does this offer also come from the miners?" asked the other, with a laugh.

"I will not disguise from you the fact," replied the stranger, with an air of mystery, "that it comes from an important personage who is deeply interested in the insurrection."

"And is this important personage so sure that he will himself escape hanging?"

"If you knew who he is, you would not shake your head so significantly."

"Indeed! Well, who is he?"

"I may not tell you."

The small man stepped forward and clapped the stranger on the shoulder, still with the same sardonic sneer.

"Shall I tell *you*?"

The man wrapped in the cloak gave a start; it was a start of both fright and wounded pride. He was prepared for neither the monster's abrupt proposal, nor for his savage familiarity.

"I am only laughing at you," added the brigand. "You little guess that I know all. This important personage is the Lord High Chancellor of Norway and Denmark; and you yourself are the Lord High Chancellor of Norway and Denmark."

It was indeed he. On reaching Arbar ruin, toward which we left him journeying with Musdœmon, he had been unwilling to intrust to any one else the task of securing the brigand, by whom he was far from supposing himself known and expected. Never, even after years had elapsed, did Count d'Ahlefeld, with all his power and all his diplomacy, discover how Hans of Iceland acquired his information. Was it through Musdœmon's treachery? True, it was Musdœmon who suggested to the noble count that it would be well to see the brigand in person; but what profit could he derive from his perfidy? Had the bandit captured upon some one of his numerous victims, papers relating to the chancellor's schemes? But Frederic d'Ahlefeld was, with the sole exception of Musdœmon, the only living being acquainted with his father's plans, and frivolous as he was, he was not quite so senseless as to expose such a secret. Moreover, he was in garrison at Munkholm, at least so the chancellor supposed. Those who read the close of this scene, without being any better able to solve the problem than was Count d'Ahlefeld, will see how much truth there was in this latter hypothesis.

One of Count d'Ahlefeld's most marked characteristics was his great presence of mind. When he heard himself so abruptly named, he could not repress an exclamation of surprise; but in the twinkling of an eye, his pale, proud features lost their expression of fear and astonishment, and recovered their usual calm composure.

"Well, yes," said he, "I will be frank with you; I am indeed the chancellor. But I hope you will be equally frank with me."

A burst of laughter interrupted him.

"Have I waited to be urged to tell you my name, or to tell you your own?"

"Tell me with the same sincerity how you found me out?"

"Have you never heard that Hans of Iceland can see through mountains?"

The count tried to insist.

"Consider me as a friend."

"Your hand, Count d'Ahlefeld," said the little man, with brutal familiarity. Then he stared the minister in the face, exclaiming: "Could our two souls escape from our bodies at this moment, I fancy that Satan would hesitate to decide which of the two belonged to the monster."

The haughty noble bit his lip; but between his fear of the robber and his desire to secure him as his tool, he managed to disguise his resentment.

"Do not imperil your own interests; accept the command of the rebellion, and trust to my gratitude."

"Chancellor of Norway, you count on the success of your schemes, like an old woman who dreams of the gown which she will spin from stolen hemp, while the cat's claws tangle her spindle."

"Reflect once more, before you reject my offers."

"Once more, I, the brigand, say to you, Lord Chancellor of both kingdoms, No!"

"I expected a different answer, after the eminent service which you have already rendered me."

"What service?" asked the robber.

"Was it not you who murdered Captain Dispolsen?" replied the chancellor.

"That may be, Count d'Ahlefeld; I do not know him. Who is he?"

"What! did not the iron casket which he had in charge fall to your share?"

This question seemed to sharpen the robber's memory.

"Stay!" said he; "I do remember that man and his iron casket. It was on Urchtal Sands."

"At least," rejoined the chancellor, "if you could restore that casket to me, my gratitude would be unbounded. Tell me what has become of that casket, for I am sure it is in your possession."

The noble minister laid such stress upon this request that the brigand was struck by it.

"So, then, that iron casket is of the utmost importance to your Grace, my Lord Chancellor?"

"Yes."

"What shall my reward be if I tell you where it is?"

"Anything that you may desire, my dear Hans."

"Well, I will not tell you."

"Pooh! you are joking! Think what a service you can do me."

"That is exactly what I am thinking."

"I will insure you a vast fortune; I will ask your pardon from the king."

"You had better beg your own from me," said the bandit. "Look you, Lord Chancellor of Norway and Denmark, the tiger does not devour the hyena. I will permit you to leave my presence with your life, because you are a scoundrel, and every instant that you live, every thought of your heart, causes fresh misery for mankind and fresh crime for yourself. But return not, or I may teach you that my hatred spares no one, not even a villain. As for your captain, do not flatter yourself that it was on your account I slaughtered him; it was his uniform which doomed him, as it did this other wretch, whom I did not murder to gratify you either, I assure you."

With these words, he seized the noble count by the arm and dragged him toward the body lying in the shadow. As he finished his protestations, the light from the lantern fell upon this object. It was a mutilated corpse, and was indeed dressed in the uniform of an officer of the Munkholm Musketeers. The chancellor approached it with a sense of horror. All at once his eye rested on the pallid, blood-stained face of the dead. The livid, half-parted lips, the bristling hair, the discolored cheeks, and lustreless eyes could not disguise that countenance from him. He uttered a fearful shriek: "My God! Frederic! My son!"

Doubt not that hearts seemingly the most hardened still conceal in their innermost recesses some trace of affection unknown even to themselves, apparently hidden by vice and passion, like a mysterious witness and a future avenger. It may be said to exist, that it may some day make crime acquainted with grief. It silently bides its time. The wicked man bears it in his bosom and is unconscious of it, because no ordinary affection is sufficient to pierce the thick crust of selfishness and iniquity which covers it; but let one of the rare and genuine sorrows of life appear unawares, and it plunges a sharp-edged sword into the dark regions of that soul and probes its lowest depths. Then the unknown sentiment of love is revealed to the wretched criminal, all the more violent for its long repression, all the more painful from his lack of sensibility, because the sting of misfortune was forced to stab the heart more deeply in order to reach it. Nature wakes and casts aside her chains; she delivers the miscreant to unwonted despair, to unheard-of torments; he feels, compressed into a single instant, all the sufferings which he has defied for years. The most various pangs rend him simultaneously. His heart, burdened by dull amazement, revolts to find itself a prey to convulsive agony. He seems to experience the pains of hell while still in this life, and something beyond despair is made clear to him.

Count d'Ahlefeld loved his son without knowing it. We say his son, because, being unaware of his wife's guilt, as such he regarded Frederic, the direct heir to his name. Supposing him still at Munkholm, he was far from prepared to meet him in Arbar tower, and to find him dead! But there he lay, bruised and bleeding; it was he, impossible to doubt it. His emotions may be imagined when a realizing sense of his love for his son unexpectedly pierced his soul, together with the assurance that he was lost to him forever.

All the sensations so inadequately described in these pages burst upon his heart at once like so many claps of thunder. Stunned, as it were, by surprise, terror, and despair, he cast himself upon the ground, and wrung his hands, repeating in woful accents: "My son! my son!"

The brigand laughed. It was horrible to hear such laughter mingled with the groans of a father looking upon the dead body of his son.

"By my ancestor Ingulf! you may call, Count d'Ahlefeld, but you cannot wake him."

All at once his cruel face darkened, and he said in a melancholy voice: "Weep for your son, if you will; I avenge mine."

The sound of footsteps hurrying along the gallery interrupted the words upon his lips; and as he turned in surprise, four tall men, with drawn swords, rushed into the room; a fifth, short and stout, followed, bearing a torch in one hand and a sword in the other. He was wrapped in a brown cloak, like that worn by the chancellor.

"My lord," he exclaimed, "we heard your voice, and hastened to your assistance."

The reader has doubtless recognized Musdœmon and the four armed retainers who formed the count's escort.

As the torchlight filled the room with its ruddy glow, the five new-comers paused in horror-stricken dismay; and it was indeed an awful sight. On the one hand, the bloody remains of the wolf, the disfigured body of the young officer; on the other, the father, with his wild eyes and frantic shrieks; and beside him the fearful monster, turning on his assailants a hideous front, indicative of dauntless surprise.

At the sight of this unlooked-for reinforcement the idea of vengeance took possession of the count, and roused him from his despair.

"Death to that brigand!" he cried, drawing his sword; "he has murdered my son! Kill him! kill him!"

"Has he murdered Mr. Frederic?" said Musdœmon; and the torch in his hand did not reveal the slightest change in his countenance.

"Kill him! kill him!" repeated the frantic count.

And the whole six rushed upon the robber. He, surprised by this sudden attack, retreated toward the opening which overhung the precipice, with a fierce roar, expressive rather of rage than fear.

Six swords were directed against him, and his eyes flamed forth greater fury, while his features wore a more menacing expression than those of any of his aggressors. He had grasped his stone axe, and, forced by the number of his assailants to confine himself to defensive action, whirled it round and round in his hand so rapidly that the circle described, covered him like a shield. A myriad sparks flashed from the point of his assailants' swords as they clashed against the edge of the hatchet; but not a single blade touched him. And yet, exhausted by his recent battle with the wolf, he lost ground imperceptibly, and soon found himself driven close against the door opening upon the abyss.

"Courage, friends!" shouted the count; "let us hurl the monster over this precipice."

"Before I fall, the stars themselves shall fall," replied the brigand.

But the aggressors redoubled their ardor and their assurance as they saw that the small man was compelled to descend one step of the flight which overhung the abyss.

"Good! one effort more!" cried the lord chancellor; "he needs must fall; push your advantage! Wretch, you have committed your last crime. Courage, men!"

While with his right hand he continued his fearful evolutions with the axe, the brigand, without deigning a reply, with his left hand grasped a horn which hung at his belt, and raising it to his lips, again and again blew a long, hoarse blast, which was answered suddenly by a roar from the gulf beneath.

A few instants later, as the count and his followers, still pressing the little man hard, rejoiced that they had driven him down a second step, the huge head of a white bear appeared at the broken end of the staircase. Struck dumb with amazement and fright, they shrank back. The bear climbed the stairs with a lumbering gait, showing his bloody jaws and sharp teeth as he did so.

"Thanks, good Friend!" cried the brigand. And taking advantage of his enemy's surprise, he sprang upon the back of his bear, who slowly descended the stairs backwards, still keeping his threatening front turned upon his master's foes.

Soon, recovering from their first astonishment, they beheld the bear, carrying the brigand beyond their reach, descend into the abyss, probably in the same way that he ascended, by clinging to the trunks of trees and to projecting rocks. They tried to roll great bowlders down upon him; but before they could detach a single one of those ancient granite fragments which had slumbered there so long, the brigand and his strange steed had vanished in a cave.

XXVI

No, no, laugh no more. Look you, that which I thought so
humorous has its serious side as well, a very serious side,
like everything in this world! Believe me, that word, chance,
is blasphemy; nothing beneath the sun is the work of chance;
and do you not see herein the purpose marked out by
Providence!—Lessing: *Emilia Galotti.*

YES, a deep design often lies at the root of what men call chance. There
seems to be a mysterious hand which marks the cause and purpose of events.
We inveigh against fickle fortune, against the strange accidents of our lot,
and lo! chaos is made clear by a fearful flash of lightning or a marvellous
beam of light, and human wisdom is humbled by the great lessons of fate.

If, for instance, when Frederic d'Ahlefeld displayed his magnificent
attire, his foolish complacency, and his presumptuous pride, in some
sumptuous apartment, to the ladies of Copenhagen; if some man, endowed
with the gift of second sight, had troubled his frivolous thoughts by gloomy
revelations; if he had told him that one day the brilliant uniform of which
he boasted should cause his death; that a monster in human shape should
drink his blood as greedily as he, careless epicure that he was, drank the
wines of France and Bohemia; that the locks upon which he could not lavish
too many essences and perfumes should sweep the dust of a cave haunted
by wild beasts; that the arm which he so gracefully offered to the fair ladies
of Charlottenburg should be flung to a bear like a half-gnawed chicken-
bone,—how would Frederic have answered these dismal prophecies? With
a laugh and a pirouette; and, more frightful still, most sensible men would
have applauded his reckless conduct.

Let us consider his destiny more closely. Is it not strange to find that the
crime of Count and Countess d'Ahlefeld met with such fitting punishment?
They wove an infamous plot against the daughter of a prisoner; this
unfortunate girl by a mere chance found a protector, who saw fit to remove
their son, charged by them to carry out their abominable scheme. This son,

their only hope, was sent far from the scene of his purposed villany; and hardly had he reached his destination, when another avenging chance caused his death. Thus in their attempt to bring dishonor upon an innocent yet detested young girl, they plunged their own guilty yet adored son into the oblivion of the grave. The wretched pair were made miserable by their own hands.

XXVII

Ah, here comes our lovely countess! Forgive me, Madam,
if I may not have the honor of a visit from you to-day. I am
busy. Another time, deal Countess, another time; but to-day
I will not detain you longer.—*The Prince and Orsina.*

THE day after his visit to Munkholm, the governor of Throndhjem
ordered his travelling carriage to be made ready very early in the morning,
hoping to start off before Countess d'Ahlefeld was awake; but we have
already observed that her slumbers were light.

The general had just signed his final instructions to the bishop, into
whose hands the government was to be committed during his absence. He
rose, put on his fur-lined coat, and was about to leave the room, when the
usher announced the chancellor's wife.

This piece of ill luck confused the old soldier, who could laugh at the
fiery rain of a hundred guns, but not at the artifices of a woman. However, he
took leave of the wicked creature with a tolerably good grace, and disguised
his annoyance until she whispered in his ear with that crafty look which
would fain seem confidential, "Well, noble General, what did he say?"

"Who,—Poël? He said that the carriage was ready."

"I mean the prisoner of Munkholm, General."

"Oh!"

"Did he answer your questions satisfactorily?"

"Why—Yes, to be sure, Countess," said the much embarrassed governor.

"Did you find proofs that he was concerned in the conspiracy among
the miners?"

The general involuntarily exclaimed, "Noble lady, he is innocent."

He stopped short, for he knew that he had uttered the conviction of his
heart, not of his head.

"He is innocent!" repeated the countess, with a look of consternation
and incredulity; for she trembled lest Schumacker had really proved to the
governor the innocence which it was so much to the chancellor's interest to
deny.

The governor had had time to reflect; he answered the persistent gentlewoman in a tone which quieted her fears, for it revealed his doubt and anxiety.

"Innocent—Yes, if you choose—"

"If I choose, General!" And the wicked woman laughed aloud.

Her laughter offended the governor, who said, "By your leave, Countess, I will report my interview with the ex-chancellor to the viceroy." Then he bowed low, and went down to the courtyard, where his carriage awaited him.

"Yes," said Countess d'Ahlefeld, as she returned to her rooms; "go, my knight-errant, for your absence rids us of the protector of our enemies. Go; for your departure is the signal for my Frederic's return. I wonder how you dared to send the handsomest young man in Copenhagen to those horrid mountains! Luckily, it will be easy enough now for me to have him recalled."

At this thought she turned to her favorite attendant.

"Lisbeth, my dear, send to Bergen for two dozen of those little combs which our elegant young men are wearing in their hair, inquire for the famous Scudéry's last novel, and see that my dear Frederic's monkey is washed in rose-water every morning, without fail."

"What! my gracious mistress," asked Lisbeth, "is there a chance that Mr. Frederic will come back?"

"Yes, indeed; and we must do everything that he wishes, so that he may be glad to see me again. I must arrange a surprise for him."

Poor mother!

XXVIII

Bernard hurries along the shores of the Arlanza. He is like a
lion rushing from his den, seeking the hunters, and resolved
to conquer them or die. The brave and resolute Spaniard sets
forth. With a quick step, in his hand a heavy spear, in which
he puts his trust, Bernard traverses the ruins of Arlanza.—
Old Spanish Romance.

ON descending from the tower from whose summit he had seen
Munkholm light, Ordener looked in every direction, until he was exhausted,
for his poor guide, Benignus Spiagudry. He called him repeatedly, but
only echo answered. Surprised but not alarmed by this inexplicable
disappearance, he attributed it to some panic which had seized upon the
timid keeper, and after generously blaming himself for having left him,
even for a few moments, he decided to spend the night upon the cliff, in
order to give him time to return. Then he ate something, and wrapping
himself in his mantle, laid down by the dying embers, kissed Ethel's ringlet,
and soon fell asleep; for an anxious heart cannot keep awake a man whose
conscience is clear.

At sunrise he rose, but found no trace of Spiagudry except his wallet
and cloak, which had been left in the tower, showing that his flight had been
very hasty. Then, despairing of his return, at least to Oëlmœ Cliff, Ordener
resolved to set off without him, for it was on the next day that he hoped to
meet Hans of Iceland at Walderhog.

It has been stated in the earlier chapters of this story that Ordener had
accustomed himself to the hardships incident to a roving and adventurous
life. Having already travelled through northern Norway several times,
he did not need a guide, now that he knew where to find the robber. He
accordingly turned his lonely steps toward the northwest, no longer having
Benignus Spiagudry at his side to tell him just how much quartz or spar
each hill contained, what traditions were connected with every ruin, and
whether this or that gaping chasm was caused by an ancient flood or by some
volcanic action. He walked a whole day through those mountains which,

proceeding at intervals like foot-hills from the principal chain traversing the length of Norway, slope gradually down to the sea; so that the coast of that country is a mere succession of promontories and fjords, while inland it is nothing but a series of mountains and valleys, a strange conformation, which has caused Norway to be compared to the skeleton of a great fish.

It was no easy matter to travel in such a region. Sometimes he was forced to follow the stony bed of a dry stream, sometimes to cross, by an unsteady bridge made of a tree-trunk, over a road which torrents born but the day before had chosen for their bed.

Sometimes, too, Ordener would journey for hours without seeing any sign of the presence of man in these wild places, save an occasional glimpse of the sails of a windmill upon the top of a hill, or the sound of a distant forge, whose smoke blew hither and thither like a black plume, as the wind shifted this way and that.

Now and again he met a peasant mounted on a little gray pony, its head down, and scarcely more untamed than its master; or a dealer in furs and skins, seated in his sledge, drawn by reindeer, a long rope fastened behind, the end covered with knots, meant to frighten away wolves, as it rebounded from the pebbles in the road.

If Ordener asked this trader the way to Walderhog cave, the travelling merchant, familiar only with the names and positions of the places to which his business took him, would answer indifferently: "Keep to the northwest till you come to Hervalyn village, then cross Dodlysax ravine, and by night you will reach Surb, which is only two miles from Walderhog."

If Ordener put the same question to the peasant, the latter, deeply imbued with the traditions of the country and the fireside tales, would shake his head again and again, and stop his gray horse, as he said: "Walderhog! Walderhog cave! There the stones sing, the dry bones dance, and the demon of Iceland dwells; it cannot be to Walderhog cave that your worship wishes to go?"

"Yes, indeed," Ordener would reply.

"Has your worship lost your mother, or has fire destroyed your farm, or has one of your neighbors stolen your fat pig?"

"No, truly," the young man would answer.

"Then some magician must have cast a spell over your worship's senses."

"My friend, I asked you to tell me the way to Walderhog."

"I am trying to answer your question, sir. Farewell. Keep to the north! I can tell you how to go there, but I do not know how you will get back."

And the peasant would ride off, crossing himself as he went.

To the gloomy monotony of the road was added the inconvenience of a fine, penetrating rain, which took possession of the sky toward noonday, and increased the difficulties of the way. No song-bird dared venture forth; and Ordener, chilled to the bone beneath his cloak, saw only the goshawk and the falcon hover above his head, or the kingfisher fly up from the reeds of a pond with a fish in its claws, startled by his tread.

It was after dark when the young traveller, after making his way through the forest of aspens and beeches which lies close to Dodlysax ravine, reached the village of Surb, where (as the reader may remember) Spiagudry had asked leave to establish his headquarters. The smell of tar and the charcoal smoke told Ordener that he was approaching a seafaring population. He advanced to the first hut which he could see through the darkness. According to Norwegian custom, the low, narrow entrance was closed by a large, transparent fish-skin, tinged at this moment by the flickering red light of the fire. He knocked on the wooden doorpost, saying, —

"It is a traveller!"

"Come in, come in," answered a voice from within.

At the same instant an eager hand raised the fish-skin, and Ordener was admitted to the cone-shaped home of a Norwegian 'longshore fisherman. It was a sort of circular tent made of wood and earth, in the centre of which blazed a fire, where the purple glow of turf was mixed with the white light of the pine. Beside this fire the fisherman, his wife, and two children dressed in rags were seated at a table set with wooden plates and earthen cups. On the opposite side of the fire was a pile of nets and oars; a couple of reindeer were asleep on a bed of dried leaves and skins, which by its ample size seemed intended also as a resting-place for the family and any guests whom it might please Heaven to send them. It took more than one glance to make out the arrangement of the hut; for a thick, pungent smoke, which found but scanty outlet through a hole in the pointed roof, wrapped everything in a misty but almost impenetrable veil.

As soon as Ordener crossed the threshold, the fisherman and his wife rose, and returned his greeting in a frank and friendly manner. Norwegian peasants welcome travellers perhaps as much from a lively feeling of curiosity inherent in their nature as from their native inclination to hospitality.

"Sir," said the fisherman, "you must be cold and hungry; here are fire to dry your cloak and excellent bark bread to satisfy your appetite. Afterward your worship may be willing to tell us who you are, where you come from, where you are going, and what stories the gossips relate in your native place."

"Yes, sir," added his wife; "and you might add to that bark bread— which, as my husband says, is excellent—a delicious bit of salt fish, seasoned with whale oil. Sit down, stranger."

"And if your worship does not like Saint Usuph's[15] fare," added the man, "and will have patience for a few moments, I can promise you a splendid piece of venison, or at least a pheasant's wing. We are expecting a visit from the best hunter in the three provinces. Isn't that so, good Maase?"

"Maase," the name which the fisherman gave his wife, is a Norwegian word meaning "sea-gull." The wife did not seem in the least offended, either because it was really her name, or because she took it as a term of endearment.

"The best hunter! I should say so," she answered with great emphasis. "He means my brother, the famous Kennybol. God bless all his undertakings! He has come to spend a few days with us, and you shall drink a mug of good beer with him. He is a traveller like you."

"Many thanks, my kind hostess," said Ordener, with a smile; "but I must be content with your tempting salt fish and a bit of this bark bread. I have not time to wait for your brother, the mighty hunter. I must set off again immediately."

Good Maase, flattered by the stranger's praises of her fish and her brother, and vexed at his hasty departure, exclaimed: "You are very kind, sir. But why should you leave us so soon?"

"I must."

"Must you venture among these mountains at this hour and in such weather?"

"My business is important."

These answers roused the native curiosity of the young man's entertainers as much as they excited their surprise.

The fisherman rose, and said: "You are in the house of Christopher Buldus Braal, fisherman, of the village of Surb."

The woman added: "Maase Kennybol is his wife and servant."

When Norwegian peasants wish to ask a stranger's name in polite style, it is their custom to tell him their own.

Ordener answered: "And I am a traveller, who is neither sure of the name he bears nor of the road he travels."

This strange reply did not seem to satisfy fisher Braal.

"By the crown of Gorman the Old," said he, "I did not suppose there was more than one man in Norway just now who was not sure of his name. I mean the noble Baron Thorwick, who is to change his name, they say, to Count Danneskiold, on account of his famous marriage to the chancellor's daughter. At least, dear Maase, that's the latest news from Throndhjem. I congratulate you, stranger, upon this likeness between you and the son of the viceroy, the great Count Guldenlew."

"As your worship," added the wife, her face beaming with curiosity, "does not seem able to tell us anything about yourself, can you not tell us something about what is going on just now, for instance, something about this wonderful marriage of which my husband speaks?"

"Yes," rejoined her husband, with a self-important air, "that's the very latest news. Within a month the viceroy's son will marry the chancellor's daughter."

"I doubt it," said Ordener.

"You doubt it, sir! I assure you that the thing is certain. I have it on the best authority. The fellow who told me had it from Mr. Poël, the favorite servant of the noble Baron Thorwick, — that is, the noble Count Danneskiold. Can any storm have troubled the waters within the week? Has this grand match been broken off?"

"I think so," replied the young man, smiling.

"If that is so, sir, I am wrong. Never light the fire to fry the fish before it is in the net. But have they really quarrelled? Who told you so?"

"Nobody," said Ordener. "I merely imagined so."

At this frank confession the fisherman could not help transgressing the laws of Norwegian courtesy by a loud burst of laughter.

"A thousand pardons, sir. But it is easy to see that you are indeed a traveller, and probably a stranger. Do you fancy that things will turn out as you happen to wish, and that the sky will be clear or cloudy at your caprice?"

Here the fisherman, well versed in the affairs of the nation, as all Norse peasants are, began to explain to Ordener why this marriage could not fail to take place: it was essential to the interests of the d'Ahlefeld family; the viceroy could not refuse the king, who desired it; besides, it was said that the future husband and wife were very much in love. In a word, fisher Braal could not doubt that the match would come off; he only wished he was as sure of killing next day that confounded dogfish which infested Master-Bick pond.

Ordener was little inclined to carry on a political discussion with so uncouth a statesman, and was delighted when the arrival of another guest relieved him of all embarrassment.

"It is he; it is my brother!" cried old Maase.

And no less event than the arrival of her brother could have diverted her from the rapt admiration with which she listened to her husband's lengthy discourse.

The latter, while the two children threw themselves noisily upon their uncle's neck, quietly offered him his hand, saying, —

"Welcome, brother."

Then, turning to Ordener: "Sir, this is our brother, the famous hunter Kennybol, from the mountains of Kiölen."

"A hearty greeting to you all," said the mountaineer, taking off his bearskin cap. "Brother, I've had as bad luck in hunting upon your coast as you would probably have had if you had gone fishing in our mountains. I think I could sooner fill my game-bag if I chased elves and goblins in the misty forests of Queen Mab. Sister Maase, you are the first sea-mew whom I have caught sight of to-day. Here, friends, God keep you! but this wretched grouse is all that the best hunter in the province of Throndhjem has got in a whole day's tramp through the heather in this weather."

With these words he drew from his pouch and laid on the table a white ptarmigan, declaring that it was not worth a shot.

"But," he muttered between his teeth, "my faithful arquebuse, you shall soon hunt far bigger game. If you can bring down no more chamois or elk skins, you shall make holes in green jackets and red jerkins."

These words, but half heard, struck the curious Maase.

"Eh!" asked she; "what did you say, brother?"

"I said that there was always a goblin dancing under a woman's tongue."

"You are right, brother Kennybol," cried the fisherman. "Eve's daughters are all curious, like their mother. Weren't you talking of green jackets?"

"Brother Braal," replied the hunter, with some spirit, "I trust my secrets to no one but my musket, because I am sure that then they will never be repeated."

"There's talk in the village," boldly continued the fisherman, "of a revolt among the miners. Do you know anything about it, brother?"

The mountaineer picked up his cap and pulled it over his eyes, with a sidelong look at the stranger; then he bent toward the fisherman and said in a low, stern tone: "Silence!"

The fisherman shook his head several times.

"Brother Kennybol, the fish may be silent, but it falls into the net all the same."

There was a short pause. The two brothers exchanged meaning glances; the children picked the feathers from the ptarmigan as it lay on the table; the good wife listened, and hoped to guess more than was actually said; and Ordener studied them all.

"If you have but meagre fare to-day," suddenly observed the hunter, evidently anxious to change the subject, "it shall not be so to-morrow. Brother Braal, catch the king of fish, if you can, for I promise you plenty of bear's grease to dress it."

"Bear's grease!" cried Maase. "Has any one seen a bear in the neighborhood? Patrick, Regner, my boys, I forbid you to leave the house. A bear!"

"Make yourself easy, sister; you will have nothing to fear from him after to-morrow. Yes, it was really a bear that I saw about two miles away from Surb,—a white bear. He seemed to be carrying off a man, or rather an animal. But no, it may have been a goatherd, for goatherds dress in the skins of animals; however, I was not near enough to tell. What amazed me, was that he carried his prey on his back, and not in his teeth."

"Really, brother?"

"Yes; and the creature must have been dead, for it made no attempt to defend itself."

"But," sagely inquired the fisherman, "if it were dead, how did it stay on the bear's back?"

"That's more than I can say. Never mind; it shall be the bear's last meal. As I entered the village I engaged six strong companions, and to-morrow, sister Maase, I will bring you the handsomest white fur that ever ran over mountain snow."

"Take care, brother," said the woman; "you have seen strange things, truly. That bear may be the Devil."

"Are you mad?" interrupted the mountaineer, with a laugh; "the Devil change himself into a bear, indeed! Into a cat or a monkey, I grant you; but to a bear! Oh, by Saint Eldon the exorciser, you're worse than any child or old woman, with your superstition!"

The poor woman hung her head.

"Brother, you were my lord and master before my revered husband cast his eyes upon me; do as your guardian angel bids you."

"But," the fisherman asked the mountaineer, "where did you meet with this bear?"

"Between Lake Miösen and Walderhog."

"Walderhog!" said the woman, crossing herself.

"Walderhog!" repeated Ordener.

"But, brother," rejoined the fisherman; "I hope you were not travelling toward Walderhog."

"I! Heaven forbid; it was the bear."

"Shall you go there to-morrow in search of him?" broke in the terrified Maase.

"No, truly; how can you suppose, friends, that even a bear would venture to take refuge in a cave where—"

He stopped short, and all three made the sign of the cross.

"You are right," replied the fisherman; "wild beasts would be warned away by their instinct."

"My good friends," said Ordener, "what is there so frightful about this Walderhog cave?"

They looked at one another in stupid surprise, as if they could not understand such a question.

"Is that where King Walder's tomb is?" added the young man.

"Yes," replied the woman; "a stone tomb which sings."

"And that's not all," said the fisherman.

"No," she added; "the bones of the dead dance there by night."

"And that's not all," said the mountaineer.

All were silent, as if they dared not go on.

"Well," asked Ordener, "what else is there that is supernatural?"

"Young man," said the mountaineer, gravely, "you should not speak so lightly; when you see an old gray wolf like me, shudder."

The young man answered, with a gentle smile: "Still, I should like to know all the marvels which occur in this Walderhog cave; for that is exactly where I am going."

These words seemed to turn his three hearers into stone.

"To Walderhog! Heavens! are you going to Walderhog?"

"And he says that," rejoined the fisherman, "just as I might say I'm going to Loevig to sell my codfish, or to Ralph's meadow for herring. To Walderhog! Great Heavens!"

"Poor young man!" cried the wife; "were you born without a guardian angel? Have you no patron saint? Alas! it must be so; for you do not even seem to know your own name."

"And what motive," broke in the mountaineer, "can lead your worship to that fearful spot?"

"I have a question to ask," answered Ordener.

The astonishment of his hosts grew with their curiosity.

"See here, stranger; you do not seem to be familiar with this part of the country. Your worship is doubtless mistaken; it cannot be to Walderhog that you wish to go."

"Besides," added the mountaineer, "if you want to speak with any human being, you will find none there."

"None but the demon," rejoined the woman.

"The demon! What demon?"

"Yes," she added; "the one for whom the tomb sings and the dead dance."

"Then you do not know, sir," said the fisherman, dropping his voice and approaching Ordener, — "you do not know that Walderhog cave is the favorite abode of—"

The woman stopped him.

"Husband, do not speak that name; it brings ill luck."

"Whose abode?" asked Ordener.

"That of Beelzebub incarnate," said Kennybol.

"Really, my kind hosts, I know not what you mean. I was surely told that Walderhog was the haunt of Hans of Iceland."

A triple cry of terror arose.

"Well!—Then you do know!—He is the demon we mean!"

The woman drew her woollen kerchief over her face, and called on all the saints to witness that it was not she who uttered that name.

When the fisherman had somewhat recovered from his surprise, he looked steadily at Ordener, as if there were something about that young man which he could not comprehend.

"I did not expect, stranger, that even if I lived still longer than my father, who died at the age of one hundred and twenty, I should ever have to show the road to Walderhog to any human being possessed of his senses and believing in God."

"Surely not," cried Maase; "your worship will not go to that accursed cave; for if one only step foot inside, he must make a compact with the Devil!"

"I must go, my kind hosts, and the greatest service that you can do me is to show me the shortest road there."

"The shortest way to reach the place where you wish to go," said the fisherman, "is to throw yourself from the top of the nearest rock into the next torrent."

"Should I reach the same end," quietly asked Ordener, "by preferring a useless death to a profitable danger?"

Braal shook his head, while his brother looked scrutinizingly at the young adventurer.

"I understand," suddenly exclaimed the fisherman; "you want to earn the thousand crowns reward which the lord mayor offers for the head of this Iceland demon."

Ordener smiled.

"Young sir," added the fisherman, with deep emotion, "take my advice; give up your scheme. I am old and poor, and I would not sell the remnant of my life for a thousand crowns if I had but one day left."

The woman, with a beseeching, compassionate look, watched the effect of her husband's entreaties. Ordener made haste to reply: "It is a much higher motive which leads me to seek this robber whom you call a demon; it is for the sake of others, not my own—"

The mountaineer, who had not taken his eyes from Ordener, interrupted him.

"I understand you now. I know why you seek the demon of Iceland."

"I wish to force him to fight," said the young man.

"That's it," said Kennybol; "you are intrusted with important interests, are you not?"

"So I just said."

The mountaineer approached the young man with an air of great intelligence, and to his utter amazement whispered in his ear: "You come from Count Schumacker, from Griffenfeld, do you not?"

"Good man," he exclaimed, "how did you know that?"

And, indeed, it was hard for him to guess how a Norwegian mountaineer came to know a secret which he had confided to no one, not even to General Levin.

Kennybol leaned toward him.

"I wish you success," he observed in the same mysterious whisper. "You are a noble young man to labor thus for the oppressed."

Ordener's surprise was so great that he could scarcely find words to inquire how the mountaineer had learned the purpose of his journey.

"Silence!" said Kennybol, putting his finger to his lip. "I hope that you may gain all that you desire from the dweller in Walderhog; my arm, like yours, is loyal to the prisoner of Munkholm."

Then, raising his voice, before Ordener could answer, he added: "Brother, dear sister Maase, regard this worthy youth as another brother. Come, I think supper is ready."

"What!" interrupted Maase, "have you persuaded his worship to give up his plan for visiting the demon?"

"Sister, pray that no harm may come to him. He is a noble and worthy young man. Come, brave sir, take some food and a little rest beneath our roof; to-morrow I will show you your road, and we will set out in search,— you of the Devil, and I of my bear."

XXIX

Comrade, ah! comrade, what comrade's son art thou? From what race canst thou have sprung to dare attack Fafnir thus? — Edda.

THE first rays of the rising sun were just reddening the highest peak of the rocks upon the seacoast, when the fisherman, who had come before the dawn to cast his nets off the shore opposite the mouth of Walderhog cave, saw a figure wrapped in a cloak or shroud descend from the rocks, and disappear beneath the much-dreaded arched roof of the cavern. Struck with terror, he commended his boat and his soul to Saint Usuph, and ran to tell his frightened family that he had seen one of the ghosts which dwell in the palace of Hans of Iceland return to the cave at daybreak.

This ghost, thenceforth the theme and dread of many a long winter evening, was no other than Ordener, the noble son of the Norwegian viceroy, who, while both kingdoms fancied him absorbed in paying tender attentions to his haughty betrothed, had come alone and unknown to risk his life for her to whom he had given his heart and his future, for the daughter of a proscribed man.

Evil omens, sad forebodings, had thus far accompanied him. He had left the fisherman and his family, and as they parted, good Maase knelt and prayed for him. Kennybol and his six comrades, who had pointed out the right road, quitted him within half a mile of Walderhog, and those dauntless hunters who sallied forth to face a bear with a laugh on their lips, gazed in terror upon the fearless traveller as he followed that unhallowed path.

The young man entered Walderhog cave as he might have entered a long-wished-for haven. He felt a transport of delight as he thought that he was about to accomplish the object of his life, and that in a few moments he might perhaps shed his last drop of blood for his Ethel. About to attack a brigand dreaded by an entire province, it might be a monster, a very demon, it was not that frightful image which filled his fancy; he saw only the figure of the sweet captive maid, praying perhaps for him before her prison altar. Had the object of his devotion been any other than it was, he might have weighed for an instant, only to scorn them, the dangers in search of which he had journeyed so far; but what room is there for reflection in a youthful heart throbbing with the double stimulus of heroic sacrifice and noble love?

He advanced proudly into the vaulted cavern, which echoed and re-echoed the sound of his footsteps, not deigning even a glance at the stalactites and the century-old columns of basalt which towered above him amid mosses, lichen, and ivy,—a confused medley of weird forms, from which the superstitious credulity of the Norwegian countryfolk had more than once created hosts of evil spirits or long processions of ghosts.

With the same indifference he passed the tomb of King Walder, to which so many mournful legends cling, and he heard no voice save the long-drawn sigh of the north wind through those gloomy galleries.

He traversed winding passages, dimly lighted by crevices half stopped with grass and heather. Ever and anon he stumbled over strange objects, which rolled from beneath his foot with a hollow sound, and assumed in the darkness the shape of broken skulls or long rows of white teeth with fleshless gums.

But his soul was undismayed. He was only surprised that he had not yet encountered the much-dreaded inhabitant of this horrible cave.

He reached a sort of circular hall, hewn from the rock. Here the subterranean road which he had thus far followed came to an end, and the rocky walls were without exit, save for a few wide fissures, through which he saw the mountains and woods outside.

Amazed that he should have thus traversed the fatal cavern in vain, he began to despair of finding the brigand. A singular monument in the middle of the underground hall caught his attention. Three long, massive bowlders, standing upright, supported a fourth, broad and square, as three pillars might uphold a roof. Beneath this gigantic tripod was an altar, also formed of a single block of granite, with a round hole in the middle of its upper surface. Ordener recognized it as one of those colossal Druidic structures which he had often seen in travelling through Norway, the most amazing instances being found in France, at Lokmariaker and Karnak,—wondrous fabrics which have grown old, resting upon the earth like tents pitched for a day, and made solid by their mere weight.

The young man, lost in thought, leaned mechanically against this altar, whose stone lips were stained dark brown, so deep had they drunk of the blood of human victims.

All at once he started. A voice, apparently proceeding from the stone, fell upon his ear: "Young man, you come to this place with feet which touch the tomb."

He rose quickly, and his hand sought his sword, while an echo, clear but faint as the voice of a dying man, repeated: "Young man, you come to this place with feet which touch the tomb." At this instant a hideous face appeared on the other side of the Druid altar, a face crowned with red hair, and disfigured by a brutal sneer.

"Young man," it again repeated, "you come to this place with feet which touch the tomb."

"And with a hand which touches a sword," calmly responded Ordener.

The monster emerged from beneath the altar, revealing his thick-set, muscular limbs, his wild, blood-stained dress, his hooked hands, and his heavy stone axe.

"It is I," he cried, with a growl like that of a wild beast.

"And I," answered Ordener.

"I expected you."

"I did more," replied the bold young man; "I sought you out."

The brigand folded his arms.

"Do you know who I am?"

"Yes."

"And you are not frightened?"

"Not now."

"Then you were afraid to come here?" And the monster tossed his head with a look of triumph.

"Afraid I might not find you."

"You bid me defiance, and your feet have trampled on dead bodies!"

"To-morrow they may tread upon your own."

The little man quivered with rage. Ordener stood motionless, in an attitude of haughty calm.

"Take care!" muttered the brigand; "I will burst upon you and rend you as Norwegian hailstones do a lady's parasol."

"Such a shield would be all-sufficient for me."

Something in Ordener's eye seemed to daunt the monster. He plucked the hairs from his mantle, as a tiger might devour grass before it springs upon its prey.

"You teach me what pity means," he said.

"And you teach me what it is to scorn."

"Child, your voice is soft, your face is fair, like the voice and the face of a girl; what death will you choose?"

"Your own."

The small man laughed.

"Know you not that I am a demon, that my spirit is the spirit of Ingulf the Destroyer?"

"I know that you are a robber, that you commit murder for the love of gold."

"You are wrong," broke in the monster; "it is for love of blood."

"Were you not paid by the d'Ahlefelds to slay Captain Dispolsen?"

"What are you talking about? What names are these?"

"Do you not know Captain Dispolsen, whom you killed on Urchtal Sands?"

"That may be, but I have forgotten him, as I shall forget you three days hence."

"Do you not know Count d'Ahlefeld, who paid you to steal an iron casket from the captain?"

"D'Ahlefeld! Stay; yes, I know him. I drank his son's blood only yesterday, from my son's skull."

Ordener shuddered with horror.

"Were you not content with your wages?"

"What wages?" asked the brigand.

"Hark ye; the sight of you offends me; I must have done. You stole, a week since, an iron casket from one of your victims, a Munkholm officer, did you not?"

At the word "Munkholm" the brigand started.

"An officer from Munkholm?" he muttered. Then he asked, with a look of surprise, "Are you too an officer from Munkholm?"

"No," said Ordener.

"So much the worse!" and his face clouded.

"Enough of this," rejoined the persistent Ordener; "where is the casket that you stole from the captain?"

The little man meditated for a moment.

"By Ingulf! here's a paltry iron box that occupies many minds. I will promise you there'll not be so much search for that which holds your bones, if ever they be collected in a coffin."

These words, as they showed Ordener that the robber knew the casket to which he referred, revived his hope of obtaining it.

"Tell me what you did with that casket. Is it in Count d'Ahlefeld's possession?"

"No."

"You lie, for you laugh."

"Believe what you will. What matters it to me?"

The monster had assumed a mocking air which awakened Ordener's suspicions. He saw that there was nothing to be done but to rouse him to fury if possible, or to intimidate him.

"Hear me," said he, raising his voice; "you must give me that casket."

The other answered with a savage sneer.

"You must give it to me!" the young man repeated in tones of thunder.

"Are you accustomed to issuing orders to buffaloes and bears?" replied the monster, still sneering.

"I would give this command to the very Devil in hell."

"You may do so ere long, if you like."

Ordener drew his sword, which gleamed in the darkness like a flash of lightning.

"Obey me!"

"Nay," cried Hans, brandishing his axe; "I might have broken your bones and sucked your blood when you first appeared, but I restrained my wrath; I was curious to see the sparrow attack the vulture."

"Wretch," exclaimed Ordener, "defend yourself!"

"'Tis the first time I was ever told to do so," muttered the brigand, gnashing his teeth.

With these words, he sprang upon the granite altar and gathered himself together, like a leopard awaiting the hunter on a high cliff, ready to spring upon him unawares.

From this vantage-ground he glared at the young man, apparently seeking the best side from which to attack him. All would have been over with Ordener had he hesitated an instant. But he gave the brigand no time to consider, and threw himself violently upon him, aiming the point of his sword at his face.

Then began the most fearful fight which imagination can picture. The little man, standing upon the altar, like a statue on its pedestal, looked like one of those horrid idols which, in barbarous ages, received in that same spot impious sacrifices and sacrilegious offerings.

His movements were so rapid that upon whatever side Ordener attacked him, he always met the monster face to face, and encountered his blade. He would have been hewn in pieces at the first onslaught, had he not had the lucky forethought to wrap his mantle loosely around his left arm, so that the greater part of his furious opponent's blows were foiled by this floating shield. Thus for some moments both made useless though tremendous efforts to wound each other. The small man's fiery gray eyes seemed starting from their sockets. Surprised to meet with such vigorous and bold resistance from a foe apparently so feeble, his savage sneers changed to silent rage. The brutal immobility of the monster's features, and Ordener's dauntless composure contrasted strangely with the swiftness of their motions and the vigor of their attack. Not a sound was heard but the clash of weapons, the young man's quick steps, and the hurried breathing of both adversaries, when the little man uttered a fearful roar. The blade of his axe had caught in the folds of the cloak. He braced himself; he shook his arm frantically, but only succeeded in entangling the handle with the blade in the clinging stuff, which, with every fresh effort, wound itself closer and closer about it.

The dreadful brigand felt the young man's steel upon his breast.

"Once more I ask you," said the triumphant Ordener, "will you give me that iron casket which you stole like a coward?"

The small man was silent for an instant; then he said, with a roar: "Curse you, no!"

Ordener rejoined, still retaining his victorious and threatening attitude: "Consider!"

"No; I tell you no!" repeated the brigand.

The noble youth lowered his sword.

"Well," said he, "release your axe from the folds of my mantle, and let us fight it out."

With a disdainful laugh, the monster answered:—

"Child, you play the generous man, as if I wanted your indulgence!"

Before the astonished Ordener could turn his head, the brigand had placed his foot on the shoulder of his loyal victor, and at one bound stood twelve paces away from him. With another leap he sprang at Ordener, and hung his entire weight upon him, as the panther hangs with teeth and claws to the flanks of the royal lion. His nails dug deep into the young man's shoulders, his bony knees were pressed into his flesh, while his fierce face showed Ordener a bloody mouth and cruel teeth ready to tear him limb from limb. He ceased to speak; no human words issued from his heaving chest; a low roar mingled with hoarse, passionate yells alone expressed his rage. He was more hideous than a wild beast, more monstrous than a demon; he was a man deprived of all semblance of humanity.

Ordener tottered beneath the small man's onslaught, and would have fallen at the unexpected shock, had not one of the heavy pillars of the Druid monument happened to be just behind to sustain him. He stood therefore half overthrown and gasping beneath the weight of his fearful foe. To gain any idea of the horrible spectacle offered at this moment, it must be remembered that all which we have described occurred in far less time than is required to write it.

As we said, the noble youth tottered, but he did not quake. He hastily addressed a farewell thought to Ethel. The thought of his love was like a prayer; it restored his strength. He threw his arms about the monster; then seizing his sword by the middle of the blade, he pressed the point straight down upon his spine. The wounded brigand uttered a fearful scream, and with a sudden leap, which shook off Ordener, freed himself from his bold adversary's arms, and fell back some paces, taking in his teeth a fragment of the green cloak, which he had bitten in his fury.

He leaped up, supple and agile as a young deer, and the battle began again, for the third time, more terrible than ever. By chance there was, close by, a pile of huge stones over which moss and weeds had grown for centuries undisturbed. Two ordinary men could scarcely have lifted the smallest of these rocks. Hans seized one in both arms and raised it above his head, poising it toward Ordener. His expression was frightful. The stone, flung with great violence, moved heavily through the air; the young man had just time to spring aside. The granite bowlder broke to fragments against the subterranean wall with a tremendous noise, which was echoed back for many moments from the depths of the cavern.

Ordener, stunned and amazed, had barely time to recover before a second mass of stone was poised in the brigand's grasp. Vexed that he should seem to stand like a coward to be pelted, he rushed toward the small man, with uplifted sword, to change this mode of warfare; but the fearful missile, launched like a thunderbolt, as it moved through the dense, dark air of the cave encountered the bare and slender blade; the steel was dashed to pieces like a bit of glass, and the monster's fierce laugh rang out. Ordener was disarmed.

"Have you," cried the monster, "aught to say to God or the Devil ere you die?"

And his eye darted flame, and all his muscles swelled with rage and joy, and he flung himself with a thrill of impatience upon his axe, which, wrapped in the cloak, lay upon the ground. Poor Ethel!

All at once a distant roar was heard outside. The monster paused. The noise increased; shouts of men were mingled with the plaintive moan of a bear. The brigand listened. The cries of pain continued. He hastily seized his axe, and sprang, not toward Ordener, but toward one of the crevices in the rock. Ordener, overwhelmed with surprise to find himself thus unnoticed, hurried in his turn to one of these natural doors, and saw in a neighboring glade a large white bear at bay, surrounded by seven hunters, among whom he thought he recognized Kennybol, whose words had made such an impression upon him the night before.

He turned back. The brigand had left the cave, and a fearful voice outside shouted: "Friend! Friend! I am here! I am here!"

FOOTNOTES:

[1] M. Charles Nodier, in the "Quotidienne" for March 12, 1823.

[2] Koran.

[3] A small coin worth twelve and a half cents. The name is still in use in Louisiana.

[4] Name of the Throndhjem morgue.

[5] The Norwegian peasants build nests for the eider duck, surprise them while sitting on their young, and strip them of their down.

[6] The Odelsrecht was a singular law establishing a species of entail among the Norwegian peasantry. Any man who was compelled to part with his patrimony might prevent the purchaser from transferring it, by declaring every tenth year that he intended to buy it back.

[7] The Persian god of evil.

[8] Bark bread, eaten by the poorer classes in Norway.

[9] Blood privilege, the right to have a hangman.

[10] It is granted.

[11] The waters of Lake Sparbo are greatly used for tempering steel.

[12] Frederic III. was the victim of Borch, or Borrich, a Danish chemist, and more especially of Borri, a Milanese quack, who declared himself to be the favorite of the Archangel Michael. This impostor, after startling Strasburg and Amsterdam with his pretended miracles, increased the sphere of his ambition and the boldness of his lies; having deceived the people, he ventured to deceive kings. He began with Queen Christina at Hamburg, and ended with King Frederic at Copenhagen.

[13] The dogfish are greatly dreaded by fishermen, because they frighten other fish.

[14] The ancient aristocracy of Norway, before Griffenfeld established a regular order of nobility, were entitled "hersa" (baron) or "jarl" (count). The English word "earl" is derived from the latter.

[15] The patron saint of fishermen.